Forever My Own

Books by Tracie Peterson

For a complete list
of Tracie's books, visit her website
www.traciepeterson.com

Forever My Own

TRACIE PETERSON

BETHANYHOUSE

a division of Baker Publishing Group
Minneapolis, Minnesota

Published by Bethany House Publishers
11400 Hampshire Avenue South
Bloomington, Minnesota 55438
www.bethanyhouse.com

Bethany House Publishers is a division of
Baker Publishing Group, Grand Rapids, Michigan

Printed in the United States of America

Library of Congress Cataloging-in-Publication Data

Names: Peterson, Tracie, author.
Title: Forever my own / Tracie Peterson.
Description: Minneapolis, Minnesota : Bethany House, [2021] | Series: Ladies of the
    lake ; 3
Identifiers: LCCN 2020056579 | ISBN 9780764232374 (trade paper) | ISBN
    9780764232381 (cloth) | ISBN 9780764232398 (large print) | ISBN
    9781493431540 (ebook)
Subjects: GSAFD: Christian fiction. | Love stories.
Classification: LCC PS3566.E7717 F68 2021 | DDC 813/.54—dc23
LC record available at https://lccn.loc.gov/2020056579

Scripture quotations are from the King James Version of the Bible.

This is a work of historical reconstruction; the appearances of certain historical figures are
therefore inevitable. All other characters, however, are products of the author's imagina-
tion, and any resemblance to actual persons, living or dead, is coincidental.

Cover design by LOOK Design Studio
Cover photography by Aimee Christenson
Lake Superior cover photo by Martin Ramirez

21 22 23 24 25 26 27   7 6 5 4 3 2 1

In memory of Heidi.

Your life touched the lives of so many,
and you will be missed.
We'll see you again!

Chapter 1

Duluth, Minnesota
January 10, 1871

Kirstin Hallberg stepped from the train onto the depot platform. A bitter wind whipped at her bonnet, sending the tails of her ribbon ties dancing. She glanced to the right and then to the left, looking for her grandmother among the small number of people waiting on the platform. Would she recognize her? The long trip from Sweden was finally at an end, and she could hardly wait to see *Mormor* again. Kirstin had only been twelve when her grandparents and Uncle Per left Sweden to live in America, and she hadn't seen them since. Now *Morfar*, her grandfather, was dead, and Uncle Per had died as well, and that was why Kirstin had come to America—to take care of her grandmother. Without family here, the old woman would be all alone.

Kirstin spied a white-haired woman and man. The woman wore her hair braided and wrapped around her head like a crown. Mormor. It had to be her.

"Kirstin!" her grandmother called and waved. The couple came forward to greet her. "*Välkommen till Amerika och Duluth.*"

"I have felt very welcomed since arriving in America. I have seen so much beauty as I traveled by train. Duluth is, well, not as pretty as I had hoped." Kirstin grinned, glancing around.

"Ja, but it is not that old of a town," Mormor declared, her Swedish cadence giving the statement a singsong sound. "But just look at you, all grown up. You're beautiful! You're even prettier than your mama."

Kirstin put down her luggage and wrapped her arms around her grandmother's neck. "Oh, Mormor. I was afraid I wouldn't recognize you, but you look just as I remember." They hugged for a long time.

"I feel that I am missing out," the man who'd accompanied Mormor said.

The older woman pulled away and kissed Kirstin's cheeks. "Ignore him. He's always trying to be the center of attention."

The old man laughed. "Hardly that. You know better, Lena. I just want to meet your granddaughter. You've talked of nothing and no one else for weeks." He extended his hand. "I'm Habram Farstad. I was your *morföräldrar*'s best friend."

"Of course! I've heard you spoken of many times in the letters home." Kirstin separated from her grandmother and gave him a hug. "You've taken good care of Mormor and might as well be family."

He shrugged. "Ja, I might as well be. At least that's what I'm always telling her." He gave Kirstin's grandmother a wink.

"Do you have a lot of luggage? A trunk or two?" Mormor asked.

Kirstin shook her head, gazing around to take in all that she could. It seemed, since her arrival in America, that all she could do was gawk at the new sights. "I only have this luggage. There really wasn't much to bring. Papa gave me some money for the trip and told me I could use whatever was left to buy some of the things I'd need once I got here. I will definitely need to go shopping for fabric and other things."

"That will not be a problem," her grandmother said. "We have plenty of stores. It used to be there wasn't much available this time of year, but with the railroad now in place, we can get goods from St. Paul whenever we need them."

"That's for sure," Habram said, nodding. "Duluth used to be like living at the end of the world before the train. Especially in the winter." He leaned down and took Kirstin's luggage. "I'll go get the carriage, and you meet me out front."

"Ja, we'll do that."

Mormor and Kirstin began a slow walk to follow Habram. Kirstin gave a sigh. "I'm so glad to be off that train. It was noisy and dirty. I thought it all very exciting, but I'm glad to be here with you. My adventure is at an end."

Her grandmother squeezed Kirstin's shoulders and pulled her close. "Nonsense. The adventure is just beginning. Now that you're here, we can have a grand time. You'll see."

Kirstin suppressed a yawn. "Well, I hope there will at least be time for a rest before we venture too far. Oh, and a bath."

Mormor laughed. "Perhaps, but first we will eat. I've made some good Swedish food for you so that you won't be too lonely for home."

Lena watched as Kirstin ate her lunch with gusto. The girl seemed nearly starving.

"*Tack*, Mormor." Kirstin beamed her a smile. "I haven't eaten much since coming to America. My English is good, but I don't always understand what some of the foods are. Especially when they give them strange names. In New York I had something called *lasagna*. It was very good, but I was afraid to try it because I couldn't understand what the man was telling me about it."

"I've had lasagna too," Mormor admitted. "It's very good."

"I sometimes didn't have much choice, so I just decided not to eat. I'm so glad to be here now and know what I'm eating."

"I'm glad you like it." Mormor spooned more lingonberry jam on her granddaughter's plate.

"I haven't had *raggmunk* with lingonberries for such a long time."

Swedish potato pancakes had always been one of Kirstin's favorites when she was very little. Lena had hoped they still were.

"I'm glad you like them. Raggmunk is always good for winter food. Plenty of potatoes are available, and we put up a lot of berries this summer. One of my friends from church has a big piece of land where blueberries grow wild, and five years ago she planted lingonberries too. They are growing so well that she gave me a whole bushel to can. You won't have to do without them here."

"I wondered if the same things that grow at home would grow here in America. I remember, though, that you wrote to Mama about the lingonberries."

"Your grandmother is a mighty fine cook, ja?" Habram said.

"Ja," Kirstin declared. "The best. Mama says she learned everything about cooking from you."

"How is your mama? I bet it was hard for her to let you sail to America," Lena said as she gathered the dishes.

"Ja, Mama was worried. She didn't like the idea of me sailing after what happened to my brother Domar. She still mourns his loss."

Lena and Habram exchanged a glance but said nothing as Kirstin continued.

"When I got to America, I wrote her a letter and mailed it right away. I don't know how long it will take to arrive, but I'm sure she'll know soon that I got here safe. The ship is owned in Sweden. They would hear plenty quick if it had been lost."

"Ja, no doubt that's true." Lena gave her granddaughter a smile. "Come on now, I'll show you your room, and you can wash up and rest."

"Don't you need help with the dishes?"

"Not this time. I know you are tired from the long train ride. There are many changes of trains between here and New York."

"Ja. Many."

Lena led Kirstin from the dining room and down the hall to the narrow stairs hidden behind an equally narrow door. "Your room is upstairs." She climbed ahead of Kirstin, and Habram brought up the rear with Kirstin's luggage in hand.

The stairs opened right into a small room that Lena had set up as a sitting area. Beyond that were two doors, one to the immediate right and one straight ahead.

"You can have the room over there," Lena said, pointing straight ahead.

Kirstin opened the door. "Oh, it's lovely. So perfect."

Lena watched as Kirstin made her way around the room, touching the mirrored dresser and then the quilted bed cover. "I made that quilt special for you when I heard you would come. We worked on it together, me and the ladies in the neighborhood."

"I love it. Blue and green are my favorite colors." Kirstin examined the quilt. It was done up in a series of stars and pinwheels.

"It's my welcoming gift to you," Lena said.

Kirstin hurried back to her grandmother and hugged her tight. "I love it, and I love you for making it for me."

"*Jag älskar dig, dotterdotter.*" *I love you, granddaughter.* Lena smiled and gently pushed Kirstin away. "Now, you wash up and rest. I'll come get you if it gets too late."

Kirstin kissed Lena's cheek and stepped back to the bed. She pulled down the covers and positioned the pillow just so.

"There's water in the pitcher and soap in the little dish behind the bowl," Lena explained. "And the hand towels are hanging just under the window. Later tonight you can have a proper bath downstairs."

"You have wooden shutters just like at home." Kirstin ran her fingers over the carved and painted designs. "It almost feels like home."

"This is your home now for as long as you like." Lena turned to Habram. "Just leave that luggage and come with me. I'll pour you another cup of coffee."

"Ja, another cup sounds good. It's mighty cold today."

Lena led the way downstairs and smiled at the sight of three sets of dishes awaiting her attention by the sink. She loved to have company. Being alone was so lonely. The house was always too quiet when the others were gone. She preferred having people in the house and extra work every day compared to being by herself.

Of course, Per had not been dead even a year. Her only son had been killed in a logging accident five years after Lena lost her beloved husband, Jürgen, to sickness. How she missed them both. If not for Habram and the boys, she might have died from a broken heart.

"When will you tell her about her brother?" Habram asked in a hushed tone.

Lena took his coffee to the table and shook her head. "I don't know. It's a great deal to tell."

"Ja, but it must be told."

She nodded. "Ja. It must be."

Kirstin awoke and glanced around the room. She had been traveling for weeks—a month and a half, actually—and it was almost surprising to find that the room wasn't moving or rocking in some manner. Ships and trains were in constant motion, and she had definitely wearied of the movement.

She snuggled down beneath Mormor's quilt and sighed. It was good to be here. She could feel it. It was the right thing to do—a thing of God, as her father might say. When they'd learned that Uncle Per had died, there had been a frenzy of conversations to decide what was to be done. Mama had concluded that they should write to Mormor and send her money to come back to Sweden. After all, they'd only gone to America because Per wanted to buy farmland and take a wife. They had heard about the cheap land in America, where a man had only to dream a dream and it would come true. In their area, the Crown and the noblemen owned the land. Papa had rented his piece for many years and even owned his house. It was one of the ways some noblemen rewarded their most faithful tenants. But Papa would never own the land.

But Mormor had written back, declining the offer. She didn't want to leave America, where her husband and son were buried. She called it home now, and Sweden was but a distant memory. So the frenzy began once again to decide the best course. Mormor could not live by herself, after all.

Each of Kirstin's siblings discussed what they might do, except for the youngest, Brita. She was only twelve. Kirstin's brother Härse had a well-established business making furniture and had no desire to move to America, even given the possibilities of expanding his business. Their sister Svena was married and expecting her second baby. There was no money for the little family to even consider moving so far away.

That left Kirstin, who was more than happy to be the one to solve the problem. All her life she had liked being in the position of helping people fix what was wrong and manage difficult situations. Although she had never married or had children, she gave advice to her friends and family who had. Most of the time the advice was sound, because Kirstin paid great attention to everything around her. When the old women talked, she listened. She'd made it her life's ambition to be wise. She wanted one day to be that old lady all the people sought for answers to their problems. Even now the idea made her smile.

When she announced that she was very much up for an adventure and would love to go to America, her parents had been surprised but saw the sense of it. For Kirstin, it was not only a way to care for her grandmother, but also to leave a part of the past behind. Sweden was full of painful memories. Perhaps none so painful as the loss of her elder brother Domar.

She had been close to him, and the fact that she hadn't been able to fix the problems that drove him away still haunted her all these years later. Never mind that she'd been a child when the problems arose. Kirstin felt a sense of failure. Domar had always been there for her, even when others felt he wasn't there for anyone. He was something of an outcast, refusing to be intimidated by authority or put in his place. Domar felt the rules were for everyone else, not for him. He drank too much on occasion and ran his mouth in such a way that he embarrassed his family and sometimes really hurt them. But when he sobered up and returned to his senses, he was always sorry for the harm he'd done and always sought to right his wrongs. If anything could be said of him, he was honest to a fault. That was why it was so hard when no one believed him.

Kirstin stretched and got up. It was dark, even though she was certain it couldn't be all that late. She wasn't sure what Mormor's routine was for the evening, but she figured she'd best join her and see what she could do to make herself useful.

As she passed the other upstairs room, Kirstin couldn't help but peek inside. Despite the darkness of the room, she could see it was another bedroom with a more masculine look to it. This had likely been Uncle Per's room. She smiled at the scent of cologne that hung in the air. She remembered Uncle Per as something of a dandy when it came to cleaning up on a Saturday night. Poor Mormor. No doubt she missed him terribly.

At the bottom of the stairs, Kirstin opened the door and stepped out. She paused to look down the hall. She'd been too tired earlier to pay much attention to the layout of the house. To the right it appeared there were other doors lining the darkened hallway. Perhaps other bedrooms or a sewing room. Mormor had mentioned a proper bath, so perhaps she had a bathing room. There were framed pictures on the hallway wall.

Landscapes that could have been Sweden. They were small and of no real significance to Kirstin. Perhaps they'd been gifts.

Kirstin glanced to the left and started for the dining room. The oak floor was polished to perfection, and despite the only light coming from a lamp on the dining room table, it still gleamed. She passed through the dining room, where they had eaten lunch, and took a moment to glance at the flowered wallpaper and an unlit lamp hanging over the table. Mormor had lit the single lamp on the table, no doubt to give Kirstin enough light by which to navigate, but hadn't lit the overhead lamp in order to be frugal. That was typical of Kirstin's family.

The kitchen came next, and Kirstin smiled at the similarity it held to her mother's in Sweden. Here there was plenty of light. Mormor had probably been working in here recently, because Kirstin could smell something baking in the oven.

White cabinets with carved trim attracted her attention. Little hearts and flying bluebirds decorated the edges, just as they did the wooden shutters in her room. No doubt her grandfather had carved and painted them. It brought cheer to the impeccably clean kitchen. There was a huge woodstove and an icebox and a long wooden table, also painted white, on which a person could prepare an entire *smörgåsbord*. A small table with four chairs sat to the far side by the window. Kirstin could almost imagine her morfar and Uncle Per taking a casual meal there with Mormor.

From outside the house came laughter. It sounded like Mormor and Mr. Farstad. It hadn't been hard to see that Mr. Farstad was sweet on her grandmother. The affection that shone in his eyes reminded Kirstin of the way Papa looked at Mama.

Not wanting them to think she'd been spying on them, she hurried away from the kitchen door and into the lighted living room. A fire burned in the hearth, and Kirstin made her way over to warm herself. The clock on the mantel showed half past five. Goodness, she had slept a very long time.

The front door opened, and Mormor stepped inside, looking over her shoulder to wave good-bye. "Yes, yes. We'll be ready. Never fear," she called. She turned back and spied Kirstin at the fire. "Ah, you're awake. How did you sleep?"

Kirstin shrugged. "Given I was in bed for nearly four hours, I would say quite well."

Mormor laughed. "Well, good. You'll be nice and rested so you can tell me all about the folks at home." She shrugged out of her coat and hung it on a peg. Next she bent to remove her boots. "I'm so glad you were able to rest. A lot of folks find daytime sleeping difficult." She came to the fire and gave her granddaughter a hug. "It's so good to have you here."

"I'm very happy to be here, Mormor." Kirstin moved from the fire and took a seat after her grandmother claimed the fireside rocker. "Was that Mr. Farstad?"

"Ja. He's a good man."

"He seems rather sweet on you."

Her grandmother's eyes twinkled. "*Ja, det är sant.*"

"Of course it's true. I'm glad you aren't trying to suggest otherwise."

Mormor chuckled. "You were always a very observant child."

"Well, I'm a child no more." Kirstin smiled and eased back in her seat. "I thought maybe I'd be the one to find romance in America, but now I see it shall be my grandmother."

Mormor chuckled and shook her index finger. "Don't be so sure. There are many men in Duluth. Mr. Farstad has a son, as you might recall. He's quite handsome and just the right age to take a wife. I've often thought it would be nice to have him in our family."

"I do recall he has a son. He has two daughters also. You told us in a letter about them living in Kansas—married to farmers—and Morfar taught Mr. Farstad and his son how to make those small sailboats."

Mormor nodded. "The Mackinaw boats. Ja. They used to work all together when the boys were free from their other jobs. Those were happy times." She seemed to drift off in thought for a moment. "But there will be happy times again now that you're here."

Kirstin noticed a long piece of jute attached to a nail on one side of the wall. It went along the wall to the other side, where it was again tied to a nail. There was some sort of twine hanging from the jute and tied together to make a diamond pattern. "What is that?"

"I'm making gill nets. I earn my keep by making them for the fishermen. I sell eggs too. Out in the shed I have twenty hens. They are all good layers, except in the winter. The lack of light makes them lazy, so I threaten to eat them." She laughed and slapped her knee as if she'd just told a great joke. "Habram put in a very small stove to keep them warm in the winter, so I just point to it and tell them they'll go in the pot if they don't lay eggs." She looked at the net on the wall. "The gill nets are something I learned to do after I arrived here."

"What do the fishermen do with these particular nets?"

"They set them in the water and catch whitefish or herring, depending on how big I make the holes."

Kirstin perked up. "I forgot you have herring in the lake. How wonderful. We can pickle and can it."

"Ja. We'll have some for breakfast tomorrow."

"It'll be just like being home."

"This is your home now. You are welcome to do what you like with your room, and if you want to change something in the house, just talk to me."

"No, the house seems perfect. Like a Swedish cottage. You even have the steep roof and traditional trim. I'd love to get a tour and see it all, when you have time."

"We can do that right now." Mormor got to her feet. "Come, I'll show you all there is. Even the chickens."

They toured the house with Mormor pointing out little things of interest. When they reached the bedroom she had once shared with her husband, she stepped aside. "You see that bed? Your morfar made it for me when we came to America."

Kirstin admired the four-poster bed. Mormor hadn't put up a canopy but rather left the bed open. "Don't you get cold without the curtains?"

"Sometimes I use them in the winter, but I forgot to put them up this year, so I just added more covers." Mormor smiled and ran her hand down the pine post. "Sometimes when it turned cold before we got the curtains up, your morfar would pile on the covers so that I could hardly move. I told him to stop or I wouldn't be able to get out of bed. He said that was the way he liked it. He thought we should stay cuddled up all winter."

Kirstin giggled. "That's a rather risqué thing to tell your granddaughter."

Mormor shrugged. "I suppose it's all in how you take it. He was a good man to me and always showed me such love. You should remember that we were a love match. We did not marry because of convenience or necessity. We fell in love in school, and that love only grew stronger through the years. He was a good husband and provider."

"I'm sure he was, Mormor. I loved Morfar very much. He was so much fun. He would play with us children and always brought us sweets to eat."

"And he loved God. That saw us through both hard times and good. He used to spend time every night before bed in prayer. I did too. Prayer is so important, Kirstin. Always remember to pray."

"I do, Mormor. I love God very much. Mama used to tell me that God should come first before anyone else—even our husbands. She said if we put God first, our husband's place coming next would be just right, because you want a husband who works hand in hand with God."

"Ja. I taught her that."

Kirstin smiled. "I know. She told me. And your mama taught it to you."

"And no doubt her mama taught her. It's good for a family to put their trust in God. Always remember that, Kirstin. No matter what else you say or do, God must come first."

Mormor continued the tour by showing Kirstin a sewing room that also doubled as the laundry room in the winter and a bathing room when baths were needed.

"We'll get the tub out and prepare lots of hot water for you to take a bath after supper."

"That sounds wonderful." Kirstin followed her into the hall.

"This is the linen closet. I keep all the bedding and towels here. Your morfar built it right into the wall so that it would be convenient for everyone to use."

"That was very smart."

"And this was Per's room," Mormor declared, opening the final door.

Kirstin stepped into the decidedly masculine room. "But I thought his room was upstairs. The room I'm not using."

"No, this one was his." Mormor offered no explanation of the room upstairs. "He liked to stay close to us in case of trouble. In the early days there were problems occasionally. He and Morfar always kept a loaded gun handy. I'm sure Mr. Farstad could tell you all about it sometime, if you ask."

Kirstin nodded, but what she wanted to ask about was the room upstairs.

Chapter 2

A few days later, after a wonderful breakfast of pickled herring, boiled eggs, and rusks and butter, Mormor told Kirstin it was time for her to learn how to make the gill nets. Kirstin followed her grandmother to the living room, where Mormor had laid out the jute rope and twine.

"I have three orders, and all are pretty big. We'll make them in sections, and then the men can attach them to their net stands." She put all her things in order, then smiled. "You can see the net I've been working on."

"Ja." Kirstin surveyed the piece hanging on the wall.

"I have nails where I can secure the head rope. We tie it up like this." Mormor took a long piece of sturdy jute and attached it to one nail and then to another midway down the wall. "The net will come down from this."

Kirstin watched as her grandmother picked up the twine and cut a piece about eight feet long.

"I cut a few of these, but you need to learn how to do this too. I like to use pieces about this long, but you can cut them different lengths if you prefer," Mormor said, holding up the pale-colored twine. "Fold it in half, then, with the top where it's folded, you'll attach it to the head rope like this."

Kirstin watched as Mormor took the looped top and put it behind the head rope. Then she drew both strands through the loop and pulled them through. "This is a cow hitch and secures the strands to the head rope. You put up as many as you need for however tall you want to make the net. You can always add on. It's easy enough to do. I like to make them about five feet high at a time and then add to them depending on the order and the total length the fisherman wants it."

Together Mormor and Kirstin put up the strands. It seemed to take quite a bit of time just cutting the pieces the same length, but finally Kirstin got them done and attached to the new head rope.

"Now comes the fun," Mormor declared. "You're going to make triangles and diamonds." She took hold of the first length of twine. "We don't do anything with this first strand, not yet anyway. You take the second and third strands and gauge how big you want your triangles by how close you have your cow-hitched pieces apart. This net will be for whitefish, so we'll put the strands about two inches apart. Then you knot the second and third strands together like this."

Mormor showed Kirstin how to tie the pieces and snug them down to make the right size. That seemed simple enough. Mormor then took the next two strands and tied them to-gether, then continued down the line in rapid succession. When she finished, there was a row of triangles all along the head rope.

"For the next line you can now take that first strand and the second and do the same. Then third and fourth, and so on down the line." She went to work, and Kirstin could see how quickly the diamond shapes were formed.

"That's all there is to it." Mormor reached the end of the strands and stood back. "Do you think you can manage?"

"I do. It's much simpler than I thought. How marvelous. I can help you make these for sale."

"Between that and the eggs, I get by just fine. Folks in our neighborhood here on the river are good. We take care of one another. We women can food and quilt together, and most of the men work the lake and are good to bring the widows fish and sometimes other meats."

As if to prove her point, someone knocked at the door.

It turned out to be Mr. Farstad. Kirstin wasn't surprised. He extended a brown paper–wrapped package and grinned.

"*Vad är det?*" Mormor appraised the package.

"A pork roast. I traded for it at Johnsson's farm. I thought we might enjoy it tomorrow."

Mormor looked at Kirstin. "We usually take our meals together since we are both alone."

"But what about Mr. Farstad's son?" Kirstin had been curious about Mr. Farstad's son since her arrival.

"My Ilian works at the same lumber camp as—" Mr. Farstad stopped abruptly and cleared his throat. "He works with his friends up north about thirty miles from town. He lives at the camp, as the lumbermen do. So I am alone usually, and your grandmother kindly cooks for me."

"And Mr. Farstad often brings me things to cook for us."

"Ja, but tonight is special. Tonight, we do not work. We are going to a restaurant where they will do the cooking and the cleaning up. Your grandmother agreed to it yesterday, and I

24

made all the arrangements. It's my treat." He grinned from ear to ear. "We will eat there at five thirty. It's called the Brewery because they make beer there as well." He turned back to the door. "I gotta go now. I have work to do even if we can't run the dredger. We got repairs to make."

"Why can't you run the dredger?" Kirstin asked.

Mr. Farstad chuckled. "The ground, it is frozen solid. We had to stop working on our canal because it was too hard to dig, and the water, it is frozen. Makes it too hard on the equipment. But we'll get that canal built, by golly."

Kirstin shook her head. "What canal?"

"Oh sure, you wouldn't know too much about that. We are making a canal so that the ships can come straight into Duluth without having to first go past Superior, Wisconsin," Mr. Farstad said.

Mormor nodded. "The town has been fighting with those folks in Superior. They don't want us to have our own way in from the lake. They think it will cause problems for the bay and the breakwaters. They think they're superior." She laughed at her joke.

"All these words I don't understand." Kirstin switched to Swedish and put her hand to her head. "I thought my English was good, but apparently I have a lot to learn. What is *breakwater*?"

"You're doing just fine," Mr. Farstad declared. "You just keep asking, and we will teach you. The army came and built some breakwaters—sort of like walls in the water—to protect the coast and the harbor. Some have been destroyed, though, because Lake Superior is a fierce beast at times."

"And Superior, Wisconsin," Mormor added, "doesn't want

us to succeed. They didn't want Duluth to get the railroad, and now they don't want us having a ship canal for direct access into our own harbor."

"Well, that hardly seems right," Kirstin replied.

"That's the way we all feel. Folks ought to be able to do with their own land what they want." Mormor nodded at Mr. Farstad. "Thanks, Habram, for the roast. We'll enjoy it for sure tomorrow."

"I already checked, and Mr. Bemford said we can use his carriage and horse. I'll come by for you at five fifteen. It's pretty cold out there, so you'd better dress warm." He headed for the door. "I might be back early, Miss Kirstin, and if I am, I can show you the boat I'm working on."

"A Mackinaw boat?" she asked.

"Ja. Just like your morfar used to make."

"I would love to see it." Kirstin remembered letters Mormor had written detailing what Morfar was doing with his latest boat. It would be fun to have Mr. Farstad show her one.

Mormor saw him out and put the roast in the icebox before settling back to work on the nets. Kirstin could see a gleam in her grandmother's eyes that only seemed to appear when Mr. Farstad was around.

"He's a good man, ja?"

Kirstin's grandmother gave a nod and began knotting strands of twine. "Ja, he's a good one, to be sure." She changed the subject. "Tell me about everyone at home. How is your little sister, Brita?"

"Brita was great when I left, although she was sad that I was going. We are pretty close despite the years between us. She's just starting to like boys and would ask me for advice."

"And you would give it."

"Of course. That's what God has given me to do—give advice and fix problems." Kirstin smiled. "I know more than most, not because of experience, but because of following the Bible. I try to listen to people rather than talk all the time. You taught me that, Mormor."

"And it has made you pretty wise. Your mor, she writes all the time about how you manage people like so many sheep. Always trying to steer them down the right path. I think maybe people have been hard on you for being so smart, ja?"

"Sometimes." Kirstin shrugged. "They mostly misunderstand my reasons. They think me nosy or bossy, but in truth I just like order and sensible decisions."

"What of emotions and romance?" Mormor asked with a glint in her eye. "How is it that you aren't married? What was wrong with those boys?"

"Some wanted to marry, but I did not want them." Kirstin smiled and worked on her knots. "Mama always told me I'd know the right one when he came along, but none of them were right, as far as I could tell. Most of them were too concerned with their own plans to hear what I might like, and most didn't care a fig about God and church. They drank too much and swore too often."

"Well, your mor is right. You'll know the right one when he comes along, but just remember not to be too proud. If God has given you wisdom, that is good, ja. But you must be careful not to offend with your confidence. Some people . . . they cannot understand this confidence. Especially in one so young."

Kirstin frowned. "I know people think that sometimes, but I try never to be proud."

"Good," her grandmother said, smiling. "Then you will no doubt attract a husband sooner than you think."

"Sometimes I think he won't ever come." Kirstin sighed. "But I have put my trust in God, and He takes good care of me." She didn't bother to add that despite her trust in God, she was dying of loneliness. She wanted very much to be married—to have a dearest friend in a husband. She longed to feel the warmth of a man's arms around her to reassure her when times were hard—when she was afraid. All her family had been there for her, as well as God, but this was different. She longed for the companionship that only a husband and wife could know. And not just the physical aspect, but that close oneness that came with years of trust and living together. Like her mother and father had. Like Mormor and Morfar used to have. After all, what was the sense of having so much wisdom if she had no family of her own with which to share it?

"Tell me about your mor. Is she happy?" Mormor asked.

Kirstin considered the question for a moment. "Sometimes." She saw her grandmother frown and hurried on. "Ja, for the most part she is happy, but she's never gotten over losing Domar. She misses him every day and goes to the cemetery, where they put a stone for him at the family plot. She says a mother never gets over the loss of a child."

"Ja, that's true."

Kirstin glanced at her grandmother. "Did you lose children too, Mormor? I mean, besides Uncle Per."

"I had a stillborn baby before your mor was born. We called him Bjorn. He was born looking so beautiful and perfect. The doctor had no idea why he had died. When we put him in the ground, I wanted to follow after him. I was so heartbroken." There were tears in Mormor's eyes, so full of loss.

"I'm so sorry. I didn't mean to make you sad. Losing Domar, especially given the situation, has haunted Mor all these years. But she should never have doubted him and believed the worst of him. That was wrong. They should never have forced him to leave Sweden." Kirstin turned back to her work. "When I have children, I will always believe in them, even if they do terrible things—I will love them and never send them away."

"Your mother knew how difficult it would be for everyone if Domar stayed in the village and lived as one who was shunned. Have you never considered how hard that would have been on her?"

"You want me to have sympathy for Mor, and I do." Kirstin pushed back her long single braid. "I have great compassion for Mor and Far. They have suffered for their decision, but that is the consequences of what they chose to do. They sent Domar away to live here with you, and instead the ship sank, and he was forever lost to us. At least until we are all called to be together with Jesus."

Mormor smiled. "I'm certainly glad to see you have kept your faith in God."

"'The fear of the Lord is the beginning of wisdom: and the knowledge of the holy is understanding,'" Kirstin murmured, remembering the Proverbs nine verse.

She knew there weren't words enough to explain how she might very well have taken her own life when Domar died if not for her faith in God. She had never been as close to any of her siblings as she was with Domar. Härse and Svena were closer in age, but Domar had spent more time with Kirstin.

Domar had taken her on walks and taught her to fish. Domar had read to her before she had much interest in books. Oh, and the long talks they'd had. Domar had confided all his dreams for the future, and Kirstin had done likewise. At least until he was forced to leave. Yes, it was God alone who got her through that horrible time and the terrible accusations put upon her brother.

"My faith in God is everything to me, Mormor. Everything."

After helping Mormor into her seat at the table, Habram assisted Kirstin with hers As he'd promised on the ride over, the restaurant was quite nice. Each table was decorated with a linen tablecloth and napkins, as well as a lighted lamp. It made the room bright and cheery. At the end of the room was a large stone fireplace. At this time, however, it was blazing with a wealth of large logs, and on the spit a roasted pig was being slowly turned over the flame. The aroma was impressive and made Hambram's stomach rumble at the thought of what was to come.

"This was so nice of you, Habram. I haven't eaten here since the last time you invited me." Mormor spread her linen napkin on her lap.

"I've never eaten anywhere like this," Kirstin admitted. "We never went to restaurants back in Sweden."

"Well, we will treat you right here in America," Habram declared.

"It can get a little smoky in here with all these lamps," Mormor added. "Hot too, but on a night like this, no one will complain."

A waitress soon appeared, listing off a few meals they had to offer that evening. They all agreed on beef stew, baked apples, and rye bread with butter.

"Lots of butter," Habram requested.

"Will you have beer to drink?" the waitress asked.

"No, we'll have that hot apple cider you make." Habram looked at Kirstin. "You'll like it. It warms you clear through. Perfect for a night like tonight." As if on cue, the wind picked up and rattled a nearby window.

"It sounds perfect."

"So, do you think you will like Duluth?" Habram asked Kirstin as the waitress returned to the kitchen. He had been observing her all evening, and she seemed quite content. He knew that would please her grandmother.

"I do. It's very pleasant, even with all the snow and cold. I've always loved the cold. Far said I'm a winter baby through and through. In fact, I arrived in America on my birthday, December thirtieth."

"We'll have to celebrate it tonight, since you had no one to cheer you on the day," Habram declared. "We'll have some cobbler with our supper."

"No, we don't need to fuss." Kirstin shook her head. "The people I befriended on the ship were good to me. We had our own little celebration. Now, tell me what spring is like here. When will it come?"

Mormor patted her hand. "Spring is late, like in much of Sweden, but so lovely. A lot of wildflowers grow in the fields, and I usually plant a few of them in pots to keep things pretty around the house."

"We plant some vegetables too." Habram toyed with his silverware. "But we won't be able to stir the dirt until much later. Maybe even as late as May. Some years it stays so cold that the ground is frozen through until it's nearly time for summer." He chuckled. "Which is why we aren't dredging the canal right now. The ground is frozen solid."

"So your canal must wait."

"Ja, and folks in Duluth are not happy about that." Habram paused as the waitress put their tankards of cider on the table. "You be careful, there, Kirstin. It'll be plenty hot."

Kirstin nodded and lifted her mug to blow on the liquid.

Habram toasted the ladies with his tankard. "To the two prettiest gals in town." He tested the drink. "Ah, just right. I like it hot." He watched as Lena and her granddaughter sampled the drink. The expressions on their faces showed their approval. "It's good, ja?"

"Ja," Kirstin replied. "*Det är bra.*" She tried it again and then put the mug down. "Very good. Mr. Farstad, tell me about your canal. Are you the one digging it?"

"No, my good friend Major John Upham is doing it. He owns the company and has dredged all around this area. He knows what he's doing there, by golly. He's going to make us a good canal, despite what Superior folks say."

"Why are they so against the canal?" Kirstin asked.

The waitress appeared with a tray holding three big bowls of stew and smaller bowls of baked apples. She deposited these and went back to the kitchen. When she returned, she brought the bread and butter, as well as salt.

"Ah, now we eat." Habram took the bread and butter. "This is good."

The waitress placed the salt on the table. "If you need something, just give me a wave."

"Ja, we will do that." Habram looked everything over to make sure it was in order.

"Will you say grace for us, Habram?" Lena asked.

"Of course I will." He bowed his head and blessed the food. He also prayed blessings on Lena and Kirstin and the boys who were logging and the boys digging the canal. "Amen."

"Amen," Lena declared loudly, while Kirstin merely whispered.

"When do you think you can start work again on the canal?" Kirstin asked as she took up her knife and fork to cut the beef.

"As soon as the thaw comes. Maybe April. There's still some work happening to shore up and strengthen the sides. We're going to have a good canal, and it won't cause all the problems they're worried about."

"With the breakwater?"

"You remembered the word." Habram beamed her a smile. She was a smart young woman. Lena had told him that even at a young age Kirstin preferred the company of older women to those her own age.

"I want to learn better English," Kirstin said. "Far said he wanted all of his children to speak several languages, but especially English."

"Maybe one day your folks will come to America," Lena replied.

"I don't know," Kirstin said, shaking her head. "Mor has been afraid of ships and big water ever since Domar died." She reached for a piece of rye bread. "But we won't talk of that now. Tell me more about your canal, Mr. Farstad."

Habram smiled. "It's going to be a great thing. It will make

Duluth rich because the ships will sail right into Duluth and won't have to go to Superior first."

The wind again rattled the windows. He could see that Lena was getting concerned.

"Maybe we could have them pack up our food so we can take it home to eat," he suggested.

"Take it home?" Kirstin laughed. "Whoever heard of such a thing?"

"Sometimes it's best that way when the storms come up quick," he explained. "It might give us a terrible snow and make it impossible to get the horse and carriage home."

"Ja, he's right. Sometimes the weather here can be quite bad. The restaurant is good to help us. We just have to bring back the dishes," Lena declared. "We can take it home, Habram. That will be good."

Habram signaled their waitress. She arrived at the table looking rather harried. "You want to take it home?" she asked.

Lena and Habram nodded, and Kirstin followed suit. "Ja," Habram replied. "Before the snow makes it so we have to live here in the brewery." He chuckled and turned to the ladies. "Which might not be so bad."

Lena rolled her eyes as she often did when he made light of bad situations. "It will be better for all of us that we get home and build up our fires."

Habram knew she was right, but he loved her company and wasn't at all eager to be without her. "Ja. We'll go home."

Chapter 3

Kirstin listened to the wind howl all night long. Every time she woke up, it was raging and her windows were rattling. She had known storms like these in Sweden. Sometimes they went on for days, making it hard to take care of the animals and other chores around the farm. The wind could make a person feel exhausted. The constant howling could even drive a man to madness.

She missed her family and the farmhouse Far and the boys had built for them. Everyone had built it, truth be told, even Mormor and Morfar. It was while building that house that Kirstin had learned how to drive nails and sand boards for the floor. It had been such a milestone in their family. They couldn't own the land, but the nobleman who did own it gave them permission to build their own house—and that they did own. It was a moment of true pride for her father.

Tossing and turning throughout the night, Kirstin dreamed of home and of her trip to America. She had been a little afraid of the ocean crossing, knowing it had taken the life of her brother eleven years earlier. She was so relieved when land came in sight again that she thought she might kiss the dirt as some of the other immigrants had.

When morning came, Kirstin was surprised to awaken to silence. The wind had stopped, and it seemed the world was at peace once again. She went to her window and opened the shutters to have a look. The sun's reflection on the snow blinded her and made it impossible to see much. The sun felt warm through the window, but not warm enough. Shivering, she pulled on her red robe and made her way downstairs. She hoped Mormor had stoked up the fire, but if not, Kirstin would do it herself.

She found Mormor sitting in the rocker, warming herself by the hearth. A ball of yarn was in her lap, and knitting needles clicked as she worked on what looked to be a shawl.

"Come get warm," Mormor said. "I tried to keep the fire going strong all night, but I sleep too hard come morning. It's a cold house today."

"That's all right. I don't mind at all. The quilts were very warm." Kirstin moved closer to the fire and held out her hands. "I should have thought to come down and check on the fire, and I certainly didn't mean to sleep so late. After all, I'm here to help you." She turned and warmed her backside and glanced toward the shuttered windows in the living room. "How much snow did we get?"

"Only a few inches. I guess it was more wind than anything, which is just fine by me. I didn't want Habram to have to shovel too much."

"He would do just about anything for you." Kirstin grinned. "You have a beau, Mormor."

Her grandmother chuckled. "We have both been lonely, so it's good to have a friend."

"Does Mr. Habram's son ever visit?"

"Ja, and he stays with me. Not with Habram. They have too many problems, and neither has patience to work it out with the other. Ilian holds a grudge against his father."

"Well, maybe I can help him see the good in reconciliation. I love to bring folks together. Especially family. It's so important that we not forsake our family."

"That is true, but maybe just give it some time. People tend to resent strangers interfering in their business."

"Ja, I know you're right, so I won't be a stranger." Kirstin turned again to warm the front of her body. Now the extra room upstairs made sense. "Does Ilian use the room upstairs when he comes to stay?"

Mormor glanced up from her knitting. "Ja. He uses that room. I'll have to give him Per's room when he comes next time. It wouldn't be good to have you two upstairs alone. Who knows what kind of horseplay might come about?" Her tone was jovial and not at all accusing.

"*Horse-play*? This is an American word?"

"Ja. It means you like each other and maybe steal a kiss or snuggle on the sofa."

"Mormor! I am a good Christian woman. I don't horse-play."

The old woman chuckled. "You will, one day."

Kirstin felt her cheeks flush but didn't know if the cause was Mormor's words or the fire. She turned her back to the fire once more. "What would you like me to do today? Should we make more nets?"

"Maybe later. I planned to clean this morning. I've already put the roast on to cook all day. We'll have a nice meal tonight. But first you eat. There's oatmeal on the back of the stove and cream on the back porch. If you want something sweet, there's brown sugar or honey. Nothing fancy, but filling."

"Sounds perfect, and I can definitely help with cleaning."

Kirstin went to the kitchen and took a bowl down from the cupboard. She scooped up oatmeal, then found the cream and sugar.

Returning to the fire, she looked her grandmother. "May I eat it here by the fire?"

"Of course. We do not stand on ceremony here."

Kirstin sampled the cereal, then gave it a gentle stir. "Where would you like me to start with cleaning?" She looked around the room.

"Well, first you can help me gather the eggs. There won't be very many. Only a few of my hens like to lay in the winter. Habram will bring us more milk from his cow. He doesn't use much for himself and generally gives it to me to make things that I share with him."

"Why don't you two marry?" Kirstin hadn't meant to blurt it out, but now that she had, there was no sense trying to take it back.

Mormor refocused on her knitting. "The Lord hasn't told us that it's time yet. We will wait for His timing."

"So you are in love." It was more statement than question. Kirstin had never thought for even one minute that she'd come to America and find her grandmother on the verge of remarrying.

"We love each other well enough. More importantly, we take care of each other." Mormor smiled.

"So you really didn't need me."

"That isn't true," Mormor said, stopping her work. "When I heard you were coming, I was so happy. Habram was too."

"I was so happy to come. I missed you so much. All those years without you and Morfar and Uncle Per were so empty. A girl needs her grandmother."

"I missed you too. I never really wanted to leave Sweden, but Per wanted to own land and find a wife. Your grandfather thought it would be a great adventure to see America."

"And was it?"

"Ja. Our entire life was a great adventure. At first I wasn't sure why God would have us be here, but when that became apparent, I was glad we were obedient."

"And what was the reason God wanted you here?"

Mormor looked rather hesitant. "I'll tell you by and by, but for now my mind is full to overflowing with how happy I am that you are here to be a part of my life in America. I'm so blessed. You are important to me, and I will cherish our time together. You'll see. It will be the very best thing for all of us."

By afternoon they had washed the walls and inside windows and wiped down all of the trim and shutters. They had also swept and scrubbed the floors after strategically moving the furniture around the room in order to do small portions at a time. At noon they ate pickled herring and boiled eggs with Swedish rye bread that Mormor had made. After that they got to work again, and just as Kirstin finished polishing the kitchen table with lemon oil, a knock sounded on the front door.

"That's probably Habram," Mormor called from the kitchen. "Go ahead and let him in, but tell him to take off his boots. I'm not going to let all this cleaning be for nothing."

Kirstin nodded and opened the door with a smile. "Good afternoon, Mr.—" She halted. It wasn't Habram.

"Well, good morning to you, pretty miss. Is your . . . is Mrs. Segerson home?"

"Ja. You may come in, but take off your boots," Kirstin said, glancing down at his feet. "We just cleaned."

"Of course." He took the chair just inside the door and began to pull his boots off one at a time. "And I'll hang my hat and coat on the peg like before."

"What is your name? I'll tell my grandmother that you've come."

"Mr. Jordan Webster. She knows me."

Kirstin went into the pantry room at the back of the kitchen. "Mr. Webster has come to see you."

Mormor dusted off her hands. "Pesky man. Seat him to the table. I'll bring the coffee."

Kirstin returned and found Webster standing by the kitchen table. "Have a seat there, please. Mormor—my grandmother is bringing the coffee."

"Yes, I see her now. Mrs. Segerson, good afternoon."

"Ja, it is, and very busy too. Would you like some coffee and cake?"

"I would. Your refreshments are always the best in the neighborhood."

"Then have a seat."

He sat at the table like an obedient schoolboy. Kirstin wondered what this man had to do with her grandmother. She remembered nothing mentioned of him in Mormor's letters. Then again, perhaps he was a new visitor from the past few months.

Mormor brought him a cup of coffee and a slice of *smörkaka*—

butter cake—then went back to fetch cream and sugar. "Join us, Kirstin." It sounded like a command, so Kirstin went to get herself a cup of coffee and sat with them at the table. She sipped her coffee, then poured a generous amount of cream in the cup. Mormor made coffee like Far did—strong enough to strip the morning from his eyes, as he always said.

"How have you been, Mrs. Segerson?"

"Since you were here last week?" Mormor smiled and glanced at Kirstin. "I am doing very fine. My granddaughter has come to live with me. So you see, I am not going to sell my house anytime soon."

Mr. Webster looked at Kirstin and gave her a smile, seeming to ignore the latter comment. "And where have you come from, Miss Segerson?"

"My name is Hallberg," Kirstin corrected. "Miss Kirstin Hallberg. I came here from Sweden, where my parents still live."

"Ah, well, it's very nice to make your acquaintance. And you've come to live with your grandmother?"

"Ja." Kirstin couldn't help but wonder what he was up to. Mormor had mentioned something about selling her house. Perhaps Mr. Webster wanted to buy it. At least, that was what she felt was implied. "And why have you come to see my grandmother, Mr. Webster?"

He chuckled. "I like a woman who speaks her mind. I have been trying to get your grandmother and her neighbors to sell me their properties. You see, I want to build a very fine hotel on this land."

"But then where would they live?"

"Well, I would pay them a fair price, and they would buy new property."

"Mr. Webster doesn't seem to understand that we have no interest in moving from this place. This is our home and neighborhood. We helped build one another's houses. We help each other every day and are the best of friends. We wouldn't have that if we moved away," Mormor interjected.

Kirstin looked at the handsome stranger. His dark hair and blue eyes were captivating and quite beautiful. He had long eyelashes for a man. Mor would say he was too pretty for a boy and that those lashes were wasted on him. Kirstin smiled at the thought.

"You seem very happy today, Miss Hallberg."

"I'm always happy, Mr. Webster, though that is hardly your concern." She nodded toward his cup. "Would you like more coffee?"

"Yes, please."

Kirstin went to the stove, where the pot was warming on the back. What manner of man was this that he would pester Mormor about buying her house even when she'd made it clear she had no desire to sell?

"Here you are." She put the coffee on the table as he pushed back his empty cake plate.

"We're very busy with our cleaning today, Mr. Webster," Mormor began. "I am sorry to keep disappointing you, but I cannot help you. We have talked in the neighborhood, and no one wants to move."

"Yes, but many assure me they would sell and move if you did."

"So you see," she continued, "we aren't interested in leaving."

"But, Mrs. Segerson, there are so many beautiful properties available to which you could move."

42

"Perhaps you could use those properties for your luxury hotel." Mormor got to her feet. "I'm afraid I must finish my work in the pantry. Kirstin will show you out."

"Please. Just listen to reason. I don't want to do this in such a manner as to force your hand."

Mormor frowned. "You do what you feel you have to do, Mr. Webster. Good day."

Kirstin had never seen anyone in her family be quite this dismissive with someone. She sat momentarily surprised by her grandmother's reaction and wondered what she should do. Thankfully, Mr. Webster got to his feet.

"I suppose I have worn out my welcome."

Kirstin rose and nodded. "I don't think Mormor wants to sell her house." She smiled. "I'm sorry."

"So am I. I'm afraid it won't bode well for these people. I might have paid them a decent price, but now they'll be lucky to get half of what I would have offered. When I'm done meeting with the town council, the people here will be sorry for not having been more cooperative."

Kirstin frowned. "You sound almost threatening, but it must be my poor English. A gentleman would surely never be so inconsiderate."

"I am a gentleman, Miss Hallberg, but I am not a fool. I'm used to getting what I want, however, and I intend to have this land. You can tell that to your grandmother." He finished pulling on his boots and reached for his outer coat and hat.

Kirstin had no idea what to say to him, so she said nothing. There was nothing that would offer him comfort anyway. Once he was gone, Kirstin locked the door in case he had any ideas of returning and letting himself into the place.

"Mormor, who is that man, and why is he being so firm about taking your house?"

"He wants everyone's land in this area. He has it in his mind to build some sort of lake resort, even though we're in the bay and river area. It's on the water here, yet protected, and with his desire to build several floors, he says people will be able to see the lake quite nicely and yet be right in the city at the same time. He's pushy, and it will get him nowhere."

"Well, he seems to think it will. He said to tell you that he's used to getting what he wants and he intends to have this land."

"Folks have all sorts of intentions, but they are often unrewarded. He'll have to have his disappointment and move on."

"He sounded menacing there at the end. You don't think he means to cause anyone physical harm, do you?"

"Oh, I don't think so. He's spoiled. You can tell his folks probably never denied him." Mormor finished dusting the rows of jars holding her canned meats. "I'm sure he'll get over it."

Another knock sounded at the front door. Kirstin put out her hand as Mormor started for the door. "I'll get it. Maybe he forgot something. I wouldn't want you to have to deal with it."

Kirstin made her way back to the front of the house and opened the door as she glanced at the row of pegs beside her. Mr. Webster hadn't left anything behind that she could see. When she turned back to the door, she found her brother Domar staring at her, open-mouthed.

"You . . . but you're . . . you're dead." Kirstin felt her breath catch.

The handsome young man standing behind her brother gave him a punch in the arm and laughed. "You hear that, Domar? You're dead."

Her brother shoved the man away. "Don't be cruel. Can't you see this is a shock to her?" He turned back to Kirstin. "I didn't expect you either. I'm sorry for the shock. I truly am. Where's Mormor?"

Kirstin backed up, but she couldn't speak.

Domar eased past her. "Mormor, are you here?"

Their grandmother emerged from the pantry and looked first at Kirstin and then Domar. "Oh dear. I wasn't expecting you this week, Domar."

The handsome man who'd accompanied Kirstin's brother stepped into the house in order to close the door.

"You boys take off your boots. We've been cleaning all day," Mormor commanded.

Domar immediately undid the lacings on his boots, but the man beside Kirstin hesitated.

"What are you waiting for, Ilian?" Domar asked.

Kirstin looked back and forth between her brother and the handsome man as her vision blurred and tunneled to black.

"I think your sister is going to faint."

That was the last thing Kirstin heard.

Chapter 4

"Well, there you are. You've made her faint," Mrs. Segerson told Domar. "I wasn't expecting you until next week, and I haven't had a chance to tell her you're still alive. Ilian, bring her to the kitchen table. I'll get some smelling salts."

Ilian looked down into the face of the petite woman he held. Her honey-brown hair had been plaited into a single braid, but bits of hair had come loose. He found himself tempted to sweep them away from her face as she slept.

He brought her to the table and then, not knowing what else to do, took a seat still holding her in his arms.

"This should wake her up." Mrs. Segerson waved the open bottle of ammonia under the girl's nose.

Domar's sister sputtered and gave a sharp jerk to get away from the smell. Ilian held her tight. "Whoa, now. Don't be fighting so."

She opened her eyes and grew still. "Who are you?"

Ilian chuckled. "I'm the man who caught you before you hit the floor. Ilian Farstad."

"You're Mr. Farstad's son, ja?" She shook her head as if trying to regain her senses.

Ilian forced himself not to frown. "Ja. That's who I am."

"Domar?" she whispered and grabbed Ilian's arm. "Is he . . . did he . . ." She sat up slightly and looked around.

"He's here." Ilian kept his voice soft so as not to startle her.

"I'm so sorry, Kirstin. I didn't get a chance to tell you that Domar is alive," her grandmother apologized, taking the seat opposite Ilian and Kirstin. "I was going to tell you soon, since they planned to come here next week. I didn't know they were coming today."

"The wind caused a lot of problems, and the boss sent us for more chains," Domar explained.

Ilian said nothing. He rather liked the feel of Domar's sister in his arms, and she seemed not in the least hurry to move. In fact, she was gripping his arm rather tightly. Of course, she had just seen a ghost.

She finally found her voice. "How can you be alive?"

"Why don't you tell her the full story, Domar?" Mrs. Segerson suggested.

Domar nodded. "What do you know about what happened . . . with Willa and Olaf?"

"Your friend Olaf put her in the family way but said it was you," Kirstin answered. "Everyone turned against you, even Mor and Far."

"So you pretty much know what happened," Domar replied.

"No, I don't. You died on the ship coming to America. That's what I know." She looked at Ilian as if he might offer answers.

Ilian shifted his weight and hers. "Let him explain."

Kirstin looked back at Domar. It seemed she still didn't register that a complete stranger was holding her. Not that Ilian minded.

"Olaf and I were very close, as you know," Domar began. "Willa too. We were all dear friends, but then Olaf and Willa began spending more alone time together, and she became . . . pregnant."

"What a word," Mrs. Segerson said, rolling her eyes.

"With child," Domar corrected. "But it so terrified Olaf because he knew his father expected great things of him, and Willa was from a poor family. So even though he loved her, Olaf ran away and blamed me. He told Willa's father that I was the one responsible. When Mr. Bergquist came to demand I marry Willa, I told him I was not the father and would not marry her. That started the whole problem."

Kirstin nodded. "But you weren't the father." Her voice was barely a whisper.

"Ja. It's true, I was not. But not even Mor and Far would believe me. No one but you."

"But they do now. Olaf told everyone he lied. At first everyone thought he was just saying that for your sake, but when the baby was born with Olaf's red hair, they knew better. I was so mad at Mor and Far that I was very unkind." Kirstin seemed to be getting over her shock. "I told them they were wrong not to believe in their son."

"No one in Sweden rallied behind me, save you." Domar smiled. "You were always faithful, Kirstin, and I appreciate that more than you will ever know. When they made me leave town, you were the only one I regretted telling good-bye. I was so hurt by the others that I didn't care about leaving everyone and everything."

"What about the ship and the wreck?" she asked, loosening her grip on Ilian's arm.

Domar shrugged. "The ship hit a bad storm. We were nearly to Nova Scotia and thought we'd be all right. They pressed on, thinking it the best they could do, but it was too much for the old ship. She began to break apart when we were still five miles out. Five miles can seem like five hundred when you're on the water and you're being lashed by wave and wind. It soon became clear all hope was lost, and the ship was abandoned. I was blown from the deck into the water and felt certain I was meant for a watery grave, but one of the sailors managed to get me to safety. He and I alone survived. The rest of the lifeboats capsized."

"Yet you let us believe you were dead." Her tone was accusing.

"He had good reason, don't you think?" Ilian asked.

She looked at him for a moment, then seemed to realize all at once that she was being held by a man she didn't know. "What are you doing?" She pushed him away and got to her feet.

"Be nice to him, Kirstin. He saved you from hitting the floor," Domar said, smiling. "It's not his fault you fainted."

"I fainted because the dead had come back to life." She took the chair between Ilian and her grandmother, then nodded at Ilian. "Thank you for catching me."

Ilian raised his brows and grinned. "I assure you it was my pleasure."

Kirstin ignored him and focused on her brother. "It's been nearly eleven years. You let us believe you had died. How could you be so cruel?"

Domar sobered. "I thought it was for the best. No one believed me when I gave them the truth. Why should I be honest with them about my survival? I figured they'd all be happy to have me out of their lives."

"But Olaf confessed that the child was his. He made things right and married Willa, despite his father being less than pleased. They're quite happy now and have four children."

"I'm glad he did the right thing, but it was too late for me. The villagers didn't give me a chance. They called me a liar and shunned me. They shamed our parents and spoke badly of them. You have no idea the horrible things they said in judgment. They didn't care about the truth. Even our parents chose to believe someone else over me."

Kirstin bit her lip for a moment. "But, Domar, you were a rather wild young man. You liked your drink and acted selfishly at times."

"I did. But I always admitted my wrongdoing. I never lied, and Mor and Far knew that full well. Yet they chose not to believe me when I told them what was going on. They didn't encourage anyone to believe me. Only you did. That's why when Mormor told me you were coming, I was glad. I've always wanted you to know I'm alive."

"Mormor, how could you do this?" Kirstin asked, turning to her grandmother for an answer. "You kept this from your own daughter, knowing the pain Domar's death caused her. How could you do that?"

"I made Domar a promise." Mrs. Segerson looked at the smelling salts in her hand rather than face her granddaughter's accusing stare. Ilian felt sorry for her. Lena Segerson had been nothing but kind to him, even though she had a great friendship with his father, whom Ilian despised.

"What kind of promise?" Kirstin demanded.

Mrs. Segerson hesitated for several long moments.

"Please, Mormor. Tell me so I can understand. My mother has mourned the loss of her firstborn all these years. She has hated herself for not believing him and has blamed herself for his death. How could either of you be so heartless? I was angry at Mor and Far and our brother and sister as well. Brita, of course, was too little to blame Domar, but the others knew better. It tore our family apart, and yet the two of you did nothing."

"They didn't deserve anything else. They sent me away," Domar replied.

Kirstin got to her feet. She looked at her brother and then grandmother and finally turned to Ilian before resettling on Domar. "You were hurt by what they did. I understand that fully. I was hurt by it too. But while they acted out of ignorance, you *chose* to put a knife in your mother's heart. How could you?"

"They put that knife in my hands, Kirstin. They told me they never wanted to see me again. Told me I was dead to them. So I left, and when the opportunity came to be dead, I was only fulfilling their own words. Now I am truly dead to them."

Kirstin shook her head, and Ilian saw tears in her eyes. "But they learned the truth and were sorry. They wanted to tell you so, but because they thought you were dead, they could not."

"And I count that as justice. A person should never pass judgment on what is not theirs to judge. Yet an entire village passed it on me, and still you think me cruel." Domar crossed his arms.

"I do." Kirstin seemed to calm a bit. "I think you and Mormor were both wrong for keeping this secret, and I hope you do not intend for me to keep it, because I will not. I've watched our mother suffer. Would you like to know what she did after

51

you left? She spent every day in prayer for you. When word came that the ship had gone down, she took to her bed in such sorrow and grief that I thought she might die."

Ilian saw Domar's face pale. The grief in his expression was evident. For all the times that they had spoken of the past, Ilian doubted his friend had ever really considered the pain he'd caused his mother by denying her the truth.

"When we were finally able to get her to at least sit in a chair, she had already lost so much weight that her nightgown was ready to fall off her shoulders," Kirstin continued. "I had to alter all her clothes. She would barely take broth, and the doctor told us she might well die from her sadness. And lest you think I agreed that what they had done was right, I was at constant odds with them. I boldly spoke my heart before we learned about your death, and even afterward, I used it as a reminder that we dare not judge one another. I am still angry at them for not believing you. Still angry at them for turning you away, but now . . . now I am angry at you for letting us believe you were dead. I don't know that I can ever forgive you for this." She frowned as tears slipped down her cheek. "Nor you, Mormor, for you know the pain of losing a child, and yet you let my poor mother endure it for herself."

She turned and stormed from the room, sobs breaking from her as she fled for the stairs. Ilian looked at the pain-stricken faces of his friends. He didn't like the way Kirstin had treated her grandmother and brother, but he could understand her reasoning. He had his own issues with family. He had never forgiven his father for the way he'd treated his mother. All Ilian's mother had ever wanted was to return to Sweden, and yet his father had never allowed her that dream.

"Well, she's right, you know," Mrs. Segerson said, staring at the wall. "I deserve her anger."

"No, Mormor, this wasn't your fault. It's mine, and I will speak to her once she calms. She doesn't understand what it is to be abandoned. She doesn't know the pain I endured. Coming to America was a choice for her. I was given none. This has been a joy for her, but it was a nightmare for me." Domar looked at Ilian. "I'm sorry you had to be in the middle of this."

"Think nothing of it. I have my own problems, as you well know."

"We are all sinful beings," Domar's grandmother stated. "We deserve wrath, but God's mercy gave us love."

Ilian didn't think much of God's mercy. It was never evident in his mother's life, nor his. God, at best, was indifferent. Domar's life proved it, as did his own.

⁓

Kirstin sat on the edge of her bed and tried to sort through what had just happened. How could her brother be alive eleven years after they thought him dead? How could Mormor have kept this from them?

She held her head in her hands and cried. Cried for the years of loss—years that might have been filled instead with healing and joy. She cried for her mother, who had wanted to die after learning her son was dead. Life had been most cruel. How could God allow such a thing?

Curling up on the end of the bed, Kirstin let herself have a good long cry. Seeing Domar again had stirred up that time in her life when she had felt so contrary to living a Christian life. Her anger and hatred had corrupted everything. Just as she had said, it had torn their family apart. Judgment had been poured over them all, and the wrath they felt was of their own making.

"God, I don't know how to handle this. I haven't been able to handle it since it first happened, but I kept putting it aside, hoping it would get better—that I would feel less pain. Now this happens, and in a way, it's like going through it all over again. What am I to do?"

Kirstin didn't mean to fall asleep, but that was what happened, and when she woke up, Domar was nudging her shoulder. "It's time for supper," he told her.

She sat up and jerked away, still stunned at the sight of him. For a moment all she could do was stare at him in the dim lamplight.

"How did you decide to let us think you were dead?" she murmured.

Domar sat on the edge of the bed. "I read my name in a list of those who'd been lost at sea. It was startling at first, and I thought I should surely tell someone, but then I kept hearing Far say, 'You are dead to me now.'"

"He didn't mean it."

"That's where you're wrong. He did. He was so disappointed in me, Kirstin. I knew I'd failed him many times. I'd seen an inkling of that look before, when he found me drunk and helped me home, but this was different. His accusation and unwillingness to believe me destroyed the love between us. All the good times we'd had as father and son were gone. The times when I'd pleased him as a boy were suddenly wiped away in light of my shame. My death was the only thing that could ease his misery."

"No! That isn't true. He loved you. He would love you now."

"Maybe, but you cannot tell them about me, Kirstin. I do not want them to know I'm alive."

"But why?"

He fell silent for a few moments, and Kirstin thought perhaps he wouldn't answer. She knew she couldn't promise to keep his secret. She couldn't know he was alive and keep it from their mother. Kirstin had the power to save her mother from the deep sorrow that had followed her since the day she'd sent her son to America. How could she not give her that?

"If you say anything to them, I will go away," Domar said. "I will leave and never let any of you know where I am."

She stared at him and shook her head. "Why? You still give me no reason."

Domar looked away. "Because if they know I am alive, they will demand I accept their forgiveness and require I beg their pardon in return."

"And you cannot do that?"

"No. I cannot. I'd rather be dead to them."

Chapter 5

Kirstin remained in her room for the rest of the day and evening, not even bothering to come out for supper. Domar's appearance had left her confused and filled with a myriad of conflicting emotions. Added to that were her thoughts toward Mormor. How could her grandmother have let eleven years pass and not once written home to let Kirstin's mother know Domar was alive?

Even as she pondered what had occurred, she heard Domar make his way into the adjacent bedroom. He'd turned her world upside down. Did he care? Would he be able to sleep tonight? She doubted she would.

After pacing and praying throughout the night, Kirstin gave up her attempts to sleep. She dressed in layers to go for a long walk. She hardly knew her way around but figured someone could always point her back to the house should she lose her way. She knew she probably should tell someone what she was doing, but it was very early, and frankly she didn't feel like talking to anyone.

After stoking the fireplace, she slipped out the front door

and started for the road. Sounds coming from the work shed between Mormor's house and the Farstad house, however, drew her attention. It was still dark outside, but lantern light shone in the window of the workshop. Against her better judgment, Kirstin went to see who was making the racket. She'd barely opened the door to peer inside when Mr. Farstad welcomed her in.

"Don't just stand there with the door open, come in and make yourself at home."

Kirstin hesitated. "I was going to go for a walk."

"It's too cold for that. Come in, and I'll show you the Mackinaw boat." He waved his hand across the half-built boat.

"It's much bigger than I thought it would be." Kirstin stepped forward and touched the wooden side with her mittened hand. "I bet it is fun to sail."

"They are quite pleasurable, and maybe one day I can take you out in one."

"Is this for yourself, or are you making it for someone else?"

"It's for someone else," he said, moving toward the bow. "But I'll have to take it out to test its seaworthiness, and you could come with me. I figure to have it done by late March."

Kirstin nodded. She noticed the woodstove at the end of the room and moved toward it. "Do you mind if I warm up? It is colder than I thought."

"Sure." He moved toward the stove and opened its small door. "Come get warm."

She did as he instructed and was grateful. "I met your son."

"Ja, I know. I came to supper. Lena always invites me, and even though I know Ilian won't say much to me, I go. I keep hoping."

"I know it's personal, but may I ask why he won't speak to you?"

Mr. Farstad shrugged and reached for some more wood. "He has his reasons. I'm not sure I understand them completely. He doesn't think I treated his mother right. She wanted to move back to Sweden, and I wouldn't go."

"Didn't she like America?"

His back was to her as he deposited the wood into the stove, but even so, Kirstin thought his shoulders slumped a bit. "She missed her sisters. They wrote letters back and forth all the time, but it wasn't the same for her. She liked getting together with them to gossip." He straightened and met her face with a smile. "So now you know. You know too that your brother is alive. I heard you fainted."

"Yes. Right into Ilian's arms. Very embarrassing." She turned to warm her back. "Shocking too. I am still so confused and, well, angry. I know you and Mormor are friends, but I'm thoroughly shocked by what she's done and . . . mad."

"Ja. I can imagine you would be." He stepped away from the stove to give her more room. "I was a little worried when you didn't come to supper. Lena said it was the shock and that you needed time to yourself."

"It was most certainly a shock to find the brother I thought dead is in fact alive. I couldn't make sense of it and fell asleep trying. It was probably God's mercy to me. I still can't understand why anyone would do something like that to people he supposedly loved. I can't make any more sense out of Ilian treating you badly because you couldn't take your wife back to Sweden for a visit. It seems just as cruel for him to hold it against you."

Mr. Farstad's gaze grew distant as he stared across the room. "It's not an easy thing, but folks always have their reasons."

"Reasons to perpetuate hate? I don't believe God would honor that, or the lies, one bit."

"No. God hates lies."

The sadness in his tone made Kirstin realize it wasn't worth discussing. Mr. Farstad had always been so lighthearted in her company. She looked back at the boat and smiled. "Why don't you show me the boat? It looks quite grand, or I'm sure it will be once it's finished."

"I'll show you the workshop first. Your morfar built it, and this was his favorite place—unless, of course, he could be by your grandmother's side. He always said, though, that this place made him happy."

"Why was Morfar so happy?"

Mr. Farstad showed her around the workshop. "He liked to work out here. He'd bring out a pot of coffee to keep warm on the stove, and the neighborhood men would come and share their news. There was always someone here with him." He pointed to half a dozen chairs. "Usually quite a few someones."

Kirstin imagined it for herself. She remembered her morfar being quite the talker. He'd never met a stranger and would help anyone who asked. "He had a bigger shop back in Sweden, and the same thing happened."

"He was always happiest in his shop, your mormor used to say."

"I remember him helping my brother Härse make furniture. Once they made me a dollhouse. It was quite nice and had a little table and chairs and beds and all sorts of things. Mor and Mormor made tiny curtains and rugs. Oh, and quilts for the beds. My dolls lived in luxury. I passed it down to my sister Brita when she turned five."

"A very nice present, I'm sure." He maneuvered to the side of the boat. "I build boats when I can. I always have someone who wants one, and they are quick to make. I get the wood locally. We have good wood here."

"What kind do you use?"

"You see there?" He pointed to the center of the boat. "I used oak for the keel and keelson, but most of the rest is pine and white cedar."

"It makes everything smell so good. I love the smell of wood. It reminds me of being a child. My brother was always making furniture. He and Morfar would make some of the most beautiful things."

"Ja, I remember your morfar talking about that. Your morfar was so talented at making these boats. He was always busy. Sometimes he would just make someone a canoe. But he liked the Mackinaws best of all. And the fishermen love them because they're swift and easy to maneuver."

Kirstin ran her fingers lightly along the planks. "It looks like a fat canoe."

Mr. Farstad laughed. "The men sometimes joke about them being 'expectant canoes.'"

His laugh made Kirstin giggle. "I suppose that makes sense. Mormor used to write about how fast Morfar could make them."

"Oh ja. He and I working together could build one in three weeks. Sometimes less. I think I was more of a liability then. I've seen your morfar work very fast indeed when there was a need. He would be out here for twenty hours at a stretch, catch a few hours' sleep, and then get right back to it. Once a man paid him to have the boat ready in two weeks. We both worked on that one, and your grandfather earned two hundred dollars for the boat. He was a wonder, your morfar. I sure miss him, by golly."

Kirstin nodded and felt the heaviness of all that was happening wash over her once again. Shaking her head, she moved back to the stove. "It's not right to have these secrets, Mr. Farstad."

The older man joined her, his expression wary. "Sometimes secrets must be kept. To tell them might make you feel better, even vindicated . . . but it might devastate someone else."

She thought his choice of words strange. Was that why she wanted to tell her folks about Domar? To feel vindicated? She was the only one to believe in him—to hold a continual trust in him. She'd been very proud of that. Was that her biggest reason for wanting to write to Mor and Far? Just so she could show off being right? No, surely it was more in keeping with her desire to fix wrongs and make them right. It wasn't personal. Or was it?

"But what about the pain those secrets have caused? Domar doesn't have to go home or ever see anyone back home again. But it would ease our mother's sorrow to know he lives." A single tear slid down her cheek.

"But maybe it wouldn't ease Domar's sorrow."

Kirstin frowned. She hadn't considered that. "I don't know. I can't imagine his sorrow is greater than Mor's."

"A comparison need not be made. One sorrow is not less important than another. Maybe you should talk to him more about it before you make up your mind. Sometimes people keep secrets for the greater good of everyone."

She wiped at her damp eyes. "You sound like someone who knows."

Mr. Farstad nodded. "I am. I have my secrets and my pain."

Mormor was fixing breakfast when Kirstin walked into the house. Without a word, Kirstin hung up her coat and hat and took off her boots. She put on the little slippers Mormor had given her, then put on her apron so she could help with the work.

"What would you like me to do?" she asked.

"Slice the bread and get it toasted. Thank you."

Kirstin did her best to make even slices of the sourdough loaf. She wasn't sure what to say to her grandmother, so she said nothing.

"I know you're very upset," Mormor began as she cracked eggs. "I know this has come as a great shock."

"It has."

"I remember the day Domar showed up here. We all thought him dead, and yet there he stood in the flesh. I was so happy to see him, and all I could think about was letting your mor know that he hadn't died. When he told me I couldn't say anything to her, it pierced my heart."

"Then why did you do it? Promise not to tell?"

Mormor sighed. "I suppose it was my selfishness. I didn't want to lose him again. I knew it wouldn't hurt her any more than she was already hurt if I said nothing."

"It will when she learns you've known for eleven years and said nothing."

"Ja. I suppose that's true enough, even though she wouldn't have seen him during that time, and he would never have written to her or accepted her letters. The rejection of her son would have been a terrible thing to go through. At least with death, she knew it wasn't his fault."

"No, it was her and Far's. It was the village's fault. They are the ones who sent him away. So they all live with the guilt of their actions."

"Good." Domar's voice startled Kirstin.

She whirled around to find him and Ilian standing in the doorway. She turned away and went back to work preparing to toast the bread.

"I hope it gives you great satisfaction," she murmured.

"Does that mean you'll keep my secret?" Domar asked.

She turned back to look him in the eye. "No. No, it doesn't. It means I will pray on the matter for one month and then decide. I will give you that much and only that much."

"Well, it's kind of you to at least consider my side of the situation."

She drew a deep breath. A part of her wanted to hurt him as she'd been hurt, as she knew their mother was hurting and would hurt even more when the truth was known. She met her brother's gaze but said nothing.

"Breakfast is nearly ready. Will you both head back to camp this morning?" Mormor asked.

"Ja." Domar took his seat at the table and reached for the coffeepot. "There's a lot of logging to be done. We're hoping to clear that one field I told you about. Mr. Morganson said he has great plans for it. He also has great plans for Ilian."

"A promotion?" Mormor asked.

"That's the rumor." Domar nudged Ilian's side. "He's earned it, that's for sure. Morganson says Ilian is the best man he's got."

Ilian plopped down at the table. "He says that about you too."

"I hope that goes well for you, Ilian. I know you are a hard worker." Mormor turned her attention back to the eggs she was scrambling in the skillet. "We'll have breakfast ready in a few minutes."

Kirstin helped get the meal on the table. Whatever Mormor asked of her she did without complaint—in fact, without a word to anyone. When the door opened and Mr. Farstad entered, she smiled at him and stopped long enough to pull out a chair.

"It's good to see you again so soon," he said.

"Good morning, Habram," Mormor declared, bringing a platter of sausages to the table.

"Good morning. I see you have my plate ready." He chuckled and took the big platter.

"You will have to share this morning," Mormor admonished.

Kirstin retrieved the jam and butter, as well as the toasted loaf of bread. She placed them near Ilian, still unwilling to look Domar in the eye. Life was certainly not turning out as she had thought it might.

"Let's sit and pray," Mormor suggested.

Kirstin watched as her grandmother bowed her head. She seemed so at ease—even content. How could she go on with life as if nothing had changed?

Well, for her nothing has changed. She's had Domar with her the last eleven years. She isn't battling with what to do about his secret.

Kirstin glanced to her left and found Ilian watching her as the others prayed. She felt unable to look away. There was sympathy in his expression and such depth of longing in his pale blue eyes. What was it he longed for? Perhaps reconciliation? She heard Mr. Farstad end the prayer and glanced away. It was only then that she wondered why Ilian hadn't bowed his head to pray with the others.

After breakfast Mr. Farstad left. He bid a good day to Kirstin and her grandmother, then wished the boys a safe journey as he pulled on his boots. Then, without another word, he exited the house. It seemed to be his routine, as if he knew the only way he was tolerated sharing their table was to say very little.

Mormor asked Domar to go with her to her room, leaving Kirstin with Ilian as he put on his boots. She began to gather the dishes rather than try to make small talk.

"I know you're upset," Ilian said, breaking the silence. "Your brother is too. His pain is great."

"Good. Maybe he'll give some consideration to what I'm going through." Her words sounded harsher than she'd intended. She sighed and refrained from an awkward apology.

"Maybe you should try to think of someone other than yourself."

She stopped mid-step and turned. "Maybe you should take your own advice. I'm sure your father might appreciate the effort."

His eyes narrowed and turned hard. "Maybe you should mind your own business."

She gave him a hint of a smile. "Again, maybe you should take your own advice."

❧

"I think she'll come around in time, Domar," Lena told her grandson. "At least I hope so. I don't want to lose you now that your morfar and uncle are gone."

"I won't leave you deserted, Mormor," Domar promised. "No matter what, I will be here for you."

"Have you reconsidered letting your folks know the truth? Maybe Kirstin is right and it's time to tell them."

Domar frowned. "I don't know why it would matter after all these years. It would only reopen old wounds. They can't undo or unsay the things they said."

"And you cannot forgive them?"

He shook his head. "I don't know how."

"Maybe you should pray and ask God. Forgiveness sometimes takes work."

"Don't you think I know that? Don't you think if it were possible for me, I would have been able to do it before now?" He walked to the window and pulled back the curtain. "I've tried, Mormor. I've tried to give it to God, but for some reason I just can't." He let the curtain fall back into place and raised his hand as Mormor opened her mouth to speak. "Please don't tell me that the Bible says if we don't forgive others, God won't forgive us. I know what the Bible says, and it troubles me day and night. I don't want to defy God. I don't want to hold this hatred and anger in my heart. I honestly don't."

"Keep taking it back to God, Domar. One of these times, maybe you'll finally leave it with Him." She came to him and kissed his cheek. "I am praying for you, just as I always have."

"I want to pray for you, but I'm sure God isn't listening to me. I'm sure He thinks me defiant, although that really isn't my heart."

"Domar, God knows what is in your heart. Just talk to Him. He loves you dearly, just as I do. As your mother and father and sister do. Your entire family loves you, even little Brita who has no memory of you."

"I hate that I've hurt them."

Lena knew better than to admonish him for his actions. God was the only one who could help him see what needed to be done. "I will keep praying for you."

He kissed her head and hugged her close. "Thank you. It blesses me to know that someone is. Especially now that I've earned Kirstin's hatred."

Lena pulled back. "She doesn't hate you, Domar. She might hate what you've done, but she could never hate you."

Chapter 6

"You're awfully quiet, Ilian," Domar said as they drove back to the logging company. "I hope Kirstin didn't upset you too much."

"No. She didn't. I'm sorry she troubled you. I know how difficult family can be."

"She didn't really trouble me. I was so happy to see her again that it didn't matter that she was mad at me. I've always wished there was a way to communicate with her and not the others, but I knew if I wrote to her, then everyone would demand to know what was in my letters so they could keep an eye on me through her."

"Have you thought about telling your folks the truth?" Ilian asked.

"Do you think about reconciling with your father?" Domar shot back.

"Sorry. I shouldn't have said anything."

Domar gave a heavy sigh. "I think about it all the time. You know that. It's hard to ignore their existence, but the ocean between us helps. My mor and far might very well regret their choices now that they know the truth about that baby, but I doubt they would be very mindful of passing judgment on others if they didn't have my loss there to remind them. It might save someone else from being falsely judged in the future. Save someone else the pain I had to endure."

Ilian focused on the team of horses as he drove. "Sometimes I think about making things right with my far, but I don't understand him and probably never will. He had the power to give my mother the one thing she wanted—the only thing that would have made her happy."

"People don't always care what will make someone else happy." Domar stared ahead at the road.

"Yeah. Like I said, I don't understand folks like that."

"Just as I will never understand my family. Kirstin was the only one who stood beside me, and she was just a child—barely thirteen. She was so certain of my innocence that I knew as long as I lived that there would never be anyone who believed in me as much as she did. I can't bear the thought of giving someone else a chance to betray me."

"Is that why you won't choose a girl and marry?" Ilian asked. "It wouldn't necessarily have to end in betrayal." Ilian maneuvered the team of horses across a narrow bridge. "Get on up, boys. That bridge isn't gonna hurt you." The nervous animals seemed reluctant but kept moving.

"I know you're right, but I suppose with this matter so unsettled, it makes focusing on a mate seem unimportant."

"But I thought it *was* settled. You made your choice, Domar. What's unsettled about it?"

His friend sighed. "I don't know. I thought things were settled too, but seeing Kirstin and hearing her talk about Mor— well, it doesn't feel settled anymore."

"Do you worry that Kirstin won't keep her word?"

Domar met Ilian's gaze. "No. That's the one thing I don't worry about. Kirstin is loyal through and through. She would never betray me. She won't say a word unless she first makes it clear what she plans. I believe once she thinks all of this through, she'll agree with me and say nothing."

"I hope so. That kind of loyalty is hard to come by."

Domar nodded. "It is."

"She's very outspoken," Ilian said after a few minutes of silence.

This caused his friend to chuckle. "She reminds me of you."

"What?" Ilian looked at him as if he'd suddenly sprouted wings. "I'm not outspoken."

"Right. You just feel the need to share your mind all of the time."

Ilian laughed. "Only when I'm right. Which is pretty much all the time. Still, I thought she was . . . well . . ."

"Very pretty?" Domar suggested.

Ilian saw no need to lie. "Of course, but there is something else about her."

"She's a godly woman. Mormor tells me her faith is quite strong."

"She didn't bow her head to pray."

"And for you to know that means you didn't bow yours." Domar grinned.

"You know how I feel about God. He's a marvelous Creator who has given us great bounty. I practice kindness and humility toward His creation. I believe He is present in everything and therefore I have no need to pray. I can simply move through life in a sort of continual understanding of His presence."

They fell silent after that and rode for miles without saying a word. Ilian thought of Domar's sister and the loyalty he spoke of. She seemed to have no difficulty standing up to her brother, and Ilian liked that about her. She'd stood up to Ilian too and hadn't done it in a mean way, but rather made it clear that she knew her own mind and heart. She wasn't afraid of everything, like so many women Ilian had met. And he couldn't forget how she had felt sitting on his lap. Small but firm.

"Will you really leave . . . if she decides to tell your folks that you're alive?" he asked.

"I don't know." Domar gazed out into the snowy woods. "I never really thought about their pain being something ongoing. I figured once I was dead, I was dead. It's hard to think of my mother pining away."

"I watched mine do that."

"I remember. Barely, but I do. Her unhappiness was so great."

"And Far never cared. At least you care about it, Domar. If you can save her from it, I urge you to do so. Now that you know your mother's pain is continual, I urge you to make peace. Knowing the truth makes a difference in my eyes. If you know your mother is suffering because of something you're doing— you need to make it right."

"Your father is suffering because of something you're doing. What's the difference? You aren't rushing to make it right."

They hit a hole, and the wagon bounced, throwing them against each other. Ilian straightened and shrugged. "My mother is dead. Far can't make it right for her, so why should I make it right for him?"

"It's no different, even if your mor is dead. Kirstin made me think, and then Mormor had her words as well."

"About forgiveness again?"

"Yes." Domar shook his head. "It's always about forgiveness. Mormor always says it's such a liberation of burdens when we forgive those who've wronged us. I just don't see how forgiving those people back home—and my family—will make me feel any better. I lost them all. At least, I lost what I thought we had together."

"I guess you won't know if you don't try, and it's not like they will know anyway. You could just tell God you forgive them and let it go at that."

"But I have to mean it," Domar said, pulling up his wool collar. "I have to mean it in my heart." He shook his head. "And I just don't know if I honestly do."

~∽~

They reached the camp nearly two hours later. Everyone was busy at work. The goal was to clear this section of forest and then build a new shelter for the draft horses and a bunkhouse for the men. It would be their northernmost camp. Ilian knew the plan was for him to run this part of the company. The boss had been training him and Domar for over two years. Ilian would be in charge, and Domar would be his right-hand man. Mr. Morganson had said he'd never met two men who worked better together, and he wasn't about to break up such a rare team. Ilian was grateful for that and glad that their boss recognized what an asset he had in them. Especially since Ilian had been at this for a long time. Only leaving to fight in the war had taken him from logging, and he intended for nothing to take him from it again.

He supposed he was one of the few who saw his work as more than a job. He'd started as a feller, cutting down the huge cork or white pine trees. Next he'd trained as a sawyer, waking up each day to a newly sharpened saw and pail of lard oil. The sawyers trimmed the felled trees into logs. The oil was sprinkled generously on the blade to cut the pitch and allow for smoother sawing.

Ilian had even worked loading the logs on the skids, sometimes piling them as high as a second story on a house. Loaders—or groundhogs, as they were often called—were the best-paid men in the camp because the job was so dangerous and required exacting skills.

"Glad to have you boys back," Morganson said, coming out to meet them as Ilian stopped the horse and set the brake on the wagon. "I need everyone on loading. We've got to get these logs to the railroad."

"Sure, boss," Domar said before Ilian could.

Ilian wasn't at all fond of the job of loading, but he was good at it. Being a "sender-upper" of the huge logs took precision and much attention to detail. It was easy to lose control and have things end in tragedy.

"You want these chains unloaded first?" Ilian asked Morganson.

"No, leave them. I'll get some of the new boys to take 'em. Hallberg, grab a cant hook and help with loading. We've got a hundred tons to move. Let's get it done."

"Yes, sir!" Domar jumped down from the wagon as a young man no older than fourteen approached.

"O'Sullivan," Morganson addressed the young man, "you drive this team to where they're loading and tell the boys to use the new chains in the back."

"Yes, sir!" the boy replied and climbed into the wagon seat. He took up the reins and waited for Ilian to dismount.

Ilian hit the ground and looked at his boss. "New boy?"

"Yup. That's Big Bart's son. He finished up his education and came to learn the business. He doesn't look like much, but the kid is strong. Smart too."

"That's good. He'll need to be." A light snow had started to fall, and Ilian glanced at the overcast skies. "The roads looked good coming in. The boys must have dragged them early. Looks like you got more snow here than in Duluth."

"Been doing nothing but snowing," the grizzled old man groused. "That's why we're in a hurry to get those logs moved. We need to get them to the railroad and load them up. The cars are waiting on the siding."

"We'll manage it." Ilian pulled on his work gloves.

The men went to work on the huge load of logs. As Ilian fell into the rhythm of the work, his mind kept going back to his conversation with Domar and then further back to his time with Kirstin. She really was something else. She had totally captivated him. He couldn't really explain the effect she'd had on him, but it was like nothing he'd ever experienced before.

He supposed it might have to do with the fact that he hadn't been around any young women in a long time. He had avoided any kind of emotional entanglement, knowing he had no desire to marry and end up in misery like his parents.

Kirstin was different than most of the women he'd known, however. There was a strength and even wisdom in her that seemed unnatural for someone so young. Ilian liked that about her, as well as the fact that she seemed completely open and honest. She spoke her mind and said what she meant. There didn't seem to be any pretense with her.

Ilian heard the snap of the chain, but it didn't quite register. One of the men yelled a warning, and then Ilian saw the logs

74

cutting loose from the stack. Standing alongside the skids, he never had a chance to get fully clear. He tried to make a jump for it, but he was much too slow.

The first log knocked him face first to the ground and rolled right past him. Ilian tried to catch himself. The sound was like a low rumble—not at all frightening unless you knew what the rumble meant. Pain tore through Ilian's right arm as a second log and then a third ripped by.

At first Ilian thought he'd escaped the worst of it, but as one final log rolled from the wagon, the tail end of it landed on him hard, mid-thigh. As his pain increased, Ilian knew he was in real trouble. He heard the men yelling and saw them make a mad dash for him. The pain increased, and Ilian heard the snap of his own femur. The pain surged upward. He wanted to pass out but fought to keep conscious.

"Ilian! Don't move. We're going to get you free."

He grimaced and panted for air. "Can't . . . can't move."

Domar came to take hold of his shoulders. "Work together, fellows. On the count of three."

Ilian saw the men take hold of the log that pinned his leg. It was no wonder he hurt so much.

"I'll pull you out when they manage to lift the log," Domar told him.

Ilian tried to nod, but his world was closing in. He had to fight to keep awake. He had to.

"One," Domar began. "Two." The men gave Ilian one last glance. "Three."

Ilian felt the weight lift. He let out a roar. Pain shot through every part of his body. Then he lost the fight and gave himself to the darkness.

"Ilian. Time to wake up."

Ilian opened his eyes to find his mother standing over him. She smiled, and because it happened so rarely, Ilian smiled back. "What time is it?" he asked, yawning.

"Nearly dawn. You said you wanted to be awake before first light."

"Yeah." He threw back the covers and got to his feet. "The men are leaving at dawn."

"I wish you weren't going to this dreadful war. It'd be so much better if we were back in Sweden."

Ilian pulled on his trousers. "Mor, we've talked about this. Everyone has to do their part. Slavery is an abhorrent thing."

"And well I know it. Your father has kept me as a slave for all these years. He's never once cared about my happiness. Just my work."

"Well, when I get back from doing my duty, I swear I'll take you back to Sweden to visit your sisters. This war won't last long. We'll have the South put in its place in six months, mark my word. I'll be home before you even have time to miss me. Maybe Far will let you go visit the girls in Kansas." He pulled on his shirt.

"He won't let me go anywhere. You know that as well as anyone."

"Well, right now that may be for the best. Who knows where battles might break out?" He buttoned his shirt, then pulled up his braces. "I promise, Mor, when this is over, I'll take you wherever you want to go. I've been saving up my money. We'll have enough for a grand journey."

"You're a good son." Mor came to stand next to him as he dug through the drawer of his dresser for a pair of wool socks.

"I think I packed my last good pair of socks."

"I'll fetch you one of your far's. He won't miss them."

Ilian felt his leg. There was a strange dull ache that was growing to a fiery sensation. What was wrong with him? He looked down but couldn't see anything. Everything had turned cold and dark. Mor had said it was nearly dawn, but it didn't look that way now.

He didn't know why, but he felt compelled to lie back on the bed. When he heard a noise, he opened his eyes and saw a beautiful young woman. Her hair was the color of dark honey, more brown than red or gold, yet there were highlights of each.

She smiled. "You're going to be late."

"Late? Why am I late? Where am I going?"

She laughed. "The doctor is waiting for you." She turned to leave.

He shook his head. "Kirstin?"

She glanced over her shoulder and smiled. Ilian jumped up from the bed to follow her but found he couldn't move. What was wrong with him?

"Lie still, Ilian."

He opened his eyes and at first saw only pine trees overhead and snow coming down through the branches.

"Don't move, Ilian."

He felt hands pressing against him. "Domar?"

"Yes, it's me. You've been hurt, and you must lie still. Here, take this." Domar put a small medicine bottle to his lips. Ilian drank the liquid.

"What happened?" he asked as Domar pulled the bottle away. "Where's Mor . . . and your sister?"

"Your mother is dead, and Kirstin is back in Duluth. That's where we're headed."

Ilian closed his eyes. He wasn't even sure that Domar was real. "What happened?" The effects of the medicine were starting to take hold. Domar's image grew blurry.

"Just rest. We can talk later, but for now you have to stay still. Your arm and leg are broken. Doc set the bones as best he could and splinted both to keep them immobile, but you have to be completely still. The medicine will help."

"Your arm and leg are broken," Domar had said. Ilian tried to register the words and what they meant.

Broken. He was broken.

⌒

Domar was glad that Ilian was once again asleep. The camp doctor had seen that he had plenty of laudanum for the trip to Duluth. The situation was grim, the doctor had told them. Ilian's femur had suffered a compound fracture. The doctor had done his best to clean and stabilize the leg for the trip, but there was no telling what might happen. He'd admonished Domar to keep Ilian as still as possible. The wagon driver was told to go slowly and keep the wagon from jostling about too much.

Just before they left, the doctor told Domar that if Ilian's femur moved too much, the bone would slip out, and the doctors in Duluth would have to reset the bone once again. Not only that, but too much movement might damage the artery. If that happened, Ilian would bleed to death in a matter of minutes.

The very thought left Domar feeling hollow inside. Numb. What would life be without his good friend?

The last thing the doctor did was pack Ilian's leg and arm in ice. It was so cold outside that Domar doubted it would melt. He shivered, pulled his coat collar up, and watched Ilian sleep.

The trip seemed to take forever, but they had to take it slow, with all the snow and dangers to Ilian. If Ilian died, Domar would never forgive himself.

I seem to have that problem with everyone else, so I might as well be hard on myself too.

He sighed and kept his gaze on the roadway. Morganson had admonished him to stay in Duluth until he knew for sure how Ilian was going to make out. The driver was instructed to stay only long enough to hear what the doctor had to say and then get back to camp.

"You have to live," Domar told his sleeping friend. "We need you. You're the best man we have." He smiled. Their boss had often commented that if he could only have a dozen men like Ilian, the entirety of Minnesota would be logged in no time at all.

Now Ilian was hurt, and there was no telling if the damage would take his life. The camp doctor had been so worried. Domar had never seen him quite that unnerved. Of course, all kinds of debris had made its way into the wound. Doc had tried to clean out the worst of it. He'd been a battlefield surgeon during the war to free the slaves. He knew his job very well, having seen hundreds, if not thousands, of gruesome injuries. He'd told them that many a man lost his leg not from the actual bullet but from the bits of cloth and dirt that had gone into the wound. Often those were the things that caused infection.

"A lot of times it's just the luck of the draw," Doc had told them.

Domar whispered another prayer for Ilian and tried to relax. He didn't believe in luck. He'd certainly never had any. It was hard enough just to hold on to his belief in God, given all that had happened. God seemed harsh and cruel and had definitely turned His back on Domar years ago.

"What good is it to trust someone who never gives you a second thought?"

"Did you say something, Domar?" the driver asked, looking back over his shoulder.

Domar shook his head. "Just wishing we could go faster, but I know it would probably kill Ilian if we did."

The driver nodded and turned his attention back to the road. "It'll be another hour or so."

Another hour. Domar looked down at Ilian. He was so pale. He'd lost some blood, though not much, but Domar knew the shock to his body was most likely taking its toll. Maybe praying wasn't a bad idea. Pray for Ilian and for himself. Life had changed dramatically for them both, and the road ahead was not going to be easy.

But when had it ever been?

Chapter 7

"I know this has been hard on you, Kirstin. I know you don't understand the choice I've made." Lena passed a plate of pickled herring to her granddaughter.

"No, I don't." Kirstin took the plate. She glanced at the fish, then set it aside. "I don't know if I'll ever understand any of this."

"I'm not sure I understand it either. It wasn't an easy choice. I weighed it very carefully and prayed about it a great deal. I think, when it came down to it, your morfar and I wanted only to offer Domar a good home with what few family members he'd accept. He lived with us for a short time after he arrived. The room upstairs by yours was his. Your uncle Per thought we should say something to the others but later changed his mind after a long talk with Domar. I suppose whatever the boy had to say was persuasive. After a while our situation became commonplace, but even so, I hurt for your family not knowing the truth."

Lena watched as Kirstin buttered a piece of toast and dipped the edge in the yolk of her egg. She glanced up before taking a bite. "I tried to pray about it last night, but I almost felt like the prayers were blocked. How could God ever honor a lie? Domar has put us all in a bad position. He has asked us to sin along with him. That isn't right."

"No, I agree. Believe me, I carry my fair share of guilt. I haven't outright lied to your mother, but keeping the secret of his being alive has been a terrible burden."

"She'll be so hurt when she learns the truth. She'll feel so betrayed by you . . . by him."

"Much like Domar felt when they sent him away, I imagine."

Lena watched her granddaughter wrestle with her thoughts. Lena knew she hadn't made the perfect decision. She knew that whichever choice she would have made with Domar, someone would feel hurt and betrayed.

"If you tell his secret, he will leave us. It will forever destroy the relationship you could have with him. He will disappear and go far from here, and never again will we know whether he is dead or alive."

"Then we must convince him to tell it himself. We must help him see that it's wrong and that he needs to end this deception." Kirstin picked up her cup of coffee. "He needs to understand the pain that he's caused."

"And you think he doesn't already know? You think no one has pointed this out?" Lena asked as she picked at her food.

"I'm sure you have, Mormor, but he's acting like a child blinded by his own pain. He needs to put that aside and see the truth, and I intend to help him see it. I intend to get him to change his mind. I have thirty days. I promised to keep his secret that long. No longer."

"You know he doesn't come here that often."

"He'll be here next week. You said so yourself. That is when his regular visit was planned."

"Yes, but then he won't return for a month. You can hardly think you'll turn him around in one visit."

Kirstin smiled for the first time that morning. "God can do the impossible. He can change Domar's heart. He can make Domar forgive."

Lena returned the smile. "Do you think God imposes the wishes of one of His children on the other?"

Kirstin's smile faded, and she looked down at her plate. "This one time, I hope He does."

"Tomorrow we will enjoy a smörgåsbord supper. Everyone in the neighborhood will bring food to welcome your arrival," Mormor announced later that morning before leaving the house for nearly two hours to go spread the news.

Kirstin had used the free time to sew and wash clothes while keeping an eye on the sourdough bread Mormor had put in the oven. She found sewing and laundry gave a person a great deal of time to think and pray. But no matter how much she did of either one, she couldn't seem to find any peace of mind. The current situation was impossible.

She heard someone at the back door even before the knocking began. Kirstin dried her hands on her apron and went to see who it might be. She was shocked all over again when she found her brother waiting on the other side.

"Domar." Would she ever get used to seeing his face again? "Where's Mormor and Mr. Farstad?"

"Mormor is visiting friends. I don't know where Mr. Farstad is. Why are you here?"

"There was an accident." He looked so grave. "Ilian's hurt. He's in the hospital. I've been there all night, waiting for them to stabilize him."

"When did it happen?" Kirstin could see the matter was serious.

"Yesterday. We had just returned to camp and started our work. They were stacking logs to drive to the railroad, and a chain snapped. The logs came loose, rolled off the sled, and broke Ilian's leg and arm. The arm isn't too bad, but the break in his thigh tore through the skin, and he could lose the leg or worse."

Kirstin's hand went to her mouth. "Will he . . . is he . . . going to die?"

"I don't know. He's badly injured, and the doctor said the shock of it could cause further problems. They've had to set the bones and stitch up the wounds. They splinted the leg and put him in traction until the stitches come out in a week or so. Then they'll cast the leg."

"And when they do that, will he be out of danger?"

Domar shook his head. "All I know is that Ilian is in a lot of pain, so the doctor is giving him medicine to keep him asleep. I was told to find his father and let him know the situation so that he could come and see his son—just in case the worst were to happen."

"This is terrible." Kirstin reached for her coat. "I'll help you find Mr. Farstad."

"No, you stay here in case they come back. I know the neighborhood and where Mormor has probably gone. I'll be back in half an hour."

Kirstin felt so helpless. "Of course." She put her coat back on the peg. "I'll pray."

Domar nodded and headed back out. Kirstin didn't know when it had started snowing again, but it was coming down steadily in great huge flakes. Had there been nothing else to do and no worry about Ilian, she might have liked to sit at the window and just watch.

"But there's no time."

She quickly finished rinsing and hanging the remaining laundry on the line Mormor had run in the dining room. Poor Ilian. She had only just met him, but already she had plans for him and Mr. Farstad to come together and put the past behind them. It didn't really matter that such a thing wasn't her job. She knew it hurt Mr. Farstad, and she had come to care for him because he cared for Mormor. If there was a way she could help Ilian and his father reconcile, that was what she would do.

"There's plenty to be done here," Kirstin murmured to no one. Her entire life she had tried to be a mediator and set things right. She had lectured many a soul back in Sweden about what they'd done to her brother, and most sought forgiveness. Kirstin had always pointed out that the forgiveness they needed was from God, since Domar was dead.

Only he wasn't.

It wasn't long before Mormor returned without Domar and Mr. Farstad. Kirstin worried Domar hadn't found him, but Mormor assured her all was well.

"Domar is going with Mr. Farstad to the hospital. They'll both return here tonight to let us know what's going on."

"How terrible for this to have happened. I'm just as sorry

as I can be." Kirstin let out a heavy sigh. "Do you think Ilian will die?"

Mormor shrugged as she hung up her coat. The snow had left it quite wet. "There's no way of telling. This is a very bad situation."

"We should cancel tomorrow's supper."

"No, the smörgåsbord will be a good time to catch everyone up on what has happened and how Ilian is doing," Mormor assured her.

"I've been praying for him. I thought this situation might even cause Ilian and his father to come together again."

Mormor nodded and started to take off her boots. Kirstin hurried to help her. "It's possible," Mormor replied, "that this will allow father and son to see beyond their past, but I have my doubts. There is such a deep wound between them. I've never really understood why Habram's lack of money to take his wife back to Sweden for a visit should cause Ilian to hate him. After all, that trip is extremely expensive, and Ilian knows it full well. For years he was saving to take her back himself, so he knows it's not without challenge."

"Why did they come to America?" Kirstin asked.

"I know only that Habram wanted a new start. He's never been a rich man. I remember him once telling me that he had to have help getting here from Sweden. I don't know why his wife let it be such a contention between them. She obviously didn't want to leave Sweden, but her husband felt it was necessary, so she should have tried to work through her sorrow and anger, but she didn't. I used to try to talk to her and share Scripture, but she was such a hard woman. She wanted no part of my comfort nor sympathy, and she definitely wanted nothing to do with God."

"I suppose Ilian loved her a great deal." Kirstin pulled off her grandmother's boot and then replaced it with a woolen slipper.

"Yes, he did. To the point that it did great harm to his relationship with his father. The two were forever at odds. Such a sad thing. Sadder still, his mother encouraged the separation between them. I had never seen such a thing in all my life until I watched how Sarah Farstad divided her husband and son."

"But why would a mother do that? What would it gain her?" Kirstin was just as confused as her grandmother. She helped with the other boot and slipper, then straightened. "I must say, we are two very torn and heartbroken families."

"Maybe that's why we've fit so well together. Ilian has long been Domar's best friend, and Habram and your morfar were dear friends, and now Habram and I are close. Maybe it's because we understand the pain that comes with families."

"And secrets."

Mormor looked at her for a moment, then nodded. "And secrets."

Domar stared down at his friend as he slept. Some of the cuts and bruises from the accident were more apparent now. After the accident, he had focused only on Ilian's arm and leg, but now Domar could see that Ilian had been injured in other ways as well. There was no doubt he was going to be dealing with this for a long while.

The doctor was keeping Ilian heavily sedated because of the intensity of the pain. It was hard to imagine what he was going through. They'd both suffered their injuries over the years, but never anything like this.

"He looks so peaceful. It's hard to remember he's in such a bad way," Habram declared. "Does the doctor think he can save the leg?"

"He said there's a good chance because Ilian is so strong and healthy. But he also said Ilian will probably always walk with a limp." Domar frowned. That wouldn't go over well with Ilian.

"Why haven't they put that hard cast on yet?"

"The doctor said there's too much swelling. The bones are set and splinted temporarily until they can get the swelling down and, in the case of the leg, the stitches out. Then they'll put the casts on his arm and leg. The arm will probably be cast in a day or two. The leg will be at least a week before he casts it. Meanwhile, the traction keeps the leg bones from shifting. That, along with the pain, is the reason they are keeping him heavily sedated. Dr. Moore said bones start healing almost immediately, so he doesn't want it to heal badly and have to be rebroken."

"Ja, that makes good sense." Habram took a seat on the metal chair by the bed and shook his head. "I wish he'd forgive me so we could be close. He doesn't realize how mistaken he is to hate me. I've never held the wrong he did me against him. I've always forgiven his misjudgment."

The words pierced Domar's heart. The issue of forgiveness was such a complicated affair. At least it had always been that way for him. God said He wouldn't forgive a person unless he forgave others, so Domar figured he was without God's grace. Others said that forgiveness was a privilege given only if the other person humbled themselves and asked. But how could a person be responsible for asking when they thought the other person was dead? He knew from things Mormor had said or read to him from family letters that there had been a lot of prayer seeking forgiveness for what they'd done to him. He had never given it much thought, however. He'd deemed it too little, too late.

He followed Habram's example and sat down. The small hospital ward was empty except for Ilian.

"He won't come home to recuperate," Habram murmured.

"He can stay with Mormor and Kirstin." Domar had already worked it out in his head. Ilian could be nursed to health by his grandmother, and Habram would be able to check on him. "I'm sure Mormor wouldn't have it any other way."

"I'll pay for his care. Whatever it takes."

"I doubt Ilian will allow that, but we'll make sure together that he has what he needs." Domar smiled. "I know you two have your issues. It seems we all do, but this is one of those times when anger and adversity must be put aside for the greater good."

"Ja. It would seem so, but I wouldn't place any bets on it happening."

"Gentlemen, the visiting hours are long over," a matronly nurse announced. "You can come back in the morning."

Domar thought Habram might protest, but instead he got to his feet. "Ja, Ilian needs a good sleep. Come on, Domar. We will go home."

"Sure thing." Domar stood and gave the nurse a nod. "You'll send word if . . ." He couldn't finish the thought. Imagining that Ilian might worsen and die was more than he could express.

"Of course," she said, her words less stern.

Domar walked from the hospital with Habram at his side. At least it had stopped snowing. They continued several blocks without a word, and then Habram began to talk in a rapid clip.

"That boy is so full of hate toward me, I don't know that even the good Lord can get him to change his mind. Ilian blames me for his mother's unhappiness because I made her move to America, but he doesn't realize she was unhappy before we ever came to America. The fact is, she was never happy with me. Her folks and mine made us marry. It was an arranged marriage, and neither of us wanted it. I agreed because I respected my parents, and she agreed because of her parents' threats to her. She was miserable even though I tried my best to make her happy and be a good husband. The girls came along, and they were such sweet babies. But it only made her resent me more, and why, I do not know. She wanted so little to do with the girls. Thankfully we were still in Sweden, and my grandmother could help care for them. I just wanted Sarah to love her children and me, but . . . she didn't."

"I'm sorry. That couldn't have been easy."

"No. But it was all we had. Then Ilian came, and I thought he and I might be close. I thought as father and son we would do much together, but Sarah . . . well, she never wanted that. She wanted Ilian for herself."

Domar didn't say a word. He wasn't sure why Habram wanted him to know all of this, but it seemed important to him, so Domar let him continue.

"She turned Ilian against me with her lies, and still I loved her. I wish she could have been happy, because maybe then Ilian could have been happy too. But neither could forgive and forget. Sarah could not let go of her selfish desires—her demands."

Habram pulled his coat closer against the cold. Domar figured it must have been at least ten degrees below zero.

"All of my life, I've only wanted good things for each member of my family, and now poor Ilian lies in a hospital bed and we don't even know if he'll keep his leg." Habram shook his head. "I do not think Ilian could handle that. He would rather die."

When Habram went silent, Domar wasn't at all sure what to say. Partly because he knew that regarding Ilian and his leg, Habram was speaking the truth. Ilian would never allow himself to be a cripple. He would rather die, and Domar feared he would make such a thing happen if the doctor took his leg.

They reached the neighborhood, where many of the houses were wrapped in darkness. It was obvious people had gone to bed. Thankfully, Mormor's house was lit up in a welcoming manner. Domar had no doubt that she and Kirstin were waiting for word, and frankly, it would be good to talk some of it out. He knew Ilian's future would rely heavily upon each person being willing to lend a hand. Soon enough he'd have to return to work, but he couldn't leave unless he knew everything there was managed.

"Come on to our house," Domar said as Habram started to turn toward his own darkened home. "Mormor will have kept supper for both of us on the stove."

"I'll go start a fire in my hearth first and then join you," Habram replied. "Tell her all that we know, and I'll be there shortly."

Domar nodded and watched the tired old man trudge up his walkway through unbroken snow before turning for home.

Kirstin met her brother at the door. "How is Ilian?"

"He's resting. The doctor is keeping him asleep so that he doesn't have to endure the pain."

She frowned. "I imagine the pain is quite great."

"Ja, I think it must be." Domar sat down and unlaced his boots. "Where's Mormor?"

"She's ironing clothes in the dining room. We've been taking turns to keep busy." She looked him over from head to toe. "Were you at all hurt when the logs broke loose?"

"No, I wasn't nearby." He frowned and put his boots by the door. "I can't believe this has happened. Poor Ilian. He was just about to be promoted too."

"Is that you, Domar? Habram?" Mormor asked as she came into the kitchen.

"Habram will be here shortly. He went to start a fire and get the house warmed up." Kirstin helped Domar out of his coat, then hung it on the peg. They heard Habram whistling as he came up the walk.

Kirstin hurried to open the door before he had a chance to knock. "Come in. We have supper for both of you."

She stepped back, and Habram entered. "Supper sounds and smells good." He quickly rid himself of his winter gear.

Mormor was already bringing the food to the table. "Kirstin, get the bread and butter."

"Ja." Kirstin hurried to the counter to retrieve the food.

"We want to hear all the news, but we will let you eat first and then hear what you have to say," Mormor declared.

They all sat at the table, and while Kirstin ate a piece of bread and butter, Mormor sipped a cup of tea. Domar and Habram ate like they'd been starved for weeks and happily took seconds.

When they'd finished, Mormor brought them some warmed apples, raisins, and rice in a brown sugar sauce. "Will he live?"

Kirstin figured that was the most important thing to know.

She frowned at the way her eyes threatened to dampen with tears. She didn't even know Ilian very well, and she was already mourning his possible loss for Mr. Farstad's sake.

Ilian's father poured himself another cup of coffee while Domar took it upon himself to answer the questions.

"The doctor believes he's stable for the time being. He may well take an infection, and that will determine a lot. They can't be sure just yet about the blood flow through the leg. If that has been compromised, he will probably lose the leg."

"How awful. The poor boy. His kind cannot function without a leg." Mormor shook her head and reclaimed her seat at the table.

"The worst of it is his leg." Domar picked up his coffee. "Compound fracture mid-thigh. They cleaned out the wound and put the bone back in place. It hadn't been set exactly right at the logging camp, but the hospital surgeon set it properly and splinted it. They also put him in traction, so hopefully it will stay in place. They can't cast it until next week."

"But why?" Kirstin asked.

"Too much swelling, and then there's the stitches. You can't put the cast on until the stitches come out, or you'll never be able to get them out. At least that's what the nurse said."

"He'll stay with me. With us," Mormor declared. "I can care for him here. He can have Per's room downstairs, and Kirstin will help me."

"I admit I hoped you would say that," Habram said, bowing his head. "We know he would never accept my help."

Mormor put aside her teacup with a smile. "Well, maybe having to rest a long time to heal his leg will heal other parts of him as well. One can never tell what God has in mind."

Kirstin smiled to herself. It really was the perfect solution. With Ilian under their roof, she could work to encourage him to heal the situation between him and his father. Now the accident made perfect sense. Sometimes God used situations to get a person's attention. Perhaps this was the only way He could get Ilian's.

The next evening the house was full to overflowing with people for the smörgåsbord. The house itself was hardly big enough to host such a large dinner gathering, but folks were content to move from room to room, holding the plate they had brought from home and visiting as if they hadn't seen one another in months.

Kirstin was introduced to one person after another but only remembered the name of her grandmother's dear friend, Metta Sandberg.

"I am so pleased you are here," Metta declared with a broad smile. "Your mormor talks about you and your family all the time. We know Domar, of course, but it is wonderful to know you too. And look how pretty you are. Your eyes are so blue— like the fjords in the old country."

Mrs. Sandberg continued to fuss over Kirstin, telling her she was too skinny, encouraging Mormor to fatten her up. The women brought her samplings of everything they'd made just to make sure their concerns were heeded. Kirstin enjoyed all of the Swedish and Norwegian dishes and was delighted with the surprise of receiving a recipe card for each dish. It was a neighborhood tradition to welcome new women, be they single, married, or widowed, with written copies of their recipes.

"What's the news on that Webster fella?" one of the men asked Habram as he joined Kirstin for the first time since the party started.

"He's still being pushy, but we all just need to stand together and tell him no. He can't do anything without all of us in agreement to sell to him. He needs all of the land."

"It's foolishness," the man replied. "He wants to make a fancy hotel with a park for the rich. This is a working town. Doesn't he understand that the water is important to us for our living?"

"Apparently not. He has his ideas, and that's all that seems to matter to him." Habram put his arm around Kirstin. "But let's forget him for a while. Have you met Lena's granddaughter?"

Kirstin let Habram introduce her around to his friends. She tried to remember the names as best she could but knew in the morning she wouldn't be able to recall more than one or two. Still, they were good people, and she liked all of them very much. Most were older folks, and she especially loved the stories of old people and their wisdom. She had learned so much from folks like these. It pleased her to know that her grandmother lived in such a neighborhood.

By the time Kirstin crawled into her bed for the night, she was still stuffed with food and blessed by the kindness of her grandmother's friends. She loved how much they adored her grandmother. No matter the age, from young to old, the people in the neighborhood thought Lena Segerson was the finest of Christian women. They had praised her for everything from her cooking to her sewing and even praised her for singing in the church choir.

Kirstin couldn't help but smile at the memory. These were

such good people, and she was going to enjoy getting to know them better.

But amid those pleasant thoughts, Ilian's situation came to mind. She hoped he would accept Mormor's offer for him to convalesce at her house. Kirstin thought it would be the perfect way to fix things between Ilian and his father. As she drifted off to sleep, she found herself making plans. Not only for Ilian, but for Domar.

All she needed was time to convince him he should tell their mother that he was alive. Kirstin believed that absolutely everything else would fall into place if she could just get that one thing done. She didn't know why it seemed that everything else hinged on it. After all, the Farstad family troubles and the Hallberg issues were two completely different affairs. The two families weren't joined in any way at all, but if Mormor and Mr. Farstad's interest in each other continued, they very well might be.

Kirstin smiled at the thought. Mormor and Mr. Farstad deserved to be happy.

Her mother deserved to be happy too, but that thought didn't make Kirstin smile. It was a worrisome matter that wouldn't be easily resolved. If Kirstin gave her mother the news, she would both hurt and fill her with joy. Worse, if Kirstin told the news, she would forever lose her brother. Just when she'd gotten him back. Why did this have to be so hard? Why couldn't Domar see the pain he'd caused and want to fix the situation?

She sighed and pounded her pillow to make it more comfortable. She just needed to trust that God would straighten this all out.

Chapter 8

Domar returned to the logging camp the next day. He knew, despite what Mr. Morganson had said about staying, that they'd want to know as soon as possible about Ilian's situation. At least Domar would want it that way if the shoe was on the other foot.

Once Ilian was stabilized, there wasn't much sense in remaining, anyway. The doctor continued to keep him drugged to minimize movement and eliminate the pain. Ilian had no idea anyone was there, so it wasn't like it would matter to him if Domar left.

"Sounds like it's just as bad as we figured," Mr. Morganson said, shaking his head. "Poor boy, and just when things were going so well for him."

"I'm sure he'll recover. Ilian's tougher than most and has the determination of twenty men."

Morganson gave an enthusiastic nod. "That he does. I figured you'd stay in town longer and make sure they can save the leg."

"The doctor sounded hopeful but said he wouldn't know for a while. The blood flow is what's critical. I knew you were shorthanded here and figured it would be best to get back as soon as possible. Besides, my weekend off is coming up, and I need to take it if I haven't been away too much already. My grandmother has repairs and tasks she intends for me to do. Ilian and I would have done them together, but now it'll fall on my shoulders. Besides, the doctor said this week would tell us all we needed to know about Ilian's leg."

"Oh sure, that's no problem. You take your days. I just added ten new men. All have experience, so we're moving right along. The demands for wood are increasing every day. Duluth will need plenty to shore up and build the new canal and docks. It's a great time to be in business."

Domar laughed at the stout man's enthusiasm. "I'd best get to work, then."

"You have a strong team, Domar, and you're a good leader. I'm glad to have you as my man. You set a good pace for those young boys. Teach 'em right. We don't need any more accidents."

"I will. I promise."

Domar went to drop off his stuff at the bunkhouse. There was an odd sense of loss without Ilian there. They had been close ever since Domar had come to Duluth. Even though they often disagreed on a variety of issues, they had stuck it out through good times and bad because both felt in many ways as if they were otherwise alone in the world.

"By your own choice," Domar muttered to himself. "By my own choice."

The work week passed quickly, with Domar working from dawn to dusk. The camp was efficient, and they managed to get all of the work done and then some, despite Ilian's absence. The accident had scared the younger men who didn't have as much experience, and they were listening to every word told to them by the old-timers. Truth be told, the old-timers were just as worried. Accidents happened frequently. No one wanted Ilian's fate.

Domar arrived back in Duluth on Friday afternoon, having hitched a ride with the camp doctor, who was going to town for supplies and a weekend of his own. During their trip, Domar asked the doctor questions about Ilian's injuries.

"Only time can tell with these things, Domar. All it takes is a piece of missed debris, and infection can set in. Infection will spell certain disaster."

"Well, I hope they were thorough with the cleaning."

"I tried to be thorough at camp, but we're so limited in what we can do there. The hospital will have had a much better time of it. You told me the doctor said he cleaned it and stitched it. I'm sure he had the facilities to do a good job, unlike me. I sometimes feel as if I'm back on the battlefield with the conditions we have to deal with." He brought the wagon to a stop in front of Domar's grandmother's house.

"You did a good job, Doc. Even the doctor at the hospital said as much."

The man nodded. "Professional courtesy, no doubt." He smiled. "Try not to worry, Domar. You should be able to tell how things are going now that they've had nearly a week." Domar climbed down from the wagon. "I'll check in on him as well. You can ask me any questions you have when I pick you up Sunday afternoon at the hospital," the doctor said. He glanced toward Mormor's house. "Tell your grandmother I send my regards."

"I will. See you Sunday."

Domar gave him a wave and headed up the narrow path to the house. In the summer the path was lined with flowers, and he could always find Mormor out tending them in the evening hours. Now, however, it was lined with new snow piled knee high. Someone had shoveled the walk.

He knocked, then opened the door a crack. "Mormor? Kirstin? It's me."

"We're in the front room," Mormor called. "Your supper is waiting in the warmer. Come inside quick."

Domar smiled and hurried to close the door behind him. He quickly doffed his outdoor wear and left his wet boots by the door. "It's a cold one today," he said, hanging his coat on the peg. He went to the kitchen, found his food, and grabbed a fork before joining his family around the fire. "Thought I might freeze to death on the ride back from camp."

"Well, you're here now, and we keep a warm house, as you well know," Mormor declared. "We're going to need more wood, though."

"I'll take care of that tomorrow," he said. "I promise."

"It's so good to have you home, Domar. Did you have a good week?" Mormor asked.

"I did." He kissed his grandmother's head, then settled on the sofa. "It was a busy one with Ilian gone." He dug into the food but noticed Kirstin watching him. She had the same strange look on her face as when she'd first encountered him.

Kirstin caught his eye, then looked down at her knitting. "I don't think I will ever get used to you being alive." She gave him a smile. "But I'm so thankful you are."

Domar chuckled. "Me too."

"Let me get you some coffee," Mormor said, getting to her feet.

"Thank you." Domar tore off a hunk of bread. "Has there been any word on Ilian?"

Kirstin gave up on her knitting and put it in the basket beside her. "We've seen him. He's doing as well as expected. The doctor has kept him sedated most of the time."

Their grandmother returned with his coffee. "His color looks good, so we're hopeful. The arm is already casted, so there's no more worries over it except that it needs time to mend."

"We've been praying for him, just as we have for you," Kirstin added.

Domar could imagine the emphasis of her prayers for him. "Thank you. I know Ilian sometimes seems not to care about such things, but I think he knows the importance."

"What do you mean?" Kirstin asked.

"Ilian doesn't believe in prayer. He believes in a Creator but thinks that His main interest was in the creating. Ilian's mother believed that way too, and he just sort of accepted it for himself. I've talked to him many times about how the Bible clearly shows God is active in the lives of His children, but he has never had a great regard for the Bible either. He believes it's written by man and therefore fallible."

"How strange. I can't imagine thinking that way. I suppose, however, having a mother tell you such things would make them easier to accept." Kirstin stretched her arms over her head. "Still, I can't imagine God not caring about His children."

Domar was anxious to change the subject, lest it turn to his own beliefs and practices. He knew Kirstin would speak to him sooner or later about forgiveness. He wanted to do whatever he could to make it much later.

"How did your week go, Mormor? Did you get those gill net orders finished?"

She rocked her chair and smiled. "I did. Your sister is quite good. And fast. She puts me to shame with her nimble fingers."

"I think it's fun, almost a game," Kirstin said.

The fire popped and crackled, causing Mormor to take up the poker. She pushed the logs around for a moment, then added another piece of wood. "It's such a cold night. If anyone wakes up tonight, be sure to check the fire." She replaced the poker and focused again on her rocking.

"We'll make sure it's tended," Kirstin said. "You just rest easy."

They shared a pleasant evening, with Mormor catching Domar up on things related to the neighborhood and town. Domar had always appreciated her attention to detail and memory for information. When it was time for bed, Mormor kissed each of her grandchildren and padded off down the hall while Domar and Kirstin lingered by the fire.

Kirstin lost no time. "Have you been thinking about letting our folks know you're alive?"

"I think about it all the time." Domar studied her for a moment. "You look just like you did eleven years ago."

"Hardly. I was just a little girl."

"I know, but seeing you sitting here, with your hair in braids and your feet tucked up under you . . . well, it's just like I remember you at that time. You usually had a book in hand when you were sitting, but sometimes it was sewing."

"Ja. I hated to sit and do nothing."

He chuckled. "I don't think I've ever seen you truly idle."

"You're changing the subject," Kirstin said, waggling her finger at him. "And you're very good at it." She grew somber. "But I must know. There are only three weeks left for me to decide."

"Haven't you already decided? Isn't that what this is all about?"

Kirstin shook her head. "No. I'm in turmoil. Between what you've said and what Mormor has said, I see a little better why you did what you did. On the other hand, I know what has taken place since you left."

He yawned. "I'm much too tired to discuss this tonight. We can talk tomorrow or even Sunday after church. I have a lot of work to do for Mormor tomorrow."

"Very well. But we will talk." She got to her feet and put her hands on her hips. "I won't be put off much longer, Domar."

"You agreed to one month."

"Ja, but Mormor told me you won't be back to visit us for a month. I have to make my time with you count. Especially if you plan to run away from the truth rather than deal with it."

Domar thought long into the night about that statement. Was he running from the truth? Maybe it was time to tell the truth to his folks. Just let them know he was alive. But then the questions would come. Why didn't you let us know you were alive? Why did you stay away all these years? Do you forgive us for not believing you? Do you still love us?

Questions for which Domar wasn't sure he had answers.

⁓

Sunday after church was the first real opportunity for Kirstin to speak to Domar. Whether he was busy with Mormor doing repair work around the house or off picking up supplies in town, he had been too preoccupied with other things to sit and listen. Sunday, however, was a day for rest or visiting friends. Shortly after lunch, Mormor had gone out with Mr. Farstad to visit their friends, leaving Kirstin and Domar at home. Domar wanted to see Ilian before he headed back to the camp, and Kirstin had offered to walk to the hospital with him.

"Domar, you have to talk to me. I can't bear it anymore. Our parents are suffering so much."

"I know that sorrow lingers, but you must admit that the bulk of their pain is gone and now they just live with regret. Which I believe is good. It helps alter a person's rush to judgment when they live with regret."

"I believe they've learned their lesson, Domar. Mor and Far realize how wrong they were. They've been careful with everyone else, never judging them even when all the facts are known and that person admits wrongdoing."

"Well, that is progress, and all it took was losing me."

Kirstin noted the edge of bitterness in his tone. "Domar, you have always been a reasonable person. You seem to like things well ordered, and I'm sure you like people to treat you with kindness and compassion. Shouldn't you also practice kindness and compassion?"

"Believe me, I've long considered this and will go on considering it, but right now I cannot give you an answer. You must do as you feel led, but just remember that no matter what we choose, there are consequences."

"Exactly so, and are you ready to deal with your own?"

He looked at her oddly. "What is that supposed to mean?"

"What if Mor dies before you decide you can bear to confess?"

Her words obviously stung, but he refused to give in. "Then she'll know the truth, won't she?"

"And that's really how you want it?" She had always known her brother to be a gentle soul. She knew what the town and their parents had done to him had changed him—probably forever—but she couldn't believe that gentle spirit was completely destroyed. "Domar, I'm not suggesting you have to have a relationship with them. Not if you truly feel nothing more than hate for them."

"I don't hate them," he said, reaching out to help her up the inclined path.

"Then what?"

"They don't deserve forgiveness," he answered after a long pause.

"None of us do. That's not why we give it. Not why God gave it to us."

Domar let go of her and shoved his hands deep in his pockets. "So let's say I tell them or let you tell them. Then what? What is gained?"

"What is lost?" Kirstin stopped and looked at him. "What does it cost you to extend mercy in this? You forgive them, and God forgives you. You restore broken hearts and go about living your life, knowing you did the right thing. You don't have to go back to Sweden. No one expects that."

"Don't they? Our parents will. Once they know I'm alive, they will expect me to return and take up farming with Far. They'll want to show me off to the village and make everyone admit their wrongdoing. It will be a circus, and those people who feel regret will come instead to feel anger and hate. I can hear it now. The blame for having kept the truth from them. The hate that I would put my parents through such an ordeal. There will be a price to pay if we tell them that I'm alive. But if we say nothing, life goes on in peace. Yes, Mor and Far have their sadness over the child they lost, but they also have the compassion of their neighbors and friends who know they will forever owe them kindness for having driven their child to his death. Isn't that a better life for Mor and Far? If you want something good for them, isn't that the path to take?"

Kirstin had to admit he made good points. There would be terrible consequences that she had never considered. In their embarrassment over unjustly forcing Domar from the village, it was far more likely the people would be angry rather than happy at the news that he had lived only to dupe them. Mor and Far would be delighted to know Domar had lived, but eventually they might accuse and condemn him for his choices as well.

They began to walk again. Kirstin didn't know what to say and stayed silent. It wasn't an easy matter. There wasn't a simple solution, as she had presumed. She had felt able to let go of her anger the moment she learned Domar was alive. She'd felt certain their parents would beg his forgiveness and all would be made right. Now she wasn't so sure.

When they reached the hospital, Domar took her arm once they were in out of the cold. "I'm sorry."

"For what?"

He sighed. "Maybe for everything, but definitely for putting you in this position. I don't know what to tell you. I can't make you remain silent, but I just don't see how speaking out can possibly help. I'm dead to them, and I can't help but think it's kinder to leave it at that."

Kirstin thought about what Domar had said while sitting in Ilian's hospital room. He was still groggy from the medication, but he was having a conversation with Domar nevertheless.

"I want out of here. I need to get out."

"Just a little while longer, Ilian. We have to make sure you don't lose your leg."

"I'm not going to let them take my leg. Won't let them."

"Then you have to lie still and let it mend," Domar reasoned. "It won't be that long in the grand scheme of things, and then you can go and stay with my grandmother and Kirstin."

She nodded. "You'll come stay with us, and we'll take good care of you."

Ilian turned to meet her gaze. The drugs had clouded his thinking, no doubt, because in the next moment he was speaking nonsense. "You're very pretty. I like the way your lips are formed. They're full and . . . and . . . ." He closed his eyes and pressed his hand to them. "I can't think of the right words."

"Well, for now, it's best you, uh, stay quiet," Kirstin urged.

"He wants to talk about how beautiful you are," Domar teased. "Let him. It probably takes his mind off the pain. Not only that, but you are quite pretty. You grew up to be a beauty, and there's nothing wrong with that. How is it you didn't marry?"

"Why haven't you?" She gave him a raised brow and a look that suggested she'd answer as soon as he did.

He shook his head. "That's a story for another day. Right

now we need to focus on getting Ilian well enough to leave this place. It's not good for healing. You know full well Mormor could do the job much better."

"Ja. We could do a better job." She smiled down at the drugged and injured man. "And soon we will."

Chapter 9

Jordan Webster listened as the town council continued their discussion and plans for the Duluth Canal. He felt sympathy for the troubles they were facing and hoped they might feel compassion in return for his difficulties with the river-bay neighborhood that refused to sell to him. Since they were eager to see industrial growth for the city, Jordan felt confident they would see things his way. At least he hoped they would.

There was a vote on something, and it passed unopposed. Jordan hadn't really been paying attention, so he had no idea what it was for. No doubt it had something to do with the canal or the area needed for its completion. He was sure their troubles and problems with the canal would be resolved, and knowing these people, they would have their way. After all, they'd won their battle to convince the railroad to come to Duluth instead of Superior, Wisconsin, which would have been a more logical choice, given they had the bulk of lake shipping. Superior knew that losing the railroad was a devastating blow they would be long in recovering from, but to lose the profit from trade coming in off the lake . . . that would sound their death knell for sure.

"The *ayes* have it, gentlemen. Now we'll hear from a Mr. Jordan Webster, who wishes to address us on a matter of commercial land use."

Jordan stood and went to the center of the room. He glanced at the table where a group of well-dressed men sat. These were the wealthy people of the city who made decisions on behalf of Duluth. They were the men who controlled everything.

"Gentlemen, thank you for allowing me to speak. I have a situation that I believe could be beneficial to us all."

"Please continue, Mr. Webster," Roger Munger said.

Jordan had met Munger on more than one occasion. He was responsible in great part for the development of Duluth. If anyone would understand, it would be Munger.

"There is a piece of land that I desire to purchase. You'll see its position on the maps I had drawn for you." He paused to let everyone take a look. The map had come at some expense, and given there were copies for everyone, it hadn't been a cheap endeavor. "The lightly shaded area is the entirety of the land I am suggesting be quartered off for commercial purposes. The smaller portion in dark shading is the piece of land I am seeking for my particular project.

"It has become evident, in light of your intentions for the canal and the area surrounding Rice's Point and Minnesota Point, that we could benefit each other by moving out the individual homes and committing this portion of land to commercial use only. Currently there are forty residences along the St. Louis River and St. Louis Bay in this area, but the day will soon be upon us that this land will be far better purposed for the city's business use—especially once the canal is in place.

"My plans are drawn up in the papers I gave you, along with the map. I won't belabor the point or delay this meeting by going over that information, but I would request that you read and consider my proposal. If the property is set aside for the advancement of commercial usage, I pledge my support. Most of the area would be perfect for city development, and at the far end of this stretch, I would like to create an elegant hotel for those coming to Duluth from all over the world. The hotel would be close enough to water transport and the train to attract travelers but created in such a way as to be an oasis from work and travel."

"Might I interrupt?" one of the councilmen questioned. "I don't understand why you don't just purchase the land and begin to build."

"I have offered the residents there twice the value of their land, but they refuse to sell." Jordan looked away momentarily, hoping they didn't realize he was lying. "It's a very close community, mostly Scandinavians, and you know how they can be." He chuckled, but when no one else did, he moved on quickly. "There is one woman in particular who has convinced the others not to sell. She has no real reason except that she loves her neighborhood, which I understand. What she doesn't understand is that as the canal goes through and other businesses take up their places along the river and bay, her neighborhood will eventually cease to exist. I have encouraged them to move en masse to another piece of land where they can reestablish their neighborhood, and still no one listens."

Jordan continued to make his point for exactly another two

minutes and then wished them a good day. He knew the game. Leave them to read his proposal, which would hopefully stir their greed with his ideas for creating parks and shops along with other needed commercial business. Of course, there was a danger that they would sell the land to some other entrepreneur, but it was a risk he'd have to take, thanks to Lena Segerson.

It was the middle of February before the doctor began to talk about releasing Ilian to Lena's care. At first Ilian hadn't wanted to go, knowing he'd be a burden on the old woman, but the idea of being stuck in a boardinghouse or, worse still, returning to his childhood home made the choice easier.

Lena had come to visit him often, and Ilian knew she and her granddaughter would make good company. The problem, as he saw it, was that he wouldn't be able to return that favor. Between his anger at what had happened and the pain, Ilian could hardly mutter two sentences together without becoming frustrated and annoyed. Often that turned into outright rage.

Why was he still alive if he had to live with the possibility of never walking again? He thought of other bad injuries he'd had. The pain had always been bearable because he had convinced himself that it was simply a part of the healing. Once he'd healed, the pain would be gone. Now he couldn't even tell himself that, because the doctor said the pain would most likely always be with him. Especially during cold weather.

The doctor had also told Ilian he'd most likely never return to working as a logger. Ilian couldn't imagine what that would mean for his future. As an adult, the only jobs he'd known were soldiering and logging, neither of which he would be able to do right away—if at all.

His leg began to throb. Thankfully the arm pain was minimal, but the leg bothered him with clockwork precision. It was time for his medication, but the doctor was giving him less and less. The man was a firm believer in working through the pain. He had grave concerns that patients who took a lot of medicine would become completely reliant upon it and never be able to get off of it. At this point Ilian didn't care. He hurt. Worse than at any other time in his life. He felt like his leg would surely explode into a million pieces from the pressure and burning. He was in agony, and no one seemed to understand that now wasn't the time to deny him relief. Let him be reliant. All that mattered was stopping the pain.

It had only been a few weeks, he reminded himself, and the first one he didn't even remember. Mercifully, the doctor had kept him asleep or very groggy. It seemed strange to imagine people coming and going and him not knowing it, but now he would have given all the money he had for the doctor to go back to that treatment.

He heard someone crying at the end of the room. A divider had been put up to shield the other patient from Ilian and the world. Apparently he had been in a freighting accident and his son had been killed. Ilian felt sorry for the man. He kept crying out to God as if it might do some good, but Ilian knew it wouldn't. God did not bother Himself with the daily, mundane affairs of man.

Although he had never called himself such, many suggested he was a Deist, relying on logic and reasoning and holding very little regard for the Bible and prayer. Ilian's mother had believed that way too. The Bible, although a good book full of wisdom, was created, after all, by men. And even if they were inspired men, logic suggested fallibility because of its authors. Ilian knew that the counterargument was that God was the author and men were merely the secretaries who wrote down the words, and therefore the book was completely infallible. Both sides made good points, but reasoning told him that God would never trouble with such a book. Why should He? Mankind wouldn't adhere to it anyway.

Ilian liked to imagine that God was very orderly and logical. He put the world into motion with great precision. He created man to think for himself—to reason using the world God had given him. It seemed to Ilian that God was more Creator than heavenly Father. The word *father* to most implied someone who desired a relationship. God, being God, had no need for that. Not in the normal sense of man's reasoning. He was the Creator, and therefore His creation was already a natural part of Him. God was in all, and all was in God. Or something like that. Frankly, Ilian paid it little attention these days.

Then there was the whole concept of hell. Ilian didn't believe in hell, unless of course it was in this hospital bed. And he didn't believe in Satan. It wasn't logical that the Creator would create an evil counterpart. What purpose would that serve? It wasn't as if God would get bored and desire an eternal sparring partner. That made no sense to Ilian whatsoever.

However, as he got older and heard Domar talk about his beliefs, Ilian had been persuaded that perhaps the Creator of the universe wasn't quite as detached as he had believed. After all, it was logical that a Creator would have some concern about His creation—especially if, as Ilian believed, the two were intricately and eternally connected.

Strangely enough, Domar had even gotten Ilian thinking on the need for a Savior, given that mankind had put the world in such disorder. It would be quite reasonable for an orderly God to create a means of returning order to a disorderly world.

There were other issues Domar had discussed that gave Ilian second thoughts about his beliefs—his mother's beliefs. He had always enjoyed a good conversation with his friend because Domar was very systematic in the choices he had made. He hadn't accepted his faith because his elders had told him it was so. He had gone out for himself to learn and figure out what was what.

"How are you feeling today, Mr. Farstad?"

Ilian looked up to find the doctor watching him closely.

"I'm in pain. A lot of it."

"That is still to be expected, but I've come with good news. We're going to let you go home in another day or so. You'll no doubt rest much easier among your loved ones."

"No doubt. I know the food will be better."

The doctor smiled. "No doubt." He began an exam of Ilian's casted leg.

"So there's no longer a danger of losing the leg?" Ilian dared the question that had been on his mind.

"I think we are safe." The doctor pressed against Ilian's large toenail and watched the color quickly return. "I was concerned about the blood vessels throughout the leg, but it appears that you've got good circulation. It would seem God was merciful. The injuries could have been so much worse. If the artery had been crushed or torn apart, you would have died within moments, and if the veins had suffered damage, I couldn't have saved the leg. You're quite blessed."

"If God truly cares so much, He could have just kept it from happening altogether." Ilian tried to keep the sarcasm out of his voice but knew he'd done a poor job.

The doctor ignored him. "Are you continuing with the exercises we gave you? You want to keep moving your shoulder and hip joints. It may not seem like much, but you'll be glad for it when this cast comes off."

"And when might that be?"

The doctor smiled. "I think another five or six weeks. We need to make certain the femur heals completely, and then there will be more exercises afterward to strengthen and improve the mobility of your knee and ankle. You'll definitely need someone to help you for a time."

Domar's sister came to mind. Funny, he knew only what Domar had told him about her, but he felt as if they'd been acquainted for a very long time. She'd come to visit him a couple of times with her grandmother, but she usually let Lena do the talking, seeming almost embarrassed to be in such an intimate setting. The memory made him smile. Maybe she could be his exercise companion.

The doctor finished his exam. "Everything looks very promising. I know you're in pain, and I will have the nurse bring you some medication, but be encouraged. You are making steady progress. All of it points to a full recovery, although we have no way of knowing just now how strong the bones will be. A few weeks back, I couldn't even be certain you'd keep this leg, with the worry of infection. Now the prognosis is good, even if you need a cane to walk. You, my boy, have cheated death."

Ilian gritted his teeth. "At this point, I wish I could cheat the pain."

"I'll send in the nurse." The doctor departed, and Ilian let out a growl.

"Ilian." His father spoke from the doorway to the dormitory. "Are you up to having a visitor?"

"The doctor just left," Ilian replied. "Talk to him if you want news. I'm in too much pain."

A nurse swept past the old man, coming to Ilian with a bottle and a spoon. "Time for your medicine, Mr. Farstad." She looked at his broken right arm and frowned as if not quite knowing what to do.

Ilian reached out to take the spoon. "Pour it," he commanded. "Two spoonfuls."

"Yes." She was young and seemed rather overwhelmed when Ilian grabbed the spoon from her hands.

"Miss Daniels, don't let patients push you around," an older nurse declared as she joined them.

Ilian recognized her as Nurse Thompson. She was a bear of a woman and twice as mean. He hurried to gulp down his first spoonful before she could forbid it. It tasted terrible, but just having it in his mouth made Ilian feel he'd won some small victory. He held the spoon up for the younger nurse to pour another. He no sooner had that spoonful in his mouth than Nurse Thompson grabbed the bottle from the girl.

"Tomorrow you will be released, and the doctor will send you home with one bottle and no more," Nurse Thompson said sternly. "The prescription will be one spoonful every six hours—if needed. You will need to wean yourself off of this, because he will not allow a refill of the prescription."

"Can't have our patients feeling comfortable, can we?" Ilian said, handing the younger nurse his spoon.

Nurse Thompson said nothing but moved toward the end of the room and their other patient. Nurse Daniels seemed completely stunned by all that had happened and stood transfixed at Ilian's bedside.

"Come, Nurse Daniels!" the older woman shouted.

It startled the young woman, who dropped the spoon and had to hurry to pick it up before joining her superior.

For a moment Ilian just stared at his father. He had no desire for a conversation, and soon the medication would make him beyond caring that his father was even there. But for the moment, he resented almost everything about him.

"The doctor said you could go home tomorrow. That's good news, ja?" his father said.

"Ja." Except Ilian didn't have a home.

Ilian didn't know what else to say. He and his father hadn't spoken more than a few words over dinner since his mother had died, and prior to that, they had argued. All the time. Argued about why Ilian's father wouldn't take his wife home to Sweden for a visit. Argued about why Ilian didn't stay out of it and mind his own business. For a long time Ilian had hated his father, but over the years that had faded into a strange sort of pity. Ilian didn't at all understand that feeling.

"You are welcome to my house," his father said, as if he didn't already know about the arrangement.

"I'm going to stay with Lena and her granddaughter."

"Ja." His father said nothing for a moment. "You made her very happy that you didn't decide to go to a boardinghouse."

"She was kind to offer." Ilian tried to shift his weight to the right, but the pain was immediate. There was a raw place where his leg attached to the torso. He grimaced to avoid growling. At least the medication was starting to take hold.

"I'm sorry that you hurt, son." His father's words seemed genuine.

"I'm sorry that the entire accident happened. Such a stupid waste. I won't be able to work for the rest of the season. I might never be able to go back to it."

"You don't worry about a thing there, by golly," his father said, shaking his index finger at Ilian. "I know we have had our differences, but I take care of my own."

"I'll take care of myself. I have my savings." Ilian didn't have the energy to argue and closed his eyes as the medicine began to take over. "I'm pretty tired. I think I'd better rest."

"Ja, you rest. I'll tell Lena you'll come to stay with her to-morrow."

"Probably tomorrow," Ilian replied, his voice slow and drift-ing.

"Ja. I'll come back with a wagon to take you home."

Kirstin was filled with a sense of excitement as she waited for Mr. Farstad to bring Ilian to the house. He would make for a nice diversion, and the sooner she got to know him, the sooner she could help the Farstad men patch up their differences. The very idea excited her. Wouldn't it be something if after all these years of anger and bitterness, the two of them could set aside everything and come together?

Kirstin had to admit that a diversion was also a selfish desire. She needed something to take her mind off of her decision regarding Domar. She enjoyed long talks with Mormor and making the gill nets, but often she had too much time to think, and when that happened, she could only think of Domar and the mess he had created for all of them. Perhaps having Ilian at the house would help her better understand her brother. Maybe Ilian could offer insight.

A couple of the neighbors came to help Mr. Farstad carry Ilian into the house on a litter. The doctor wanted absolutely no pressure on the leg and had forbidden any kind of walking, even with crutches. Ilian was clearly annoyed and embarrassed but tolerated the older men and their help without a word. Once they had him settled in the bed in Uncle Per's room, Mormor and Kirstin went to see what they could do to make him more comfortable.

Mormor retrieved another quilt from the blanket box. "It's supposed to get quite cold tonight. I hope that flannel nightshirt is big enough in the shoulders. You and Per were nearly the same size."

"It feels fine, Mrs. Segerson."

She nodded and gestured to Kirstin. "We will be your nurses. Here's a bell to keep by your side as you sleep. You can ring it any time you need one of us."

"I hate putting extra work on you," Ilian muttered.

"You have done a lot for me, Ilian. This is the way it is for friends and family. We help one another in times of trouble and share celebrations in good times. We will have you mended in no time at all. You'll see."

He didn't look convinced and tried to straighten the pillow behind him. Kirstin stepped forward and pulled it free. "Tell me when it's just right." She leaned in toward him, careful not to touch him, and settled the pillow behind his head and shoulders.

"Thanks. That's good." He paused and settled back. "Very good."

She straightened. She wanted to brush back the dark hair that hung across one eye. It had bothered her since she'd come into the room, so without making much ado about it, she pushed it away from his face and smiled. "There, now you can see."

He looked at her for a moment. With their gazes locked, Kirstin's cheeks warmed. Ilian Farstad was quite a handsome man.

"Thank you," he said with just a hint of a smile on his lips.

"Ilian likes to play checkers, so maybe when he's settled and out of pain, you can bring the checkerboard and play a game or two," Mormor told Kirstin. She then looked at Ilian. "Kirstin is also a good reader. It helps her to practice her English, so maybe you'd let her read to you sometimes."

"Of course, Mrs. Segerson."

"You rest now, Ilian, and don't forget to ring when you need anything."

Kirstin followed her grandmother from the room, wondering why she suddenly felt like there were fish jumping in her stomach. Maybe she was coming down with something.

"Are those nets finished yet?" Mormor looked at the wall where two long nets hung.

"Almost. They need to be tied off and finished."

"Good. We need to start on some more. Mr. Landers told me he needs a new net, so we will get that started. I will help you finish these first."

They got to work completing the nets, and Kirstin found

herself thinking about Domar. It would only be another week and he'd come home. Her month would be up, and although she had prayed and prayed, Kirstin still didn't know what she would do about the situation. She'd thankfully already written Mor and Far and wouldn't be obligated to write again until she received something from them. Still, the situation nagged and nagged at her. She had to figure out what to do, and soon.

"You're awfully quiet."

Kirstin glanced up to find Mormor watching her as she wound up the new fishing net. "I was just thinking. A lot is on my mind."

"I know you are worried about Ilian, but I think this is probably about your brother, ja?"

"Ja. I know he will come next week, and I don't know what to do. I feel so bad about what happened to him, but that was eleven years ago. It seems a long time to carry his anger and revenge."

"You think this is his revenge?" Mormor asked. She tied off the ends of the net.

"Ja, in a way. He is getting back at the people who betrayed his trust and chose not to believe him. He is punishing them."

"Ja, I believe you are right. I've spent most of this time trying not to think on it at all, but you make a good point."

"He's convinced himself that this way the people will learn a lesson about false judgment. That they will go on being sorry for what they did, but it seems to me that one man cannot change another by such an action. I was thinking about this last night just before I fell asleep. I remember when I was a girl and the Lindbergs' youngest son fell through thin ice and drowned. Mor told us all that we always needed to be cautious about ice. For a year or two I remembered his death, and I was careful on the ice, but then I stopped, and the lesson was no longer important. Now I seldom ever think about him and what happened, except in this instance. I think that is how it is with Domar. Before I left for America, no one ever talked to me about him. He's been gone too long. Eleven years, and now only family remember him."

"Ja, people don't remember for long, especially if it makes them too uncomfortable. When they have to remember that their mistake ruined the life of another, they'd just as soon forget." After winding up the second finished net, Mormor took up a large ball of jute and began measuring off pieces for the new gill net.

"Ja. Maybe that will help Domar change his mind." Kirstin looked at her grandmother and smiled. "He might see that it shouldn't matter anymore."

"I hope so, for your sake as much as his. Just remember, your decision will touch many a life. Not just yours."

Chapter 10

Jordan Webster spied the pretty young lady in the stationery store and made his way over to her. He had no intention of giving up working with the people, in case the city decided against his ideas.

"Aren't you Lena Segerson's granddaughter?"

"I am. I'm Kirstin Hallberg, and you're Mr. Webster, the man who wants to buy my grandmother's house and land."

"Yes." He gave her a broad smile. "I'm surprised you remember me."

She gave a little shrug and secured the ties on her dark red knitted cap. "You're the only one who wants Mormor to leave her home."

"And who will pay her well for her property."

Miss Hallberg smiled. "No amount of money is enough when you love your home and wish to remain in it."

"I suppose it must seem that way, but this city is growing quickly, and that land is much needed for the modernization of Duluth," Mr. Webster said.

"I am not so good with my English that I understand mod . . . er—moder . . . nation?"

"Modernization. It's all about keeping up with the times, making things better."

"But how is it better if people lose their homes and have to go elsewhere? Mormor and her friends love their neighborhood."

"And they can all move together to another neighborhood."

Miss Hallberg shook her head and shifted the basket she carried. "No, I think not. Mormor is happy and wants to stay."

"But you must convince her to go," Jordan pushed, hoping to get his point across. "The time will come when that land will be needed for businesses. It's on the water, and once the canal is in place, there will be a real buildup of that area with commerce and—"

"Mod-ern-i-zation," she interjected, trying the word on for size. "Such a word."

"But a good one. Yes, modernization is coming to Duluth in a big way. Once the canal is in place, it will join with the railroad to make Duluth the center of commerce for the western end of Lake Superior. If need be, the city will take possession of the land and move them out."

She gaped at him. "They can do this?"

"They can and often have for the betterment of the entire community, rather than bowing to the desires of a few people. It's called eminent domain. The government can and will come in and take the property, even against the will of the owner."

"How is that good? I thought America was good, but not if you can steal someone's home."

"America is very good. They wouldn't take the land without paying for it. They will compensate at a fair price. But I will pay more." He could see he had her complete attention. "Your grandmother probably doesn't realize what the law allows for, but that's the truth of the matter."

She muttered something in Swedish.

"I'm sorry," Webster said, shaking his head. "I don't speak your language."

"I said, I think then they will do it without Mormor." Miss Hallberg picked up several postcards. "I must go now. I hope you have a good day."

"Thank you. I hope you do too, but I hope even more that you'll try to talk some sense into your grandmother."

Kirstin frowned. "My mormor is known to be quite sensible. I do not believe she lacks sense just because she doesn't do what you want." She paid for her cards and tucked them inside her coat before turning to him one final time. "Good-bye, Mr. Webster."

Jordan watched her go. Maybe the idea of the government coming in to force their removal would motivate Mrs. Segerson to convince her friends to sell. He smiled to himself. One way or another, he meant to have that land and to build his hotel. He would persuade the city to put in a beautiful park, and the entire area would be a lovely retreat for those visiting the city.

Kirstin went straight home, eager to tell her grandmother what Mr. Webster had said about the city buying up property whether a person wished to sell or not. Surely that wasn't true. In Sweden, people were always talking about America as if it were some idealistic dreamland where anyone could own land if they had the money to pay for it. No one ever mentioned the government being able to take it away at will.

"Mormor?" she called as soon as she stepped into the house. She slipped off her boots but didn't bother with her coat and cap. "Mormor?"

"I'm back here with Ilian."

Kirstin made her way to Ilian's room. She hadn't helped much with his care yet. Mormor had insisted that she could manage Ilian's care if Kirstin would keep the house in order.

Looking into the room, Kirstin found Mormor giving Ilian a mug of something hot to drink. He seemed quite eager for it and sampled the drink immediately.

"It doesn't taste all that good, but it will ease your pain. I learned to make this concoction back in Sweden, and it always helped with the pain," Mormor said.

"I'm willing to try most anything. There's always liquor, but I know you've never been one to keep that in your house. I don't want to dishonor you by bringing it here. I'd move first."

Mormor glanced back at Kirstin. "You didn't even take off your hat and coat. It must be something important you need to say."

"Ja." Kirstin undid the ties on her cap. "I saw Mr. Webster at the stationery store. He sought me out to talk about helping him."

"Helping him?" Mormor looked concerned. "Do what?"

"He wants me to convince you to move."

"That man has some nerve," Ilian muttered.

"I hope you told him I have no desire to move," Mormor stated, gathering her things, putting the smaller items in a washbasin.

"I told him, but he said there is a thing called em . . ." She thought for a moment. "Em . . . ant domain."

"Eminent domain," Ilian offered.

"Ja!" Kirstin nodded and came closer to his bed. "That's it. Eminent domain."

"And what is that?" Mormor asked.

"It's a means by which the government, for the benefit of the community, can buy up privately owned property for their own use," Ilian said.

"And Mr. Webster said this would be done if the people did not sell," Kirstin added.

Mormor looked worried, and a frown furrowed her forehead. "And they can do this, Ilian?"

"They can. I saw it happen with land needed for the railroad. They pay the owner the going rate for what the land is worth, and the property then becomes the government's."

"That hardly seems fair." Kirstin was frowning too. "Mr. Webster said it was for modern-i-zation."

"No doubt, but as I understand it, he wants to put in some fancy hotel," Ilian replied.

"He said he would pay more than the government, and I should convince you and the others to sell."

"It is very upsetting to think the government would force us to move," Mormor said, shaking her head. "I must talk to Habram about this. Excuse me." She picked up the basin and left the room.

Kirstin looked at Ilian. "They really can take away her land? Her home?"

Ilian grimaced. "I'm afraid so."

"America is not so good a place, then. What use is it to own property if the government can just take it? It's no better than the Crown or nobility in Sweden leasing property and then refusing to renew the lease or let it pass on in the family."

"It doesn't happen that often. If it did, people would rise up and make the government change the laws."

"They can do that?"

"Ja. It isn't easy, but it does happen."

"How? When? Can we do it now?"

"They make amendments," he said, smiling. "Those are legal changes to the Constitution."

Kirstin put her hands on his arm. "Stop. I will never learn it all. It's too much."

This made Ilian chuckle. "I'm sure in time you'll figure it all out and maybe even want to become a citizen."

"A citizen of America?" Kirstin had never really thought about what the future might hold for her in that regard. She was a Swede, and although she had come here to care for Mormor, she hadn't really planned to stay. Her curiosity got the better of her. "How do I become a citizen? Are you one?"

"I am. I was born here not long after my parents came to America, but because they weren't citizens, I couldn't be considered a citizen. So when I turned eighteen, I made it clear that I wanted to be a citizen, and later when I joined the army to fight for the Union, they made me one. A couple years ago, Congress, the men who were voted by the people to represent them, made changes to the law again. Now the naturalization law includes black people. Before that only white people could be citizens."

"It sounds very complicated." Kirstin undid the buttons on the red knit coat Mormor had given her.

Ilian nodded. "It is. That's why it doesn't get changed very often."

"So if I wanted to be a citizen, what would I have to do?"

"Live here for five years and tell the court you want eventually to be a citizen. They keep a record of that, and you have to tell them that at least three years before you can be made a citizen. And you have to have witnesses who will tell the court that you're a good, upstanding person. Maybe I will do that for you if you decide to become a citizen."

Kirstin felt her cheeks warm. She looked away as she shrugged out of her coat. "I should go hang these up." She took her cap and coat and hurried down the hall. She wondered if she would ever get used to being in Ilian's bedroom with him lying in bed. It seemed so scandalous, and yet it wasn't. He was injured, and she was just trying to help.

"Would you take Ilian his lunch?" Mormor asked. "I have it ready there on the tray. There's more in the pot on the stove if he needs it, and of course you may help yourself. I'm going to go find Habram. I need to talk to him about what Mr. Webster said."

"I hope it isn't true, Mormor." Kirstin hung up her things, then went to give her grandmother a hug. "I couldn't bear for them to force you from your home."

The older woman kissed Kirstin's cheek. "I wouldn't like that either, but perhaps God has another plan."

Kirstin helped Mormor into her coat and watched her head down the walk. The skies were the color of gunmetal, and the heavy clouds suggested more snow, and a lot of it. Kirstin sighed and closed the door.

She picked up Ilian's tray, breathing deeply of the aroma of Mormor's stew. Only then did she realize how hungry she was.

"Mormor said I should bring you your lunch. Are you ready to eat?" she asked as she entered Ilian's room.

He nodded, but he seemed less happy than earlier.

Kirstin took the tray to the bed. "Would you like me to help you sit a little better before I put the tray on your lap?"

"No. I can manage." He scooted up just a bit, his jaw clenching.

Kirstin felt sorry for him. "Mormor left to find your father. They seem to spend a lot of time together. Are you aware of that?"

He settled against the pillows and raised his arms so she could put the tray on his lap. "I know all about it." His words were clipped.

"Would like some jam for the bread?"

"No."

"You don't have to bite my head off. I'm trying to make sure you have everything you need." She didn't realize she'd spoken in Swedish until the words were out of her mouth. "Sorry," she said in English.

"I'm fine." He picked up the spoon. "I'm just fine, so you can leave."

She was surprised by his attitude but didn't want to argue with him. "You have the bell if you need me to help you."

She headed for the door and left Ilian to sulk. For whatever reason, he had turned sullen, and while she understood that he was probably in a lot of pain, that was no reason to be angry with her. Of course, she had mentioned her grandmother and his father spending a lot of time together. Maybe Ilian realized that if they were to marry, he would have to mend fences with his father in order to keep having a relationship with Mormor.

Grabbing herself a bowl, Kirstin spooned up some stew and took a seat at the kitchen table. There was work aplenty to do after lunch, so she was determined to stop letting Ilian invade her thoughts.

"I'll just put him from my mind."

Yes, he was handsome and smart, and she'd found that he could be charming. She had not minded at all when he'd held her on his lap after she fainted, but his dour behavior was most unpleasant.

"I suppose I shall have to give him a wide berth, given he's in pain," she muttered to herself.

Mormor had explained that the breaks he had suffered, especially in the leg, were quite invasive, with many nerves and tissues disturbed. "He's always had a temper, but no doubt the pain makes it harder to control his mood," Mormor had said.

Still, a person ought to be grateful to have folks around them who were willing to care for them. He didn't have to snap at her. She'd done nothing wrong.

It dawned on her that she wasn't anywhere close to putting him from her mind.

Habram skipped the small talk and asked the mayor the one question on his mind.

"Joshua, tell me the truth—is the city thinking of using eminent domain to buy our neighborhood?"

Joshua Culver had been a longtime friend of Habram's. He sighed. "I won't lie to you. It has been brought to our attention."

Habram glanced at Lena. "Do you realize how many people live in our neighborhood?"

"It's not just your neighborhood, Habram. It's all of those along the waterfront in the industrial area. We have wonderful plans for that area once the canal is finally dug through. If we get it through."

"Oh, we'll dig it out, but I don't see why the city needs to take that land from the good folks who settled it."

Culver squirmed a bit. "Habram, you know as well as I do that that area is prime land for waterfront industry. A great many shipping issues could be resolved by utilizing that land for commercial purposes."

"But people live there, and they love their homes. I live there and have since I came here. You were one of the folks who showed me that area and urged me to buy."

"I know that, Habram. And at the time it was a good idea. Now it is undergoing other consideration."

"So you would just push out all of those families. Good and godly men and women who helped settle this town when few were of a mind to stay."

"Habram, I'm not trying to force anyone to do anything they don't want to do, but this is for the good of all. Everyone's best interests are being considered."

"So your mind is made up? You will take the land against our will?"

"I'm afraid it's starting to look that way."

Habram got to his feet, and Lena rose as well. He shook his head and gave his friend one final imploring gaze. "Joshua, you must think about what you are doing to these people. They have needs."

"And if we take the land, we will pay them generously. It's a condition I insist on. Not only that, but the city will sell them

other land at a good price and lend every help we can to seeing
that if the new property has no house already on it, one will be
built quickly and at a discounted price."

"You've thought of everything," Lena said. "Everything but
how you are tearing out our hearts. Some raised their families
in those homes. Others said good-bye to loved ones there. We
have our memories of good times and bad, and it was there
that we befriended our neighbors and helped see one another
through the bad times. We will never have that closeness again.
You will put us here and there and spread us out throughout
the city, and our neighborhood will be lost to us. Our family—
gone."

"Perhaps I can find land where all of you can once again build
together. That would surely resolve the problem, wouldn't it?"
Mayor Culver looked from Lena to Habram.

"It would resolve the problem not to make us leave at all,"
Habram said, unable to hide the sorrow in his voice.

He left the mayor's office and took Lena's hand as they walked
out into snow. Heavy snow.

"I had hoped to take you for coffee and to hear all about
Ilian, but we should return home. It looks like it's going to be
bad for us."

"The snow, or the city buying up our houses?" Lena whispered.

He gave her hand a squeeze. "Both."

Chapter 11

Habram was surprised when Major John Upham appeared at his door the next day. "Afternoon, John. Come in." He swung open the door. "I have a fresh pot of coffee on the stove. Would you like a cup?"

"Sure thing." John looked at the dirty floor and then back at Habram. "You want me to take off my boots?"

"No, I have a fair piece of cleaning to do, as you've already noticed. Just sit at the table and I'll get the coffee."

"I was surprised to get your note. What is it you want to discuss?"

Habram brought the pot of coffee and two mugs. He didn't bother with cream and sugar, knowing that John drank his coffee black, just the way Habram liked it. "I have some *skorpor*, if you'd like. Lena Segerson made it."

"No, the coffee is more than enough."

"Just so you don't go telling folks I was a poor host." Habram laughed and took his place at the table just as John took his chair.

John chuckled. "Never would. You've always been a good friend."

"That's why I wanted to talk to you about my job at the dredging company. I'm of a mind to retire."

"I figured it might be something like that."

Smiling, Habram poured them each a cup of coffee. "I can't help myself. My son was injured in a logging camp accident, and even though he doesn't particularly care for my company, he's next door. Should they need a man's help, I want to be close by."

"I can understand that. It's not like we're doing much anyway. By the time we get back to digging the canal, however, your son should be right as rain."

"I know, and I'm excited to see that canal made. I can always lend you a hand then, if you need it. Just not full-time."

"I suppose I'm not going to talk you out of this, but you know I'll need you when we do the final digging. You're my most trusted worker, and you need to be a part of this. It's a moment of history, and you've earned a front-row seat not just to observe, but to take credit for participating. Superior says if we start digging again in the spring, they'll definitely file an injunction, so we've all decided that once we start up again, we need to be prepared to work fast and finish it. Night and day, if necessary."

"I agree." Habram refilled his friend's mug. "Even though I've never seen the court system move all that fast, we should be prepared for anything."

The major took a long drink. "Good coffee. Nice and strong. So, what are your plans now that you'll no longer be dredging?"

"I'll work on those Mackinaw boats more. Maybe take a few more orders. It's a pleasant sort of work, and my son may find himself needing a job. The doctor tells us he's not going to be able to return to logging. His leg suffered a compound fracture, and the doc says he'll always walk with a limp. Still, it could have been much worse. He could have been crushed and killed. It's happened to more than one man."

"True enough. I'm glad he was spared."

"I am too. I've been thanking God for it and praying Ilian will come around to spending time with me."

"If he's smart, he will." John finished off the coffee and got to his feet. "I have work to do. I suppose I need to accept your resignation, eh?" His eyes narrowed. "I'm not at all happy about this, but at your age, you've earned a rest. I accept, so long as you'll help me when we dredge the final bits of the canal."

"I'll be there. You just let me know when."

"Won't be until the harbor thaws and then some. I'm guessing the ground will stay frozen solid for a while and we wouldn't be able to dig a thimbleful. So once the thaw comes in late March or April, we'll get back to work."

Habram got to his feet and extended his hand. "Sounds good to me. Thanks for coming by."

The younger man smiled. "I look forward to finishing this final job together. I don't trust anyone more than I do you."

After John left, Habram looked out across the neighborhood toward the water. He knew they were going to lose the battle with Webster and the city, but it was hard to accept. He'd lived here for such a long time. Since his family moved to Duluth, this had been home, and now it would be his no more in just a short time.

He turned toward Lena's house. She made him happy with her love of life. She was almost always happy, seeing the positive side of even the worst situation. She was loyal too. Fiercely loyal. She had kept Domar's secret all these years because of her love for him. A love Habram felt she shared with him also, and he meant to reward it by making her his wife.

After Per passed away, Habram had been about to suggest he and Lena marry, but then the news had arrived that Kirstin was coming to keep Lena company, and he hated to impose himself on that situation. He would just bide his time. The Lord knew when it would be right. For now, he would focus on trying to mend fences one more time with Ilian.

Kirstin found sleep impossible. She knew in a couple of days, Domar would arrive and they would discuss her decision. Only she didn't have a decision.

She threw back the covers and stepped into her slippers as she got out of bed. Pulling on her robe, she kept hearing the same question in her head.

What is the right thing to do?

She made her way downstairs, and as she reached the hall, she heard Ilian moaning. His door was slightly ajar, so she went to it and opened it a little wider.

"Are you all right?" she asked in a hushed voice. She went into the dark room. "Would you like me to light a lamp?"

"No."

"How about a cold drink of water?"

"No." This time the word was delivered with more irritation.

"Sorry. I'm just trying to help."

He said nothing for a time, then sighed. "I'm sorry. I just can't get comfortable no matter how much I try."

Kirstin came closer. "I could try to help with pillows. Mormor put a ton of them in here for just that reason."

"I suppose you could try."

"I'll need to light at least a candle."

He sighed again. "Go ahead and light the lamp."

She wasted no time and found the matches. Soon the soft glow of lamplight revealed a miserable Ilian. His brow was lined with sweat despite the room feeling chilled.

"All right. Tell me where you hurt the most."

He spent the next few minutes explaining, and while he talked, Kirstin built a little nest of pillows around him. By the time she finished, he was looking at her as if she'd just pulled a rabbit from her pocket.

"That's so much better. I don't hurt at all. How in the world did you do that?"

"I listened to you." She couldn't help but smile. "I'm glad I couldn't sleep so that I could help you. It makes me feel that I at least accomplished something useful and good."

"Why can't you sleep?"

"Domar."

"Your brother? But why . . . oh, not telling your folks. Is that it?"

Kirstin nodded. "Yes. I don't know what to do. It's his right, I suppose. But I know how much it will hurt them when they find out the truth."

"So why do you want them to know? Isn't it better to leave things as they are? Maybe one day Domar will decide to tell your folks about what happened and why he made the choices he did."

"But then they'll want to know why I never said anything. They'll be mad at me."

"That will be their problem, then. They'll have feelings to deal with no matter what. I don't know that I would have done things the way Domar has, but I feel that it was, and is, his decision to make."

She met Ilian's gaze. His eyes were so blue—so persuasive in the way they held her attention. She swallowed the lump in her throat. "I guess I feel torn in my loyalties. I always knew Domar was innocent and hated that no one else believed him. It made me so mad. I've been angry at our parents all these years, but the intensity had faded until I saw Domar again. Now I feel that anger, but it's mingled with sadness and pain. I know Mor is going to be as devastated as she is happy to learn Domar is alive. She's going to be so hurt that he would do this to her, and it hurts me too that he let me believe he was dead.

"I used to visit the graveyard where Mor and Far put a marker in his memory. I would walk that cemetery for hours and weep. I missed him so much, and it broke my heart to think he never knew that the people realized the truth—that Mor and Far were sorry for what they'd done. I used to beg God to let Domar know."

"You think God would do something so trivial?"

"It wasn't trivial to me." A tear slid down her cheek, and she ignored it. "A part of my heart died when I heard Domar was dead. Now I learn he's alive and well . . . and though I'm happy and rejoice . . . I'm also deeply hurt that he would let me bear that pain."

"Maybe you should ask yourself if you could do it over, would you want to know."

She nodded. "I have asked myself that very question. Knowing the pain and anger this has caused me, would I rather not know?" She looked at the carved headboard above Ilian's head. "And I always answer the same thing."

"Which is?"

"Yes. I would rather know he's alive and get to be a part of his life and he a part of mine than to never know the truth."

"But, Kirstin . . ." His voice was barely a whisper, and she couldn't help but look down to meet his eyes once more. "Domar doesn't want them to be a part of his life. He'll never return to Sweden, and I doubt he'll be much for corresponding. Won't it just cause them more pain to be openly rejected?"

She shook her head. "I don't know. I just don't know."

"What's going on?" Mormor asked as she came into the room.

"I couldn't sleep, and when I got down here, I heard Ilian moaning in pain." Kirstin pointed toward the bed.

"She has made me most comfortable and very nearly pain-free," Ilian said from his pile of pillows.

"I can see that." Mormor chuckled. "You look like a bird in its nest."

"I suppose we were too loud and woke you. So sorry, Mormor."

"Nonsense. It's nearly four thirty. I wake up about this time every day. Your morfar and I always used to get up about this time. We'd stoke the fire in the living room, and I'd get the stove going. Then I'd climb back in bed sometimes until the house warmed up, and while I waited, I prayed."

"I'll help you get the fire stoked, but then going back to bed sounds like the best possible choice." Kirstin looked back at Ilian. "And since you're all ready for sleep, I will bid you good-night and leave you to it."

He smiled. "Thanks again for the help. I'm glad you don't intimidate easily."

Chapter 12

Ilian didn't wake up until nearly noon. He'd been so exhausted from the various parts of his body hurting that he hadn't gotten a decent sleep since the accident—until last night. He supposed he'd have to ask Kirstin to tuck him in more often. The thought brought a smile to his face. She was good company and had such a gentle touch. He found himself thinking of her all the time lately.

"Good morning," Lena said, coming in without so much as a knock. "Hopefully Domar will be with us later today. I know he's going to be anxious to see how you're doing."

"Well, I'm doing a whole lot better since Kirstin figured out how to arrange those pillows. I slept like the dead."

"And well I know it. It's eleven forty-five. You missed break-fast altogether." Lena laughed and came to help him sit up. "The doctor will be coming to see you today. I'm sure the news will be good, and maybe he'll let you get up and sit, maybe use crutches to move around. Wouldn't that be nice?"

"It would. I'm sick of this bed."

"Ja, I can imagine you are." She left the room and returned

with a basin. In it was an inch or two of water. She placed it beside him. "I'll get you a washcloth and towel." She went to the dresser nearest the door and retrieved the items. "You get all cleaned up, and I'll bring you some lunch before the doctor arrives."

Ilian went to work on washing while Lena brought him a clean nightshirt.

"I'll go get your lunch ready and be back for the basin shortly," she said.

Ilian was so grateful to Lena. She had been like a grandmother to him for more than a decade—sometimes even a mother.

Thoughts of his mother threatened to rob him of his good mood. She had been so miserable—so lost in sorrow. When he thought of his parents as a couple, he could only remember their arguing. Mor was either angry or sad every moment of every day, and always she blamed Far. Ilian had tried so hard to please her and earn a smile, but all she could say was how much she missed Sweden and her family. She talked of how they would want to see Ilian and know him. She just knew if they were to move back to Sweden, Ilian's older sisters could find good husbands, and she could show Ilian off to some wonderful young Swedish women. At the time Ilian had no desire to marry, seeing how miserable his mother and father were, and he told her so. Mor always told him that was just because they didn't marry for love.

Lena reappeared. "I'll take that basin and the wet washcloth and towel. Do you need anything else?" She began gathering the articles.

"Just lunch. It smells good."

"Chicken and dumplings. I made it thick so you could manage it."

144

"One of my favorites." Ilian couldn't help smiling. "And maybe some coffee too . . . please."

"Of course. I'll have it to you in a quick minute. You finish getting dressed, and I'll send Kirstin with the tray."

Ilian liked the idea of seeing Kirstin again. So far, besides the food being so much better than at the hospital, her company was what Ilian enjoyed the most.

"Pardon the interruption."

The cast on his arm made dressing tricky. Ilian had finally managed to put on the nightshirt and popped his head through the opening when he found his father standing in the doorway. He frowned. "What do you want?"

"I came to check on you. Lena said you had a good night's sleep."

"I did." Ilian adjusted the nightshirt and eased back against the pillow.

"I'm mighty glad to hear it. Lena also tells me we need a bar hanging down from the ceiling to help with getting you up and down. I brought the things to build it. I thought maybe I could do it after the doctor comes and you've had your lunch."

"Why don't you just leave it for Domar? He can do it tomorrow." Ilian didn't feel like fighting about it, but he also didn't want to endure his father's company any longer than necessary. He could be civil for a few minutes, but for a job that might take a good part of an afternoon, Ilian wasn't convinced he had the patience.

"Domar will have plenty to do when he gets here. I don't mind lending a hand. I know you don't want to be bothered with me," his father said, fixing him with a look that dared him to say otherwise, "but Lena asked me to handle it, and I will."

Ilian frowned. "Anything to increase my misery."

"That isn't why I agreed to it. I figure, since you aren't going to be able to go back to logging for a good long time—maybe never—you and I should talk about what you can do to make a living."

"And what do you have in mind for me?"

"You could help me make the Mackinaw boats. We wouldn't even have to work together, except to use the same tools and workshop. You know well how to make the boats, ja?"

"Yes, of course I know how to make them. But I definitely do not want to work with you." Ilian fought to keep his words civil. Just seeing his father and knowing that he was trying to plan for Ilian's future stirred his anger.

"Does it not bother you even a little that you might have died in your accident?"

"But I didn't."

"No, but you might have, and you would have left this life with the hateful anger still between us. Ilian, you are a grown man. Your hate might have been understandable and even excused in your youth, but you are thirty years old now. Isn't it time we put the past to rest?"

"Maybe if Mor were still alive." Ilian narrowed his eyes. "But she's not, and she left this world without being able to ever return to her family in Sweden."

"We were her family too."

Ilian clenched the covers in an iron-like grip. "You let her live in misery. Too selfish to spend a little money to take her home to Sweden."

"It wasn't my selfishness that kept us here. It was because I loved her that I couldn't take her home."

There was definite sorrow in his father's voice, but Ilian couldn't bring himself to stop. "Ja, that's certainly love—a love that killed her. Now go. I don't want to discuss this anymore."

Kirstin overheard the last of Ilian's conversation with his father, and when Habram came from the room, she was busy putting away a stack of towels in the linen closet. She watched him walk the length of the hall with his head hung low. It was hard to understand how a dead woman continued to cause such misery between the two men.

She finished with the towels and went to the kitchen, where her grandmother was speaking to Habram in hushed tones. He nodded and left out the back door.

Mormor looked up and smiled. "Would you mind taking Ilian his lunch?"

"No, not at all." Kirstin moved to where the tray was ready and waiting. She thought about asking Mormor why Ilian hated his father so much. Mormor had mentioned in the past that Ilian blamed his father for his mother being sad and miserable. Habram had even told her a little bit, but it just didn't add up. Mrs. Farstad had never liked America, but Habram wouldn't even consider returning to Sweden. Why?

Kirstin took the tray to Ilian's room and could see he was hardly in a very good position to eat. She placed the tray on the dresser and went to the bed. "Let's see if we can get you propped up a little better for eating."

He grumbled something inaudible.

She pulled away many of the pillows they'd used to make

his nighttime rest more comfortable. "Can you scoot up if I help you?"

"Of course." His tone was surly, and it was clear he wasn't at all concerned with being congenial.

She took hold under his right shoulder, careful not to pull his arm. "I think if you can push up on the left side with your arm and bend your good knee and push, we can get you into a better position. Then I'll put the pillows around you. On the count of three. One, two, three."

She pulled up with all her might. She could be quite strong when it was required. What she hadn't planned on was slipping on a corner of the blanket. She could feel herself teetering toward the broken arm against Ilian's chest and stomach and knew if she fell, she would land on it. In that split second, however, Ilian acted, putting out his left arm to catch her in an awkward manner—his hand pressed against her neck, almost cutting off her breath.

"Are you trying to hurt me?" he growled.

Kirstin straightened. "I'm so sorry. I didn't see the blanket on the floor, and when I moved, it made me slip." She coughed and rubbed her throat.

He gave her a momentary look of contrition, then frowned. "Did I hurt you?"

She stopped rubbing her neck. "I'm fine. Be glad I wasn't putting the tray on your lap. You'd be covered in chicken and dumplings." She smiled, hoping it might lift his mood, and reached for the offending blanket. "Your covers are quite the wreck. I'll straighten them for you after we get the pillows in place."

She went to work plumping up pillows and sticking them

behind his back. The doctor had said it was all right for Ilian to sit at an incline in bed, but not to sit up fully just yet. Kirstin was mindful of this as she maneuvered the pillows under and around his shoulders and arms.

"There, now for the covers."

For modesty's sake Ilian held fast to the sheet while Kirstin pulled the other blankets from the bed. She shook them out and adjusted them to cover him from waist to toe, leaving his casted foot out. Mormor had knitted him a toe cover so that his foot wouldn't get too cold at night, so Kirstin took a moment to adjust that as well.

"There. Now it's all put right."

Ilian said nothing. It was clear his mood was black, but Kirstin wasn't going to let him get away with it. "It's customary to say thank you when someone does something nice for you."

Ilian met her gaze. His forehead furrowed. "Thank you."

She nodded and went to retrieve the tray from the dresser. "Do you want to try it on your lap or just have it on the bed beside you? Mormor made the soup very thick, almost like a casserole, so you could eat it easier. Or I'm happy to help you."

He shook his head and snapped, "I'm not helpless."

She forgot about her English and switched to rapid-fire Swedish. "I know that, but you are in a bad way, and you don't even appreciate that people are trying to help you." She didn't wait for his answer regarding the placement of the tray and set it beside him. "You don't act grateful and instead are mean and ill-tempered. That hardly seems the right way to thank someone. Honestly, I heard you barking at your father, and now you're barking at me. I'm trying to remember you have injuries that probably hurt, but I hardly see that you'll feel better by yelling."

"I didn't yell." His voice had calmed. "I'm sorry for offending you."

Kirstin straightened and studied him for a moment. "It does offend me that you hate your father so much."

"It offends me that you don't mind your own business."

"But it is my business. I'm helping nurse you to health. Your overall well-being is of my utmost concern, and your anger and bitterness is certainly not helping you heal. Maybe if you talked about why you're so angry, it would help."

"It won't help because it won't change anything. Now, leave me alone and let me eat in peace."

"I could hear you two yelling all the way to the front stoop," Domar said, coming into the room.

"Domar! I thought we wouldn't see you until this evening." Kirstin went to him and gave him a hug. "I'm glad you're here."

"What are you two fighting about?"

"If you could hear so well, you already know," Ilian replied.

Kirstin stepped back. "I don't know why you bother to be friends with someone who can so easily push away people who love and care about him."

Ilian gave a huff. "I don't push away those people who deserve my respect and love."

"How is it that you have the right to judge who deserves your respect and love? You aren't God, and as far as I can tell, you don't even practice good sense." She folded her arms against her body and fixed him with what she hoped was a stern look.

"And neither do you." Ilian shook his head. "You need to

understand that there are things in this world that do not include you."

Kirstin looked at her brother. "I think your friend may have sustained a concussion in that accident. His mind isn't working well."

Domar laughed. "Nope. He's always been stubborn."

"Are you taking her side in this?" Ilian asked, his brows rising.

Holding up his hands, Domar shook his head. "No. Don't put me in the middle of this. I just came to say hello and see how you are after a month of pampering."

"The doctor is due in this afternoon, so I guess we'll find out then." Ilian motioned to the chair. "Why don't you keep me company while I eat my lunch?"

"Let me grab a bowl for myself, and I'll be right back."

"Good. You can take care of him when he can't handle something," Kirstin declared and headed for the kitchen.

She was completely exasperated with Ilian. How was she supposed to help him and his father put their lives back together if he wouldn't be open and honest with her about why he hated Habram so much?

"Having difficulties with Ilian, are you?" Mormor asked from where she was cracking nuts.

Kirstin heard Domar coming down the hall and shook her head. "I'm just sick and tired of people and their unwillingness to just talk. Everything has to be so secretive."

"Talking about me, are you?" Domar asked, throwing Kirstin a smile.

"I'm talking about anyone who refuses to understand that truth is better than lies."

"And exactly who is lying?" Domar asked, getting a bowl

and helping himself to the chicken and dumplings. "Not much broth, eh?"

"There's more broth on the back of the stove you can add to yours," Mormor replied. "Ilian needs it nice and thick. He has only one hand with which to feed himself, and he doesn't like to be helped or babied."

"As far as I can see, he doesn't like much of anything." Kirstin went to get her own bowl.

"He was certainly happy enough with you last night when you helped him be more comfortable in bed." Mormor grinned.

"What's this?" Domar asked, looking at Kirstin as if she had plenty of explaining to do.

"Oh, I'm not going to tell you. Everyone else thinks it's just fine to say nothing, so I will follow your example." She pushed past Domar and helped herself to the chicken and dumplings. "What I will say, however—" she paused and looked at both Mormor and Domar—"is that Habram is a very nice man, and I like him. He's done nothing but treat me with kindness and joy. If I have to pick a side, I'm picking his, because no one who acts as he does could possibly be to blame for all the anger and bitterness I heard in Ilian's voice."

"Maybe," Domar said, "it's best not to be judgmental about either one. Each man carries his burdens and cares. Some he'll share, but others he feels compelled to carry alone. Neither tears nor jeers will change the mind of a determined man."

"That is very true, Domar. It's best not to interfere," Mormor said. "That's what your morfar would have said about it. Sometimes we don't get to know everything about a situation or matter." She reached out and gave Kirstin's arm a pat. "Sometimes it's best to just let them explain in their time, rather than trying to force it."

"All I know is I was raised to tell the truth and be open with people when they asked me for explanations." Kirstin stuck her spoon into the thick soup. "The Bible says the truth will set us free, but I guess some folks enjoy the prisons they've made for themselves."

Mormor nodded. "You're right. Some do." She glanced at Domar. "For whatever reason, some do."

Chapter 13

"I think you're improving, Ilian. Your range of motion is good, so I know you've been doing the exercises I gave you." The doctor smiled and then listened to Ilian's heart. "You sound good." He straightened. "You show no signs of infection, and your blood circulation is good."

"Does that mean I can get up and start moving around?"

"Well, a little more than you have been, yes. The problem is that you've got a broken arm as well as a broken leg. You can't use the crutches in the manner you need to with just one crutch. You won't have the necessary stability, and the last thing you want to do is fall. A fall could seriously undermine all that we've accomplished."

Ilian didn't try to hide his feelings about the matter. "I'm sick of lying around."

"Well, with help and some adjustments, I will allow you to sit with your leg propped. I can show your friend Domar how to make the appropriate piece. You'll need support for the leg the full length of the cast, and it's usually best if it's made in such a way that it's attached to what you're sitting on. I'll draw it out for him."

"All right." Ilian was disappointed that he couldn't start working with crutches, but he was determined to follow orders and not lengthen his time in the casts. "When will the casts come off?"

"For the arm, just another week or two at the most. Then you'll work on strengthening it before we put you on crutches. The leg cast will be on for another few weeks. We need to give that femur plenty of time to heal. After it comes off, you'll also have to strengthen it and be on crutches for a time. We don't want to overdo it. I'll let Mrs. Segerson know that you'll be here with her probably another four, perhaps five weeks."

"So when I get the cast removed, I should be able to walk?"

The doctor frowned. "I can't tell you that for sure. As I've told you from the beginning, you may always need to walk with a cane. If the leg hasn't healed correctly, you may have limited mobility. You must be prepared for the possibilities."

"I know the future is unknown at this point, but I'd rather focus on walking and getting back to normal than consider any other possibility."

"Ilian, I don't want you to disappoint yourself. Your break was bad. We did our very best to fix that break, but the leg will always be compromised. You can't consider returning to any kind of logging work. That work is far too strenuous, and the risks are too great. You'll never be strong enough for it."

"But it's what I do for a living. Now you're telling me I must do something entirely different."

"Something far less physical. You aren't going to have the

muscle strength to climb trees and stack logs. Your forearm isn't going to hold up well to sawing or axe work."

"Well, maybe not at first, but in time I should be able to build the muscles back." Ilian waited for confirmation.

"Yes, the muscles should strengthen. I just can't be sure of that leg. I haven't seen other patients with this kind of break regain the kind of dexterity they'd need for climbing and working at the logging camps. Maybe you'll be different. For now, keep up with your exercises, and perhaps you will be the exception." The doctor glanced around and frowned. "I thought I told you to get a hanging bar of some sort over the bed." He glanced overhead. "That will help tremendously, especially after the arm cast is removed."

"It's being installed today. By the time the cast comes off, I'm sure I will have one-armed it many times." Ilian eased back against the pillow.

"Well, I'll come check on you again in a week or so. Hopefully we can remove the arm cast."

"I'll look forward to it."

"Shall I tell the others what I've told you?" the doctor asked, motioning his head toward the door.

"Please. That way maybe they'll pester you with all their questions instead of me."

The doctor nodded and gathered his medical bag. "Then I will. Ilian, I know this has been hard on you, but you are doing the best of any patient I've ever had with a similar injury. Just be patient."

"I'm trying."

Ilian watched him leave and frowned. It sounded like he was still facing a lengthy recovery. He'd have to ask Domar to pull some money from his bank savings in order to pay Lena. He wasn't about to sit around and let her take care of him for nothing. She and Kirstin had worked very hard to see that he had what he needed.

"So the doc says you're healing up nicely," Domar said twenty minutes later, bringing his tools and building materials into the room. "If you aren't too tired, I'd like to get that hand bar put in place. Mormor had a broken broom handle that I sanded down, and I think it will work perfectly. Now I just have to find the right place in the ceiling to secure the chains."

"Chains?"

"Ja, you betcha," Domar said with a grin. "I found some old pieces of chain that I saved years ago. You should never throw things away. There's always a way to repurpose them. I remember Uncle Per asking me what I would ever do with the chain, and I said who could tell." He chuckled. "But now I know."

Ilian smiled. "Well, hopefully it will be my ticket out of this bed."

Domar sobered. "Just don't be in too big of a rush. I'd hate you to have to start all over again."

"I know. Me either."

Kirstin followed Habram out to the woodworking shop. He had already told Lena he planned to work on the boat all day, and Kirstin was hoping he would talk to her about the past. Now that Ilian was feeling better, she wanted to put his focus on healing his relationship with his dad. It gave her something to put her mind on other than what she should do about Domar. With him home this weekend and her month more than up, she had to try once more to convince him to let their folks know he was alive. If not, she was going to have to make her decision on how to handle the matter.

"Mr. Farstad?"

"Hello, Kirstin. Come in out of the cold."

She looked down the long room and spotted him at the far end, where he was working on the bow of the boat.

"You've managed to get it nice and warm in here." She walked to the stove and held out her hands. "I wondered if we might talk while you work. Or I can even help with something, if you show me how."

"No, you rest and just talk. Take a seat on that chair and tell, me what's on your mind."

She wasn't sure where to begin, and she continued standing. After thinking about it for a minute, she finally posed a question. "Do you want to mend fences with your son?"

Habram stopped what he was doing and looked at her. "I've wanted that more than anything. I'm not getting any younger, and this has been between us most of his life."

"Tell me more about it . . . if I'm not prying too much." She smiled.

He shrugged and refocused on his work. "You know the biggest part of it. His mother set him against me from the day he was born. She favored him greatly and loved him more than his sisters. But especially more than me."

"His sisters are in Kansas now, right?"

"That's right. They married farm boys. We had gone to Minneapolis for supplies, and the boys were the sons of one of the businessmen we dealt with. We were in town a couple of weeks, and the girls fell in love, and the boys asked me for their

158

hands. Sighne was only sixteen, and I thought that too young to marry. The boys had plans of moving to Kansas to start a farm together. I didn't like the idea of them living so far away. However, their mama said so long as Sighne and her husband would live close to Maja and her husband, it would be all right. Maja was twenty, and the girls were very close, so they married and moved to the Kansas Territory when it opened. They have good farms and are all very happy." Despite his words, his expression grew sad. "I think Sarah just wanted to separate us. She resented our closeness."

"How terrible. For a mother not to want closeness in her family doesn't make sense to me."

"Ja, it's hard to ponder, but it's behind us now." He forced a smile. "They have stayed close to me. They write often and tell me all about their families. Someday I want to visit them. Maybe take your grandmother too."

"I'll bet she'd like that very much." Kirstin tried to be as encouraging as possible, but she wanted him to continue the story. "So that left just you and your wife and Ilian?"

"Ja. Ilian was only fourteen. He was already sympathetic to his mother and wanted very little to do with me unless it was to plead her case. But there were things he just didn't understand and was too young to know."

"What kinds of things?" Kirstin blurted, then immediately regretted it. "I'm so sorry. I know that's none of my business."

"There was always difficulty between Sarah and me. Not only was our marriage arranged, but Sarah loved another. She blamed me the rest of her life for tearing her away from her true love."

"Was that the real reason she wanted to go back to Sweden?"

"Ja, I think so. She did love her sisters and wanted to be close to them, but her heart was consumed by her love for another."

Kirstin had warmed sufficiently and moved away from the stove, finally taking a seat. "That's really hard to live with."

"Ja." Habram focused his attention on sanding.

"Does Ilian know this?"

"No." Habram stopped and turned to Kirstin. "I couldn't tell him while his mother lived. When she died from whooping cough while he was in the war, then I thought finally I could tell him this. Tell him everything."

She wondered if Mr. Farstad would refuse her closeness, but she went to him anyway and touched his arm. "And did you? Is that why he wants nothing more to do with you?"

"No." Mr. Farstad's blue eyes bored into her. "He never returned home to live again. He told me I had killed his mother as surely as if I'd put a knife in her back."

Kirstin's hand went to her mouth. She couldn't imagine anyone being so heartless. How could Ilian ever think such a thing of his father?

Habram gave her a sad smile. "He's not a cruel person by nature," he said, almost as if he'd read her mind. "He was just speaking from the pain he felt."

Kirstin lowered her hand. "I think it's time you told him the truth. Tell him before he gets the casts off and can run away from hearing it. Whatever the truth is, it will be better for the telling."

In that moment she knew the answer to her own predicament. She didn't want to betray Domar, but he was the one setting the rules regarding truth. Not her. She wanted her mother to know the truth so she could put her mind at ease—so she could ask Domar's forgiveness for having blamed him falsely.

"You have a funny look on your face. Are you all right?" Habram asked.

Kirstin looked up and met his gaze. "I just realized in saying what I did to you that I have the answer to my own ordeal. The truth will set us free. Yes, it might hurt some, but it is always good to tell the truth and deal with the consequences, even when they aren't of our own making."

Habram considered this for a moment. "Yes, but sometimes it isn't our truth to tell."

This time it was Kirstin who took a moment to consider. "But when the person responsible for speaking that truth can't or won't . . . don't we have an obligation to do so? When we know the truth and say nothing—let the lie live on—aren't we lying as well?"

Habram nodded. "You make a good point. I shall have to pray about this tonight."

Hoping he wouldn't take offense, Kirstin hugged him. "You are like a grandfather to me, and I've come to care about you very much. Please know you always have a friend in me, Mr. Farstad."

"Call me Habram. I will consider you another of my grand-daughters."

Kirstin smiled. "I'll do better than that. I'll call you Morfar."

Chapter 14

"Well, I'm heading to bed," Mormor declared. "My bones are aching something fierce, and I think the warmth will do me good."

"I'll get the warming pan," Kirstin said, getting to her feet.

Domar watched his sister, knowing that when she returned, they would talk about her decision. She had asked him that afternoon to make time to talk to her after Mormor went to bed. She had no way of knowing how her coming to America had affected him. He hadn't realized how much he'd missed his parents and siblings until he'd seen Kirstin again. Maybe it was time to give up the lie and let them know he was alive.

Mormor had talked a lot about it when he'd first come to America, but once he set down the rule that he would leave if she said anything, she gave up. He had been quite the bully about it, and now he felt ashamed. She'd only been concerned about her daughter's brokenhearted sorrow. When Domar thought of the pain he'd caused—really let himself consider it—it was all he could do to keep from racing back to Sweden on the first boat. He'd never meant to cause that kind of pain. He'd never allowed himself to even think of it. He'd been young and prideful, and his feelings had been hurt by the way not one person stood up for him except Kirstin.

He owed her more than he liked to admit.

"There, that's all taken care of. Mormor is so smart. Do you know she puts warmed rocks in her warming pan rather than embers? She had a friend whose house burned down when the bed warmer caught the covers on fire. Her friend was barely able to get out of the house. So after that, she started warming small rocks in the oven and then loading them into the bed warmer." Kirstin sat in Mormor's rocking chair. "I think that's so very smart."

"It is. I'm glad to know that. I won't worry so much about her that way."

"I don't think we have to worry about her anyway. I believe it won't be long before she and Mr. Farstad marry."

Domar chuckled. "You've come to that conclusion, have you?"

Kirstin tucked her feet under her and pulled a knitted blanket over her body. "I have. They are very much in love. That's obvious."

"Yes, I agree. It's only really happened in the last couple of years. I thought maybe they'd marry when Uncle Per was still alive, but it just never seemed to fit."

"She said they're waiting for God to tell them it's time."

Kirstin watched the fire for a moment. Domar knew she was most likely trying to figure out how to broach the subject they needed to discuss, so he opened the matter himself.

"Have you decided what you're going to do regarding my being alive?"

She said nothing for several long minutes. When she finally looked at him, there were tears in her eyes. "I have, but it pains me to tell you. There was no possibility of either choice being without pain. I think that's why I kept putting it off."

"But you're going to tell them."

She nodded and wiped at her tears. "Ja. I can't keep your lie. I'm sorry. I know that means I will lose you, and it breaks my heart in two. I just ask that you hear me out and try to understand my position."

Domar found he wasn't at all angry, nor did he want to argue with her. In a sense, he felt relief. Maybe this was what he'd needed to prod him to do the right thing. But what if it wasn't the right thing?

Kirstin drew a deep breath. "I was speaking with Mr. Farstad earlier today. We were talking about his situation with Ilian. The years—a lifetime of anger and hostility between them. Mr. Farstad said there were so many things Ilian didn't know—issues and complications that made his decisions for him. I told him maybe it was time to tell Ilian the truth. I said, 'Whatever the truth is, it will be better for the telling.' That's when I knew the answer to my own dilemma. There will be consequences, but in the long run, the truth is what will set us free."

"But there will be pain in telling the truth just as there would be in continuing to keep the truth from them." Domar didn't have much of an argument left in him. He knew she was right.

"Yes, but at least it will be done with. Your conscience will be clear, no matter where you run away to, and they will know the truth. Mor will be relieved, even if she knows she can never see you again. She'll know that you're alive and well. It will break her heart to know you'll have nothing to do with her, but again, that's a part of the consequences you have created."

"And you think that heartbreak is better than believing me gone?"

"No. Sadly, I don't think there is a winning side to this pain. I suppose that's what has made it so difficult. I think Mr. Farstad believes his situation is much the same. However, keeping the lie—feeding it and carrying it—is exhausting and dangerous. It perpetuates the bitterness and anger and will do nothing but cause harm. The truth isn't that way. The Bible says the truth shall set us free. The Bible says that Jesus is the truth. I suppose in seeking Him rather than our own desires, it ought to be clear to us how we should handle this matter, but it hasn't made it any easier for me."

"Nor for me."

Kirstin's brows came together as she considered something. Domar remembered her looking very similar when perplexed by a mathematics problem during her school years. "I wanted so much for there to be an easy answer that would please us both. I wanted to be like Mormor and say, 'Well, it's not my job to set the world right.' But if it's not my job," she said, looking up at him, "then whose?"

Domar leaned back and put his arms behind his head. "When will you write to them?"

"Not until they write to me. I sent a letter when I arrived and have heard nothing yet. It takes a long time to get mail from Sweden. Mormor says it might even be March or April before my letter reaches them. Then another few months until they can get a letter to me. That will give you plenty of time to make your plans and let us have you for a while longer." A sob broke from her throat. "I hate that I shall lose you. I only just found you again." Tears streamed down her face, and Domar knew he couldn't let her bear this misery.

"Don't cry. When you write to them, I'll include a letter of my own."

"You will?" She blinked against her tears, but the look of hope he saw on her face was unmistakable.

"I will. I won't leave you."

"But you said . . ."

"I know what I said." He sat up and reached out to touch her hand. "You've convinced me that it's the right thing to do. I don't know what's going to happen. I don't know if my heart will be forgiving. I have no idea what the future will bring, but I know it's the right thing to do."

Kirstin unwound herself from the chair and came to sit beside Domar on the couch. She hugged him close. "I love you so much. I felt certain I was sacrificing you for the truth, and it was almost worth the lie."

He chuckled. "Almost, eh?"

She looked up and kissed his check. "Almost."

Kirstin checked on Ilian once more before heading upstairs to bed. She felt lighter and happier than she had since learning that her brother was alive. She very nearly danced up the narrow steps. She prayed silently, thanking God all the way to her room.

There was still the matter of actually doing the deed and hearing back from their family, but she felt certain that the initial reaction was going to be one of such joy that nothing else would matter. In time they could deal with everything else.

In her room, she knelt beside the bed. The floor was icy, but she didn't care. "Oh, Father, thank you that Domar saw the truth. Thank you for giving me the bravery to follow through on what You told me to do. I felt that I was under such a terrible burden, and now You have lifted that off my shoulders. Help me, please, to always be willing to speak truth even when it's hard like this."

She thought of the folks at home. "Please help them to understand why Domar made the choices he did. Help them to forgive him and to offer their requests for forgiveness as well. Let the tallies be wiped out and the debts paid in full. Let there be rejoicing.

"And let Mr. Farstad . . . let Morfar share the truth with Ilian, and let Ilian be willing to receive it and forgive whatever lies between them. Let both be willing to let go of the past and focus on the future in love. Father, they need each other and can't even see it. Let them realize how much they need this alliance. Let them learn the importance of forgiveness and love."

She sighed and got to her feet. She tossed her robe over the chair and got into bed with great haste. The covers and sheets were as cold as the floor, but they would warm quickly enough. She snuggled down and smiled.

"Thank you, Lord. Amen."

Feeling greatly reassured, Kirstin all but floated through the morning chores. She knew Mormor thought her a bit tetched but said nothing. Maybe she suspected the reason for her mood, but she waited for Kirstin and Domar to tell her.

Domar spoke first. "I'm going to tell our family that I'm alive."

Mormor's eyes widened. "And what brought this about? As if I didn't already know."

"Kirstin convinced me that the truth is better than a lie. I'm tired of living with this hanging over me." Domar smiled. "And I have to admit, I had a better sleep last night than I have since coming to America."

"I'm so glad, Domar. I believe in the long run it will be for the best. It will almost be like the prodigal son coming home."

"Well, I'm not going back to Sweden. I have no desire. I wouldn't mind seeing Mor and Far again, though, and even Härse and Svena and little Brita."

"She's not so little anymore," Kirstin reminded him.

Domar smiled. "She was just a babe when I left, and I've never known her." He looked at his grandmother. "Never think I am without my regrets."

"I know you have regrets. I could see them in your eyes every time you came home."

"I truly regret making you keep my lie." He lowered his head. "I never thought of it that way. Kirstin helped me see it over this last month. I suppose I needed someone to be strong and confront me with the truth after all these years. I'm so sorry, Mormor. I pray you'll forgive me. I put you in such a bad position."

"Of course I forgive you." She patted his hand. "Just as your parents will."

"I hope so." He looked up, and his eyes were damp. "I hope so."

They ate breakfast and talked about the work yet to do.

Mormor never liked Domar to have to help her on the Sabbath. She felt it was a day of rest, but with so much needing attention before he left that afternoon, they decided to forgo church and take care of the problems while Domar was there to help. He convinced her by saying he had already had such a tender time with God the night before and that this morning he felt as if he'd been to a month of services.

As the morning and early afternoon passed in quick succession, Domar realized he only had about two hours remaining before his ride would come to take him back to the logging camp. He wanted to spend some time with Ilian and let him know what he'd decided and why. He hoped it would encourage Ilian to clear up things in his own family.

"Do you have time for a talk?" Domar asked from the doorway to Ilian's room.

Ilian looked up from the book he'd been reading. "Ja, sure. Come on in."

Domar smiled as he crossed the room. "How are you feeling?"

"Better now that I can sit in a chair."

"And that is comfortable?" Domar pointed to the board that extended from the chair Ilian sat on to another to hold his leg. Kirstin had made a long padded cushion so that Ilian wouldn't have to sit on a hard wood surface the entire time.

"Your sister is gifted in knowing where to place pillows. She tucks them here and there in places I don't even think will help, and yet they turn out to be the very thing I needed most."

"She is gifted. She's helped me in a big way too." Domar pulled up a kitchen chair and turned it around to sit on it backwards. He rested his arms atop the chairback and lowered his chin to sit on his hands. "I'm going to tell my parents that I'm alive."

"Truly?" Ilian's look of disbelief was genuine. "I never thought this day would come. But I'm glad. You know I believed you should save your family pain if you could. But what happened to them never deserving to know?"

"Well, none of us deserves the grace we're given. At least I know I don't." Domar gave his head a slight shake. "I guess as I listened to the things Kirstin said, I realized the futility of what I was doing. The sinfulness too."

"What sin? You aren't the one who rejected them by believing a lie. You didn't shun them and force them to leave their home. You're the one who was betrayed. You owe them nothing."

"I owe God everything, though—especially truth. I was reading my Bible last night. Romans 12:18 says I should live at peace with all men. I just think it's time I let the past go. I cannot change anything that happened back there. I can't. But I can change the future, and I think I'd like that. I'd like to talk to Mor again. I'd like them to know what I've become."

"If that's important to you," Ilian began, "then so be it. But don't do it just because your sister has put you in a situation of having to admit it."

"I'm not. She has offered wise counsel, and that has influenced my decision, but I'm doing this of my own free will. It's the right thing for me to make peace."

"I suppose you think I should make peace with my father as well." Ilian gave him a hard look. "Well, I can tell you I'm not going to do it."

Kirstin came in through the open door at that moment. Both

men turned to stare at her. She looked behind her and then back at the men. "What is it?"

"If you've come to persuade me I need to make peace with my father, don't even start," Ilian reprimanded.

Kirstin looked at her brother and then back at Ilian. "I didn't say anything about your father."

"I just heard that you convinced Domar to tell your folks that he's alive. That might be all well and fine for him, but it's not going to work for me."

"And what makes you think I care one whit about you? I haven't even decided whether we can be friends," Kirstin said. "And with you acting like this, my decision is rapidly being made for me."

"I can't be friends with someone who is friends with my father," Ilian shot back.

Kirstin put her hands on her hips. "Then I'll let Mormor know, and we'll get you moved elsewhere. I'm sure she has no desire to take care of someone who won't allow her to choose for herself whom she can befriend. I've no doubt she won't give up your father's friendship."

"I don't mean it that way, and you know it."

"I doubt she does," Domar interjected, "because even I'm confused by your sudden attitude."

Ilian cast aside the book on his lap. "You know how it's been between us, Domar. I don't want to be berated by your sister about renewing my relationship with Far."

"And have I been doing that?" Kirstin asked.

"No, but now that you have your brother forced into telling your folks he's alive, I'm almost certain you'll start in on me."

Domar crossed his arms. "Now get this straight, Ilian. I made my own choice. Kirstin didn't force me to do anything. You are creating a false picture for yourself if you believe otherwise. She made some good points, but I chose what I wanted."

Ilian's hard expression relaxed. "I'm sorry, Domar. I didn't mean to put you in this position. I know you to be your own man, but I also know how much you love your sister. If this is truly your decision, then please forgive me for thinking otherwise. No one wants us all to be friends more than I do."

"Well, I don't know that I want to be your friend at all." Kirstin started for the door. "I've never met anyone more selfish and hard-hearted. I'm not even sure you're capable of friendship, and I certainly won't give up my friendship with your father just because you want to go on bearing him a grudge. Grief, you won't even hear out the poor man's side of the matter. Why would I ever want to be friends with someone like that? The price would be much too high, as far as I'm concerned."

She left with both Ilian and Domar staring after her.

Domar grinned as he turned back to Ilian. "I never knew her to have a temper like that. You must bring out the worst in her."

Ilian frowned. "Would you help me back to bed?"

"Of course." Domar got up and pulled back the covers. "But if you're planning to relocate yourself to a boardinghouse, tell me now. I leave in less than two hours."

Ilian looked at him oddly. "What are you talking about?"

"Well, Kirstin is right about one thing. Mormor and your father are very close these days. You aren't going to be allowed to come between them. So if you can't handle that situation, you'd best stop living under her care. I won't have you hurting Mormor."

Ilian's jaw clenched and unclenched. "I know they hold strong affection for each other. I love your grandmother and wouldn't do anything to hurt her."

Domar nodded. "Good. I think Kirstin can fight for herself, but I won't have Mormor in the middle of it. Now, give me your arm."

Chapter 15

A week and a half later, having seen very little of Kirstin, and never without Lena present, Ilian still couldn't get her words out of his head. She acted as if the rift between him and his father was all his fault. She didn't understand how his father had betrayed and deeply hurt the wife he promised to love and cherish. Kirstin didn't know the things Ilian knew about his mother's loneliness and sorrow. She had been a perfect wife, as far as Ilian could see, and received nothing in return.

Ilian flexed his arm. The doctor had come early that morning and removed his arm cast. The weakness in those muscles surprised Ilian. Not only had he been faithful with his exercises, but maneuvering the cast itself was like lifting a weight. The doctor admonished him to move steadily but slowly as he worked toward using the crutches. Ilian was already determined to be using them by the end of the week, no matter what anyone thought. He needed to be back on his feet. This lying and sitting about was going to make him crazy, especially as the weather warmed.

But it was Kirstin who was really making him feel out of sorts. She wouldn't come to play checkers or read to him. She wouldn't speak more than two or three words when she came to help Lena change the bed and tidy the room. She was angry, and Ilian had never known a woman to be angry with him. It troubled him deeply.

"Well, I'm sure you're glad to have that cast off," Lena said, bringing him his lunch. She put the tray on the table beside him, then pulled it closer so he could reach it without difficulty. "There's a hint of warmth in the air today. Makes me think of spring and planting a garden."

"Too early for that," Ilian said, smiling. "What have you made me today?"

"Oh, this is just some of that fish and potatoes hotdish left over from last night. You seemed to like it, so I thought maybe you'd be willing to eat it another day."

"I am happy to eat whatever you give me. In fact, I have some money for you. I keep forgetting to give it to you."

"Money? Whatever for?" Lena asked as she went about looking for anything in the room that needed her attention.

"You've taken care of me for nearly two months now. You need to be reimbursed."

"Your far has already taken care of that many times over. I told him no, just as I'm telling you, but he didn't listen."

Ilian frowned. "Far isn't responsible for my debts."

"I know that well enough," Lena said, coming to stand in front of him. "He knows it too. He was just being kind, and I don't want you making him feel bad for it."

Ilian was surprised by her comment. It was very nearly a reprimand. She was starting to sound like Kirstin.

"I don't plan to make anyone feel bad for anything, but I do believe in paying my own debts."

Lena nodded. "Then you take that up with him." She gave him a broad smile. "I forgot to bring the applesauce. Let me fetch it."

"No, please wait." Ilian didn't want there to be any problems between him and Lena. "I'm sorry if I was harsh. You know things are difficult between Far and me."

"I do."

Ilian looked past her to the papered wall. "I . . . well, I am glad he kept up with the debt. I hadn't really thought about it until recently because of the pain and frustration of being bedfast. I apologize for that, because I'm sure the added cost of my being here wasn't easy for you without someone to provide for you."

"Nonsense. God provides for me and always has. And you've been very little trouble. Oh, you eat more than Kirstin and I, but Domar does too, and he gives me money all the time, well beyond what he eats. Your father is always looking out for me, even before you came to stay here."

"I know. You care about each other very much."

"We do." Lena drew a deep breath. "You'd do well to figure out how to care about each other before it's too late. Man has only so many years on this earth, and you never know which will be your last. You might think you can make things right later rather than sooner, but sometimes that isn't the opportunity we get."

"But you know how things were. You knew my mother."

"Ilian, I did know your mother, and a more bitter and selfish woman I never met."

His jaw dropped, and Lena continued.

"I can see you never expected me to say such a thing, and

usually I am not one to speak ill of the dead, but in all my time with her . . . that was what I knew of her. She had no forgiveness in her heart. No kindness toward her husband and certainly no love. It can't be easy to live without love, but your father had it from neither of you, and yet he continued to work hard to support you both and to show nothing but generosity. I never heard him raise his voice to your mother, and you know we live close enough to very nearly hear each other's whispers. Yet I heard her nag and rail at him, screaming at the top of her lungs. It was embarrassing to witness it, and I felt sorry for her, but as a married woman, she should have respected her husband and at least allowed him his dignity."

Ilian was taken aback. That wasn't what he remembered of his mother. He remembered her tears and quiet sorrows. Her misery. Oh, there were fights, to be sure, and yes, if he was honest, she started most of them and fought on long after his father wished to end it. Ilian had always told himself that was because his father didn't care enough to understand her feelings, but maybe it was because there was nothing he could say or do to make her feel better.

"I know you loved her," Lena said, coming to his side. "I don't want you to stop. But you need to rethink the past and realize she was a bitter person. She made everyone around her feel it, and if you are honest with yourself, you'll see that her bitterness is what you feel for your father. Your father never wronged you. He went out of his way to be a good man to you—a good example. He loved you very much. He loves you now. You've never even tried to embrace his love, but it's always been there for you." She patted his shoulder. "There is no worse regret and sadness than having the power to make a

thing right but leaving it undone and then finding it too late."
She didn't wait for his response but headed for the door. "I'll
get your applesauce."

Ilian continued to stare at the door even after she returned
with the applesauce and then left again. He was humbled by her
words, knowing it to be true that he'd never given his father a
chance to be right in any situation. He had heard some of his
father's point of view regarding the lack of money to travel,
the poor timing or inability to get away from work, but Ilian
had never really seen any of that as valid. They were excuses,
nothing more.

He picked up his fork and thought of Domar. His friend
would advise Ilian to take it to God, to pray about it, but prayer
had never meant much to Ilian. He'd never believed God had
actual time or interest to listen to His creation.

But maybe he'd been wrong about that. Maybe he was wrong
about a lot of things.

That afternoon Pastor Persson from the Swedish Methodist Church came to visit. In the past Ilian had wanted nothing
more than a passing nod from the preacher, but today he had
questions for the man of God.

Lena seemed just as content to set up the visitation in Ilian's
bedroom as to hold it in the living room. Even Kirstin joined
them, much to Ilian's surprise. She looked so pretty with her
hair braided down her back and covered with a simple white
cap. She wore a traditional Swedish outfit with her skirt, blouse,
and vest done in colors of blue, green, and pale yellow.

"So there, how ya doing today?" Pastor Persson asked Lena

once he was settled in his chair. "You weren't in church the week before, and I didn't see you on Sunday either. I feared perhaps Mr. Farstad had suffered a setback."

"Actually, no," Lena answered before anyone else could. "Kirstin and I were there this week, but we sat behind the De-Groots. You know how tall all those boys are, and because of Ilian, we hurried home right after the service." She grinned. "The week before, however, we played hooky. I had so much to accomplish before my grandson Domar headed back to the logging camp that we made the next day our Sabbath."

"Oh, I'm relieved to hear that. It's not usual for you to be gone. I would have come to visit last week, but I had a cold and didn't want to spread it to my congregation."

"And now are you feeling better?" Kirstin asked.

"I am. Thank you. A little hot tea and rest and I'm right as can be. Ilian, I see you have your arm back."

Ilian nodded. "I do, and it's a great relief. I'm hoping soon they'll take off the leg cast as well."

"The doctor is quite pleased with his progress." Lena got to her feet. "I'm going to check on our tea and cookies. Kirstin, why don't you come help me, and then Ilian and Pastor Persson can get caught up on all that talk men like to discuss."

The ladies left, and Ilian couldn't help but smile. "Do you have anything to talk about? If not, I have some questions."

The pastor smiled. "Go right ahead."

Ilian wasted no time. "My mother was something of a Deist, and I fashioned my beliefs after hers. I don't consider myself to be a Deist . . . really I don't consider myself much of anything when it comes to religion. I believed in a Creator. I didn't be-lieve in prayer, except perhaps to praise Him for what He had created, but otherwise I found it useless to expect He would be involved in our requests."

"I'm very familiar with the Deist way of thinking," Persson declared. "I had an uncle who practiced that way of belief."

"Then, of course, you understand." Ilian shook his head. "But Lena and her family aren't of that thinking. They believe God is active in our lives. They see prayer as a way to be in constant communication with God. They believe God sent Jesus to save us from our sins and that the Bible is a book written by men who were given words from God. I've never thought such a thing, but of late I am rather comforted to think that might be true."

"Is it so hard to believe that a Creator could have created a book of history, laws, and His desires for mankind? He is very logical in that way, no? After all, He would surely know that chaos would ensue without directions for order. The Bible is filled with logic and reason, as the Deist mind would surely appreciate."

"But shouldn't truth be subject to the authority of human reason? After all, we were created by God. . . . Is it not also true that He gave us the ability to reason for ourselves?"

"But should there not be one profound and righteous truth over all reasoning? And shouldn't that be God's truth—His wisdom?" Pastor Persson took out his Bible and opened it. After flipping through the pages, he paused. "This is from First Corinthians, chapter one. Paul is encouraging the people to be of one mind in God. He's telling them how important unity is and how little value the wisdom of the world holds. He says here in verse nineteen, 'For it is written, I will destroy the wisdom of the wise, and will bring to nothing the understanding of the prudent. Where is the wise? Where is the scribe? Where is the disputer of this world? Hath not God made foolish the wisdom of this world? For after that in the wisdom of God the world by wisdom knew not God, it pleased God by the foolishness of preaching to save them that believe.' Later, starting in verse twenty-five, Paul says, 'Because the foolishness of God is wiser than men; and the weakness of God is stronger than men. For ye see your calling, brethren, how that not many wise men after the flesh, not many mighty, not many noble, are called: But God hath chosen the foolish things of the world to confound the wise; and God hath chosen the weak things of the world to confound the things which are mighty; And base things of the world, and things which are despised, hath God chosen, yea, and things which are not, to bring to nought things that are: That no flesh should glory in his presence.'"

Ilian sat back for a moment and considered the Scriptures. "I don't think I understand."

"Logic and reasoning have no power over what is most important. Wisdom cannot save you, Ilian. Only the cross can do that. Man may reason and speak from his authority all he likes, but he doesn't realize it has already failed him."

"So we put aside my reasoning . . . . my logical conclusions. Then tell me this: I hear Domar talk about his relationship with God. Tell me why Christians believe in God as their Father, in Jesus as their Savior, and the Holy Ghost as one who counsels and offers comfort."

Pastor Persson smiled. "You want me to tie it all up in an easy-to-understand package, eh?"

"That would be very nice," Ilian said, chuckling in spite of himself.

"It really isn't that hard. Love is at the core of it all. You believe God is perhaps indifferent. The Bible tells us otherwise. The Bible tells us that God is love, and everything about Him proves that to be true. The sinful nature of man has corrupted God's creation. Sometimes the illogical reasonings of those who believe they know better are a stumbling block that creates chaos. God is love. That is at the very heart of relationship, wouldn't you say?"

"I suppose. The love of a man and woman draws them together. The love of mother and child bonds them in a way that is like no other. The love of friends for one another causes them to go above and beyond what they might do for a stranger. Love is powerful in a relationship."

The older man smiled. "God is powerful in a relationship, because He is love in its purest form. When sin entered the world and mankind was corrupted and turned from God, He did not stand by indifferent. We are His children. A parent who loves His own is not going to give them up. So God sent His son, Jesus, to give us a way to reconcile our relationship. The very source of love sent love to prove His love for us, even while we were still sinners."

The words stirred something in Ilian's heart. "And this love is what we find at the cross? A love that will have no ending?"

The pastor nodded. "How could it end? God's very nature is love. Love would only die if God died, and He cannot. He goes on forever with no beginning and no end. Jesus died on the cross as an act of love, but He rose from the grave in an even greater truth of love. His love has not only conquered death—it has given us eternal life with Him."

"Here we are, gentlemen," Lena said, bringing in a tray with tea and cups. Behind her, Kirstin carried a plate of cookies. Lena set the tray on the dresser. "Just put the cookies on the bed where they can reach them."

Kirstin came closer to Ilian. She refused to look at him, as she had before, but this time Ilian didn't mind. His thoughts were full of what Pastor Persson had just told him. It seemed to make so much sense. Sense that hadn't been there before.

Lena handed the pastor and Ilian each a cup of tea. "Were you having a good discussion?"

Ilian tensed. He didn't really mind Lena knowing about their talk, but he was still trying to understand, and he didn't need anything complicating the matter for him.

Pastor Persson smiled. "Of course. I always enjoy discussing the world around us. Ilian will be more than happy when his recovery is complete, I'm sure, and by then perhaps we can take a walk and enjoy the spring. It will be here before we know it."

"Oh, I know. I long for it," Lena agreed. "I get a hint of warmth, and I want to be digging in the dirt and planting seeds. My chickens long for it as well."

"All creation no doubt longs for it."

Ilian relaxed and sipped the tea. He didn't know if Pastor Persson understood his feelings or not, but he appreciated the man's discretion.

They chatted for another ten minutes or so until the pastor announced he should be moving on. He allowed Lena to wrap a half-dozen cookies for him to take home and then bid them good-bye.

Kirstin was left to clean up as Lena escorted the pastor to the door. Ilian took the opportunity to make his apology.

"I'm sorry for the way I acted."

She looked at him, not speaking nor changing her expression.

"I know I was harsh, and I have no right to tell you who you can be friends with. That was ungracious of me."

"It was mean and selfish," she snapped back.

He might have smiled at her spunkiness at another time, but right now he merely nodded. "You're right."

She relaxed her blank expression with just a hint of a smile.

"I hope you'll forgive me. I never meant to dictate who could be your friend. The road I've walked with my father has been difficult, but I am rethinking the past, and partly because of your influence. But I don't want to be pestered about it. I must come to it in my own way."

"I can be pushy," she murmured. "I recognize that. I like to fix things and make bad situations good."

"So can we clear the slate between us and start again? I'm not asking you to be my friend, but maybe we could be at peace with each other and work toward that possibility."

Kirstin nodded. "I'd like that."

Ilian's apology had taken Kirstin by surprise. He had never seemed like the kind of man who was willing to apologize. That afternoon she took a walk near the water. The air was still cold but not quite so bitter. She had always liked the water. Rivers, creeks, lakes, oceans. It didn't matter. Water represented the possibility of things to come. After she thought Domar had been lost at sea, she'd held it in less regard, but now she thought it was appropriate. That vast ocean had presented her with possibilities she had never thought could be. On her own trip to America, she had gazed out from the deck at the greatness of the Atlantic. For days there was no end in sight, and they were but a tiny island floating across the mass of water in search of something more substantial. She remembered feeling that was a good picture of her own life.

"Miss Segerson."

Kirstin turned at the familiar voice. "Hallberg, Mr. Webster. I'm Kirstin Hallberg. My grandmother is my mother's mother, which is why she is my mormor. If she were my father's mother, she'd be my *farmor*." She thought it very rude that he hadn't bothered to remember her name.

He smiled. "I speak no language save English. It's served me well enough over the years, but at times like these, I find such information fascinating."

Kirstin shrugged. "What can I do for you?"

"I wondered if you'd talked to your grandmother about selling."

"We've discussed the situation several times, but as she's told you, she's not interested. This is her home, and she's quite content. Besides, it's winter, and no one who has a choice would move during the coldest months."

"Well, my thought was that the residents could have until May to move. It will warm up by then for sure." He smiled as though he had just offered her a grand gesture.

Kirstin looked at the surrounding neighborhood. "The people here love their homes. Why would you take that away from them, Mr. Webster? Have you never loved something enough to fight for it?"

"That's the way I feel about my plans for the land—my hotel. I want to build something beautiful that will be valuable and special to a great many people."

"At the price of taking it away from others who love it as well? I fail to see why your interests should be more important than those of the people here before you. Aren't you rather selfish for wanting everyone else to change for your needs?"

Mr. Webster looked away as one might do when caught in the act of something illegal or, worse yet, immoral. When he didn't answer, Kirstin bid him good day and headed on down the river path.

"Wait," he called to her.

Kirstin turned, and he came toward her.

"I have made myself unappealing to the folks in this neighborhood, but that was never my intention. I offered them more money than another developer might have because I wanted to be more than fair. I wanted this experience to be as good for them as it would be for me. I don't understand why they don't see it that way."

"Perhaps because some things cannot be bought with money, sir. Their memories are here. Their children grew up here, and some of them died here. Some fell in love, and many rely on the river for their jobs. You cannot expect a man to trade his livelihood for a small, temporary fortune. These are sensible people who know it's better to go forward slow and steady. The money means very little if they cannot continue to earn a living. River and bay access is critical, just as the city believes a canal is critical. You must consider the way of the water. It's life to them."

He shook his head, and Kirstin knew he would never understand.

"I must bid you good day now, Mr. Webster. I'm sorry that you are so unhappy with us, but I suppose that's just the way it must be."

"It won't be that way for long. It's been an obstacle, but in the long run I will have my way." His tone turned angry, and his expression grew hateful. "These people don't know me well enough to realize I get what I want."

Kirstin had the audacity to chuckle. "My mormor said that of you when I first met you. She said you were like a spoiled child who'd never been told no or made to wait. You've just said as much, but stranger still, you sound proud to be that way." She shook her head. "Most men would have the good sense to be embarrassed."

She left him by the river.

Chapter 16

"There's something I want you to see," Mr. Farstad told Kirstin. "It's quite interesting."

Kirstin looked up from her poached egg and toast. "What is it?"

He laughed. "A surprise. If your mormor can spare you, we'll go right after breakfast, just as the sun is about to come up."

"I've already given my permission," Mormor said, bringing the coffee to the table. "I'll take care of Ilian's breakfast and dressing. You two don't worry about a thing. He's getting along so much better now that he can move about. He's pretty spry for such a big man."

"Did I hear my name mentioned?"

They all looked in surprise at Ilian. He stood in the dining room entryway, balancing himself quite capably on his crutches.

"Look at you!" Kirstin hadn't meant to be so excited, but she couldn't help herself. "I'm so happy for you. How does it feel?"

"Not bad at all. The arm doesn't hurt a bit. The leg is heavy from the cast, but otherwise just fine. In a few more weeks I should be right as can be." Ilian's entire demeanor was changed by this simple liberty that most took for granted.

"Well, I am most impressed," Mormor announced. "Come, we'll figure out a way for you to eat at the table."

"No, I'm not dressed. That wouldn't be right."

"It's just fine," Mormor declared. "It's not like Kirstin and I haven't seen you in your nightshirt every day for the past few weeks."

Habram got up and pulled together two chairs, while Kirstin went for pillows. She returned just as Habram was helping Ilian place his leg on the chair. "It's not all that comfortable, I'm sure," the older man said by way of apology.

"No, I don't think I've been truly comfortable since before the accident," Ilian replied.

"Well, the doctor is pleased with your healing," Mormor said, bringing another plate to the table. She had already placed four poached eggs and two thick slices of ham on the plate. "Here you go. I was going to bring this to you in bed, but it's so much nicer to have you here."

"What were you all discussing so intently when I came into the room?" Ilian asked.

"Your father is taking Kirstin to see ice stacking."

Kirstin tucked a pillow behind Ilian's back. She looked up. "Ice stacking? Someone is going to stack ice? Is that like when they harvest ice for the icehouse?"

Habram laughed. "No. It's much more amazing, and we won't say anything more about it. It's a surprise."

"You'll love it," Ilian replied, smiling at Kirstin.

She liked him better this way. Perhaps the time to ponder his life and all that he'd been through had changed him. She knew he'd spoken to Pastor Persson. The older minister had wisdom from years of study. If anyone could help Ilian better understand forgiveness and God's will for their life, it would be a man of God. Still, Kirstin had hoped to have a hand in Ilian's transformation. She liked helping people that way. It was like watching caterpillars turn into butterflies. Of course, she had gotten herself into plenty of trouble by imposing herself into the lives of others, and she had also learned more than one lesson on pride.

She didn't want to be prideful about helping reconcile folks. She just got such a great sense of satisfaction from seeing fences mended.

"Morfar, I saw Mr. Webster yesterday," she mentioned, reclaiming her seat. "I was walking in the neighborhood, and he stopped me."

"I've heard his plans with the city are very soon to be approved," Habram admitted.

"What? Truly?" Kirstin could hardly bear the idea that so many people would lose their homes. "Perhaps we should go to the next council meeting."

"Ja. Could be that might prove useful," he agreed. "There's to be one tomorrow night, but I think the decision is made. My guess is we'll have another month or so, but hardly more. I expect them to wind up business on this, because as soon as the thaw comes, the only thing that will concern them is going to be the canal."

"Habram's right." Mormor handed around the toast rack. "We must continue to pray for God's direction and to be ready for whatever His will might be. I've already started to pack things, just as you suggested, Habram."

"Do you suppose His will would ever be to move you from the place you love?" Kirstin asked, glancing first at her grandmother and then to Morfar.

"Sometimes things like that happen. It happened to Abram in the Bible. God told him to get out of his country," Morfar reminded them. "Perhaps God is saying that to us as well. I figure we need to prepare our hearts—listen to God and not worry about what man is about to do."

"I wish I could feel at peace with it," Mormor said, smearing jam on her toast. "Perhaps then it wouldn't seem so unsettled."

The older man smiled. "We're all here together, and we will fight for one another. No matter what, we have that, and we have God's mercy. It will work out." He scooted back from the table. "Now, Kirstin, if you are finished, hurry and get your boots and very warmest clothes, and we'll go see ice stacking."

Kirstin was more than a little excited about their adventure. She was grateful that Mormor had insisted she wear a long woolen cape over her coat. Having never gone to the lake, Kirstin was unprepared for the stout wind that did its best to freeze her to the bone.

It took twenty minutes to walk to where Morfar wanted them to be, but they arrived just as the sun crowned the eastern horizon. The rosy pink and orange colors, along with purples and pale reds, blended in a swirl across the sky. It was like a masterpiece painting, something drawn with exacting expertise. God's expertise.

"How beautiful!" Kirstin could scarcely look away. "It's like nothing I've ever seen."

"And you haven't even observed the ice stacking yet." Morfar pointed below to the rocky shoreline. "Look there and listen."

Kirstin followed his instructions. Down below on the shore, there were what appeared to be panes of glass pointing jaggedly to the sky. It looked as though someone had come along and stacked them there, row after row, to point heavenward. "That's ice?"

"It is. The water freezes on the surface, and then the wind blows it to shore and it breaks into great sheets."

She watched as the motion of the lake brought the ice to shore. "It looks like panes of glass for windows."

"It does," he agreed. "It's like nothing else. It will stack here for hours."

"Just listen to it. All the cracking and popping. It's almost like music." Kirstin marveled at the sight and sound. If not for the cold, she could have stood out there all day, watching and listening. "What a marvel."

"I'm glad you like it. A lot of folks find it fascinating, but some are afraid. The power of the lake is intimidating."

"It certainly is. But there's so much more. The life it gives is also amazing. Mormor told me how fishing kept folks in town alive when all else failed. She said the beauty of this place was something that always stuck with her. Sure, there are scars put on the area by man's attempts to remake it and settle it for themselves, but I remember the letters she wrote to us in Sweden. She spoke of the great forests and wildlife, the flowers and abundance, and always there was the lake." Kirstin shook her head, still overwhelmed by the riot of colors in the sky. "How could a person not fall in love?"

"It is a beauty, to be sure." Habram gave it a long look. "When I first came here . . . well, it just felt right. It felt like home, and I've always loved it."

"You love my grandmother too." She glanced at him as if to dare him to deny it. He didn't.

A smile touched his lips. "I do. She is a most precious woman, and her joy for living is unlike anything I've ever known."

"She would say that God wants us joyful. She loves the verses in James that tell us to 'count it all joy when ye fall into divers temptations.'"

"Ja. We have discussed James many times. Counting all as joy is a hard thing to do."

Kirstin nodded. "I agree. It's hard to see something like Mr. Webster's actions against the neighborhood and count that as joy."

"But we must. As the Bible goes on to say in James, 'Knowing this, that the trying of your faith worketh patience.'"

She laughed. "Ja, and 'Let patience have her perfect work, that ye may be perfect and entire, wanting nothing.' I have read it so often I've memorized it." She shivered, and the old man reached for her arm.

"We should head back."

"Oh, just a few more minutes," she begged. "I don't mind the cold."

"If you're sure."

Kirstin grinned. "I am. I have ice running in my veins, Far used to say. Being born in winter and raised in Sweden, the cold is not a bother to me. But leaving this too soon would be." She stared out at the breaking ice, absorbing the sound, cherishing the moment. "Does it always do this?"

"No. The temperature and winds have to be just right. When it comes, however, it is a wonder."

"It is. I shall always cherish this moment."

"Do you see the land just beyond this point?"

Kirstin looked in the direction he pointed. "I do. It's lovely."

"It has been suggested that this might be a good place to relocate the neighborhood. There's some access to the lake and a great stream from a creek that comes down from the north. If we work together as a neighborhood, we could certainly have what we need. Some might have a greater need to keep their businesses on the river or closer to town, but for most of us, this could suffice."

"I just can't bear to think of all of you being forced to leave. It seems so wrong, and yet I know our happiness—our joy—is in God's hands. Do you remember that little prayer they teach Swedish children, the one that starts out 'God who loves the children dear'?"

"I think so. Let's see if I remember it. '*Gud som haver barnen kär, Se till mig som liten är. Vart jag mig i världen vänder, Står min lycka i Guds händer. Lyckan kommer lyckan går—Du förbliver fader vår. Den Gud älskar lyckan får. Amen.*'"

Kirstin clapped. "Ja, exactly so. It was written for the Crown Prince of Sweden nearly one hundred years ago. 'God who holds the children dear, look after me, who is little. Wherever in the world I wander, my happiness is in God's hands. Happiness comes—happiness goes. Thou remainest our Father. He who loveth God obtaineth happiness. Amen.' Mormor taught it to me when I was young, and it was always so special to me."

"Why in particular?"

Kirstin turned from the lake and started walking toward the path. Morfar took her arm to steady her on the ice. "I suppose it was comforting to know God was watching over me, but also because of what it said about happiness—or joy, as Mormor would say. She felt it was more than just being happy—it was a sort of spiritual joy that made us complete. My joy is in God's hands. Happiness might come and go, but if we love God, we obtain true joy."

"I agree." Morfar held on to her arm as they climbed a rocky place on the path. "My Sarah never taught the children to pray. She didn't believe in it."

"How sad. I hope you did."

"I tried. I told the girls that their mother's belief was in an indifferent God, while I thought God was very much interested in all we did. I told them that God listened to our prayers, despite what others might think, and that I knew this to be personally true. The girls started going to the Swedish Methodist Church with me, and they gave their hearts to Jesus even though their mother scoffed at their choice."

"How sad to have your own mother scoff at your decision regarding God."

"I can't say I was much kinder about Ilian following his mother's beliefs. But I've thought about what you said about truth, and I plan to share all that I know with Ilian. I just wanted to tell you of my plan because afterward . . . I think he will need a good friend."

Kirstin looked up at the older man. The wrinkles in his weathered face suggested a weariness of decades, but the twinkle in his blue eyes bore proof of a liveliness that carried on and would carry him forward for many additional years.

"I will be a friend to him."

Morfar smiled. "I think you might one day be much more."

His words surprised Kirstin, but she did her best to hide her thoughts and hurried to put the focus back on Habram's problems with Ilian. "I'm glad you're going to talk to him. I have to admit to being a person who likes to fix bad situations. When I saw the problems you and Ilian shared, I wondered how I might have a part in changing things. I'm starting to see now that that isn't how God would have me be.

"After what happened to Domar, I spent a great deal of time trying to fix the hearts and minds of those in our village—in my family. Then, when the truth came out, there was some satisfaction in being right, and people thought me very wise. Now, with what's about to happen, I feel only sadness for the lost and wasted years. I know there will be pain with the truth, and for the first time, I don't want to be in the middle of trying to make this right."

"You've grown up, little Kirstin." He gave her a sympathetic smile. "When we're young, we think we have all the answers— that we have all the wisdom needed."

"Then we grow up and realize just how much we lack." Kirstin smiled.

"Ja, but don't forget your verses in James. The next section tells us that if we lack wisdom, we can ask God, and He will give."

Kirstin nodded. "Ja. He will give wisdom. His wisdom, not our own."

The following evening Habram and Lena took their seats among their neighbors at the city council meeting. It was soon called to order, and Joshua Culver spoke for several minutes as the mayor, introducing the men around him. Habram noticed the kindly Mr. Carson as well as Jordan Webster in the audience.

The council went through a handful of short reports, and then old business was introduced. "We are, I believe," Joshua began, "at that point where we will discuss the situation of Mr. Webster's request." He spoke for several minutes about what had been discussed at the last meeting. "Mr. Webster, we have considered your suggestion and found it has great merit for the city of Duluth. The waterfront properties are very important to our town's success, and those in the area pointed out by you on your drawings appear to us to be of utmost importance for the shipping industry as well as town development." He glanced around at the other council members. "Is this now new business? I get confused on that matter, but I want to suggest a vote on whether or not we should claim this portion of town through eminent domain."

Lucas Carson got to his feet. "May I be allowed to speak, sir?"

"Of course, Mr. Carson."

Carson scanned the audience and then turned back to the council. "I think, in a matter of such great importance, we should at least hear from the people whose land would be taken."

"We have heard quite a bit from them, Mr. Carson. Many have come to see me privately," Joshua said, glancing at Habram. "I am not without my own sentimentality, but the land in question is critical to the city. We've studied the situation, and you must admit that in the future, with further development of the shipyards and harbor, this land will be needed. It is best to deal with this now so we can focus on getting our canal opened."

"And the hotel will benefit the city as well," Mr. Webster exclaimed, jumping to his feet. "The plans I have are extravagant and beautiful. The hotel will bring people to Duluth from far and wide."

The mayor pounded his gavel. "There will be order, Mr. Webster. You are speaking out of turn."

"I apologize." He quickly reclaimed his seat.

"All of this has been discussed in detail," Joshua declared. "I believe we have heard all that we need to hear."

And with very little additional discussion, a vote was taken, and the motion was approved. The city would take the land. Habram and Lena exchanged a knowing glance, while around the room men grumbled and women sobbed.

Habram squeezed Lena's hand. "God still holds our future."

"Ja. He does. We will not fear the unknown."

Jordan Webster wore a look of elation. Habram wanted to slap the silly grin from his face. It wasn't right that a person's land should so easily be taken from him. He expected that in Sweden, but not in America.

As they filed out of the room, Habram heard Lucas Carson question one of the councilmen.

"What percentage of money does Webster plan to give back to the city from his hotel profits?" Mr. Carson asked as Webster approached.

"Lucas, you know this is best for Duluth," the councilman replied.

"I tried to buy their land fair and square," Mr. Webster interjected. "I offered more than the city will. They are the foolish ones for not taking it." He preened. "It's going to be great for Duluth."

Carson gave him a hard stare. "Maybe so, but what is best for these people?"

What was best for the people of this neighborhood? Who could know, save God alone? He heard the crying of the women and the angry outbursts from the men and couldn't help but wonder where God was in all of this.

"Habram," one of the men said, "is there no way we can fight this?"

"None that I know of. We must put our trust in God. He has never failed us."

"Habram's right," Lena added. "And who knows, this might turn out to be a bigger blessing than we could ever imagine." She smiled at their friends who had gathered around. "I don't want to leave my home, but I trust in the Lord and will count it all joy."

On Sunday afternoon, Pastor Persson came to see Ilian. He was surprised to see the pastor, but even more surprised to realize that he was glad the man had visited.

"You're getting around on crutches now," Persson declared. "What a great thing."

"Yes, I'm building my strength. The doctor says I may put a little weight on the leg from time to time for strengthening. I can hardly wait to be free of the cast's confines, however. I just want to break loose from it."

The pastor took a seat beside Ilian's chair. "I think we all have that feeling this time of year. Wanting to break free from our winter cocoon. There is an anticipatory sense of what is to come."

"Ja." Ilian tried not to think of the limitations he might yet have to contend with in his life. "Like being on the edge of something about to happen."

"Like the canal." The older man smiled. "There is great anticipation for the weather to warm and the canal to be built. It's all anyone in town can talk about."

"I'm sure. My father is a part of it, and I know he's anxious for it to be completed. Folks in Wisconsin don't want us to have it."

"No. Their fears give them great concern for the future. I believe we can all work together to make a good life for all. There will be plenty of need for both harbors once more people come west. Now that the war is behind us, westward expansion is on the minds of people back East. They find the scars of war worth escaping, or they long for adventure."

"I try to imagine the frontier at times." Ilian smiled. "But I've never been one who really longed for adventure. Just a place to call home—something and someone to be forever my own. I've lived in the logging camp for so many years and then on the battlefield during the war. I long for a fixed foundation—a permanent home."

The pastor nodded and leaned back in his chair. "The contentment of the soul that is born from the security of consistency."

"Ja. Consistency." Ilian thought about that word. "I believe that's a word I've often heard Lena associate with her faith. She told me once that God was the only constant in her life."

"Many people feel that way, including myself. God's consistency makes the inconsistent, constant change of the world more bearable. When nothing else offers the comfort of the familiar, I know that in God I will find contentment. He never changes."

"I am finding it more and more attractive to hear you and others speak of God as someone who is ever present. A constant, as you say. People tell me that I need Him—that I need His Son Jesus as a Savior. They tell me my sin nature cannot be made right with God unless accompanied by Jesus. You told me logic and reasoning could not save me. Only the cross could do that."

"It's true. Jesus reconciles us to the Father. When we accept His gift of salvation—His death on the cross in our place— then He goes before the Father and offers representation. As if your father knew nothing of me, but you and I had become associates. You would approach your father on my behalf and vouch for me."

"Ja, I can see that now. It's all so different from what I learned from my mother, but I can see now that her beliefs never served her well." Ilian felt a warmth in his chest. For the first time he could see God as something other than indifferent. "His love for His own creation . . . it seems real to me for the first time. Not something born out of emotion and nonsense, but out of the pride of creation—the part of Himself that He gave when He breathed life into us."

"A beautiful way to think of it. One that I can't say has come to me before, but one that will remain with me for the future." The pastor gave a knowing nod. "I believe your spirit is crying out for that oneness with God, Ilian."

"Ja. Oneness. To be complete and whole. To feel the presence of the living God . . . and to please Him. The Deist philosophy believes in practicing kindness to all, to extending a sort of generosity of spirit. When I read about Jesus—He is the very epitome of that generosity."

"He is. He could be firm with people, but always He was good."

Ilian considered that for a moment. "It once seemed like mythology to me. God the Creator sends his Son to earth to be born of a virgin. It was so similar to Greek stories of gods and goddesses that I believed it wasn't true."

"Satan loves to bring doubt to the world, Ilian. Often the deepest spiritual truths have an immediate appearance of impossibility, but when you look deeper—into the heart of the matter— you will see truth that had formerly eluded you. Your beliefs are not all wrong—they're just incomplete. There are many people who believe God indifferent. There are many who believe Him involved in every intimate detail. There are those who believe a Savior is unnecessary, and others who know there is no other way to God but through the Son. Jesus Himself told us that."

"I didn't know that," Ilian replied. "It seems to me that Jesus wrote nothing of Himself, and that made me curious."

"He didn't have to write about Himself. His very nature caused all of creation to testify on His behalf. The disciples wrote about him as well. They couldn't help it. Something deep in their soul cried out to acknowledge the wonder and holiness of God incarnate."

"I have much to learn in order to understand all that you're saying. My way obviously isn't serving me well, and neither did it serve my mother. What can I do to come closer to God?"

"We will start with confession and prayer. The Word says if you confess your sins, He is faithful to forgive. Give your heart, and He is faithful to guard it evermore."

In that moment, there was nothing Ilian wanted more than this.

Kirstin was sitting in front of the fireplace reading when Pastor Persson and Ilian came out of the bedroom. Mormor had been resting her eyes and opened them at the sound of people moving about.

Pastor Persson smiled. "Ilian would like to say something."

"Of course," Mormor said. "What is it, son?"

Ilian looked at the pastor and then at the women. Kirstin thought he looked nervous, but then he squared his shoulders and spoke. "I recognize I am a sinner in need of a Savior. I have asked Jesus to be that Savior to me."

Mormor got to her feet and went to Ilian, hugging him close. "I knew this day would come. I have prayed long and hard for your eyes to open to the truth."

Ilian nodded. "I am grateful you have prayed for me. Your kindness and love always encourage me. It was . . . well, it was so like the mother's love I needed."

Kirstin didn't know what to do. She was happy to hear this news, but it wouldn't be proper for her to hug him as Mormor had. She offered him a smile instead and said nothing.

"I told Ilian it was good to confess his need of a Savior to others and his acceptance of Jesus's sacrifice on his behalf. It helps him to be accountable when people know his decision." The pastor gave Ilian's back a gentle pat. "The lost is found, and another sinner has come home. There is great rejoicing in heaven."

"There's great rejoicing right here on earth," Mormor said. "I will make us a wonderful dinner to celebrate."

Kirstin figured this was something she could join in on. "I'll help." She closed her book and put it aside. "It will be a meal fit for a king."

Chapter 17

Official word from the city regarding the neighborhood properties came on the same day that Ilian's cast was removed. Both
had a sobering effect on the family. It was clear in both situations
there was a great deal left to do.

Ilian stumbled around a bit, trying to get his bearings. His leg
felt like it belonged to someone else. It was no longer strong
and muscular, but rather seemed skinny and weakened in such
a way that he found it difficult to gauge his steps.

"Don't put your full weight on it," the doctor admonished.
"Try it at first with the crutches still bearing more of the weight.
You can walk around like this and get used to the feeling of
using them. You will restrengthen the leg as you go, and we'll
carefully see how far we can increase your abilities."

It was disappointing not to be able to doff the cast and just
resume his life. Ilian had hoped that would be the case, and
having proof that it wasn't left him less than satisfied. Couldn't
God make right that which had been injured? Lena had said
she was praying for complete healing. Was God not listening?

"Are there any other restrictions?" Lena asked the doctor.

"He must do the exercises to strengthen the leg. Only by doing them can he hope to build up those muscles. The leg itself looks good. The cuts all healed nicely, and the bone seems straight. Now it's a matter of working to regain what was lost."

That statement stuck in Ilian's head long after the doctor departed. His father came to the house later for lunch, and Ilian thought of how much work was yet to be done with that lost relationship. He still had no real understanding of what he should do as a new Christian, but it seemed that reconciliation was always at the core of what Christianity stood for. Perhaps in time he would better understand his role in that.

"It's going to be announced with letters coming to each of the families tomorrow," Far was saying to Lena.

Ilian had only given the conversation a fraction of his attention, but he knew the city had decided to take the residents' properties along the bay and river.

"How long will we have to get out?" Lena asked.

Kirstin brought coffee to the table as well as the butter dish. "Yes, how long? Do we have to move in just a few days, or are they giving us weeks, or longer?"

"Thirty days, I believe I heard them say."

Ilian could see that his father was upset. There was so much to do and so little time. At least now with his cast removed, Ilian would be able to be of use. How much use was yet to be determined.

"A house cannot be built in that short a time," Lena declared. "I suppose we shall have to get rooms at a boardinghouse or hotel."

"Or buy a tent," Far added. "I could order them from St.

Paul. There is a good tentmaker there. Oh—there is a man named Mr. Lucas Carson who was at the council meeting. He works for Jay Cooke and has pledged to help us. He felt that the way things were done was unnecessary. He doesn't appear to like Mr. Webster much more than the rest of us do. Remember the land I pointed out to you when we went to see the ice stacking? He owns it. He has arranged for a meeting tomorrow for anyone who wishes to see the land and discuss purchasing it from him and building a new house."

"That's encouraging. It seems Mr. Cooke has only good things in store for our little town," Lena replied. "I, for one, would like to hear from Mr. Carson and see what he has in mind."

"I knew you'd feel that way. I thought perhaps all four of us could go. I'll see if I can borrow Mr. Bemford's carriage. I'm sure he won't mind. Mr. Bemford has already made clear that he's moving back East to live with his daughter. He won't have any interest in the meeting."

"That sounds good. You let us know, and we'll be ready." Lena touched his shoulder. "Can I get you more to eat?"

"No. I have to get that boat finished. The fewer things we have to move, the better."

"I wonder . . ." Ilian started, then paused. Everyone looked his way, making him uncomfortable. "Uh . . . that is . . . could you use a hand?"

His father smiled. "Definitely. The faster we finish the boat, the sooner I can get to packing up the tools."

Ilian nodded. "I'll get my boots on and join you."

Far got to his feet. "We're going to be very busy. Before I get to the boat, I'm going to go talk to Mr. Bemford."

"We are also going to need some crates for packing," Lena reminded him. "I wonder if you might be able to find us some."

"I'll find them, or we'll make them," Far replied. "Mr. Carson said he has materials we can use—things left over from railroad shipments."

"Mr. Carson sounds like quite the generous soul," Kirstin murmured.

"He's a good man, to be sure. He worked hard to get us the railroad, and I believe he and Mr. Cooke are putting a great deal of money into the canal and other improvements. They believe in Duluth and want it to be a wonderful city."

"Well, God bless them both," Lena replied. "The world needs more men like them."

Kirstin wasn't sure why, but she felt drawn to the workshop where the Mackinaw boat awaited completion. She ran her hand along the side of the hull, amazed at how smooth it had been sanded. Her people had all been farmers, although her brother was a furniture maker, thanks to training from their grandfather. Both of Kirstin's grandfathers had enjoyed working with their hands—building and creating.

The door opened, and Kirstin watched Ilian hobble through. He seemed to focus on each step as if it took all of his effort and strength.

"Are you all right?" She went to him. She could see the muck that coated the lower half of the crutches. Spring was making a mess of things.

"It's difficult to get around out there. With the ground starting to thaw, I'm having trouble with my footing. It's like learning to walk all over again."

"Come sit. I'll get the stove going." She went immediately to the stove and opened the door. There were a few embers still burning, and with some kindling, she was able to build a fire. Soon the warmth began to spread, and she smiled. "There, now we'll be cozy." She left the door open to let out the maximum heat.

"It's nice. Thank you."

"Have you come to work on the boat?"

"Ja. I figured we must be about this work, or it won't get done in time."

"In time to be thrown off the property?" She frowned and looked away. "Sorry, but I'm not very happy about this. Poor Mormor. She lost Morfar here and Uncle Per, and now she'll lose her home—the only one she's had in America. It seems so unfair."

"It is unfair, but much in life can be." Ilian rubbed his thigh.

"Is it hurting you?"

He nodded. "A bit. More of a dull ache than full pain. The doctor said I would probably notice it when storms were coming up. I suppose we'll see some rain or snow later."

Kirstin moved away from the stove and toyed with the tools on the workbench. "I'm sorry you're hurting."

"It's all right. I'll be fine."

Silence fell between them. Kirstin wanted nothing more than to quiz him on his decision to become a Christian, but she didn't want to make him too uncomfortable.

"You seem anxious. Is it the move?" Ilian asked.

"Partly." She didn't look at him but continued to touch one

tool and then another. Morfar usually kept a very neat work-shop, but it was evident he'd left without putting things away that morning.

"What else is troubling you?"

She stopped and looked at him. His expression was full of compassion and kindness. He didn't look at all condemning or teasing.

"I suppose everything feels a little out of hand." She forced a smile. "All the packing and the moving. Domar doesn't even know what's happening yet."

"He'll learn soon enough. Far told me there's going to be an agreement between the logging camp and the sawmill. They're going to keep the product local for the new houses—the ones that will be built for those who want to move to the new loca-tion. It's something else Mr. Carson arranged."

"And for those who don't wish to move?"

Ilian shrugged. "You know as well as I do that the people will have to move. Where they go will be entirely up to them."

She nodded. "It makes me very angry. I don't approve."

He chuckled. "I'm sure the mayor of Duluth is heartbroken at your lack of approval."

Kirstin couldn't help but smile. "I know. I'm being silly, and that's not something I'm usually accused of being."

"No, I can well imagine not. You've always been very seri-ous since I met you."

"You say it as though you don't approve."

"I think seriousness is a wonderful quality. There's nothing worse than for a young woman to be addlepated and nonsensical. A man could never rely on such a woman as a mate."

"No, I don't suppose he could." Kirstin turned away from

him. The questions she longed to ask were still very much on her mind. "Was your mother . . . a serious woman?"

"Oh yes, but I'm sure you already knew the answer to that. My mother was unhappy, and that led to her being quite serious."

Kirstin turned. "But not with you. You were her pride and joy. Morfar—your father—told me that. He said you were the one thing that gave her joy."

Ilian stared at the crutches he still held. "I was, but it was never enough to make her truly happy. I tried. I wanted very much for her to be happy, and if not that, then at least content."

"I'm sorry she wasn't. It seems so strange to me that she couldn't find even one thing to rejoice in. Your father wanted so much for her to be happy. He told me so." Kirstin crossed her arms. "I don't expect you to believe that."

"I suppose I deserve that. I haven't been very open to hearing anything negative about her."

"Nor anything positive about your father." She waited a moment for him to explode, and when it didn't happen, she pressed on. "He cares very much for you. You must see that."

"I do. I guess I've always known it. It was just much too easy to push him aside on her behalf."

"I don't mean to judge her harshly, but what kind of a mother would want to alienate her child from their father? That seems so wrong to me. We were never allowed to speak ill of either parent. The other would never have tolerated it."

"Ah, yes, but your parents loved each other."

Kirstin grabbed a wooden chair and pulled it over next to Ilian's chair, then took a seat. "You're right, of course. I think love always makes a difference." She felt her heart skip a beat as his gaze lifted to meet hers.

"Love is everything. Pastor Persson told me that the Bible speaks of God being love. I suppose that means that when we love each other, we are inviting God into the relationship in some way."

"I believe you are right." Kirstin smoothed her skirt. "Look, I want to say something and not offend you. It's only because I have come to care for your father—and for you—that I would even risk it."

"All right. You have my permission to say whatever you wish. It's the least I can do, given all the care you've given me."

"It was my pleasure to help." She folded her hands together. "Ilian, now that you've made peace with God, I hope . . . that is, I want very much for you and your father to start anew. To put aside the past and . . . well, forget . . . forget . . ." She couldn't bring herself to say it.

"My mor?" he asked.

The next thing she said would either destroy the frail bond they'd just formed or strengthen it. "Not her . . . not exactly. But her unhappiness. Her discontent." Kirstin looked up and found him watching her, his expression stoic. "Please don't get me wrong. I never want you to forget her or her love for you, nor yours for her. But I feel that so long as her anger and bitterness is allowed to come between you and your father, you'll never be able to move forward. You cannot make her happy now, so dwelling on it seems a wasted effort."

He said nothing, and for what seemed like hours, Kirstin waited for him to speak. She thought about continuing to talk, to tell him she knew what it was to allow her parents' thoughts and feelings to influence her. Or maybe even to say how she had often stood up to those thoughts and feelings. But she didn't. She felt awkward and almost wished she'd stayed silent.

Ilian finally spoke. "I appreciate what you've said. I suppose I always feel like I might betray my mother's memory if I try to work things out with my far."

"Your far told me that she never loved him. That theirs was an arranged marriage."

"That's true. They were forced to marry by their parents. I don't really know why. Perhaps there was money or land involved. I cannot say. But I do know Mor said that she never loved Habram Farstad and never would." He sounded so sad and resolved that Kirstin almost lost her nerve.

"How terrible to never be loved by your wife." She bit her lower lip, afraid she might cry.

"It would be terrible. The worst thing possible."

"I've said enough. I just . . . I hope you and your far will try to start fresh. We'll all be moving elsewhere, so it will be a new start for all. Then there's the possibility that my mormor and your far will marry."

"I think there's more than a possibility of that." He chuckled.

She smiled and felt a bit of the tension leave the room. "Yes. I think so too."

"And because of that and, well, frankly, my own personal reasons, I would like for us to be friends."

Kirstin felt a shiver run down her spine. "Friends?"

"Yes. I told you once that I wasn't asking you to be my friend, but now I am. You have more than proven yourself worthy of friendship, even during those times when I did not."

She nodded and lost herself in his icy blue eyes. "I'd like that very much. I'd like to be your friend, Ilian."

"Well, well. What is this?" Habram asked, coming into the room. "I have not one but two new assistants?"

Kirstin laughed and got to her feet. She went to embrace the older man. "I have been keeping Ilian company while we waited for you. Were you able to secure the carriage for tomorrow?"

"Oh, ja. We will be able to travel in style."

"Good. I'll let Mormor know." She stretched up on tiptoe and kissed the old man's cheek before hurrying from the workshop.

"She's quite a girl," the old man said, turning to Ilian.

"Ja, she is for sure."

Far sobered. "So, what can I do for you, Ilian?"

Ilian shook his head. "Nothing for me. Like I said at breakfast, I want to work on the boat . . . with you."

Habram Farstad smiled. "I'd like that very much, son. As Lena always says, 'Many hands make light the work.' I need to finish this boat as soon as possible. It's nearly complete, and if we both get to work on it, I can give it to the new owner and have the money we'll need for the move. Lena and Kirstin are not women of means."

"I have money we can use for the move as well. I owe them much."

"Ja. We both do."

Chapter 18

By the middle of April, a great deal of progress had been made. Mr. Carson had arranged for a large work crew to build houses, and already the homes in the new neighborhood were in various stages of completion. Not only had Mr. Cooke agreed with Mr. Carson's request to provide discounted help and materials, but he had approved rentals to those who felt they simply could not purchase their own place.

Kirstin and Lena worked night and day, packing their belongings. "I think it's a good thing I did not bring many clothes when I came to America," Kirstin said as she helped Mormor pack items from the shed.

Lena held up a piece of twisted metal. "I don't even know what this is, but I cannot imagine needing it. I suppose I shall put it in the pile for Domar and the boys to figure out."

"Morfar is busy again with the dredging company. I know he's excited about the canal, but I wish he could be here with us. He always seems to know exactly what is good to keep and what should be thrown away."

"He is," Mormor admitted, "a very wise man."

**Harrison County
Public Library**

Kirstin smiled to herself. She was convinced there would be a spring wedding. "And Domar will be home this Friday. I've really missed him. And, of course, there's the letter."

A letter from Sweden had arrived the day before. Kirstin had both looked forward to it and dreaded it. Overall, it proved to be good. Her mother and father were relieved to know she was safely in America and thankful that she was making her way to Duluth. Kirstin had sent her first letter from America prior to reaching her grandmother and had written another shortly after arriving in Duluth. Mor didn't reference that second letter, however, so Kirstin assumed she had sent this reply prior to its arrival.

"I have spent so much time trying to write my letter to Mor about Domar." Kirstin shook her head. "Sometimes I wonder about the good of telling them, but then I remember how all of my life I've been taught to tell the truth. Truth was always such an important thing, and when I was little, I knew without a doubt that truth was always expected." She folded a piece of canvas to put in the crate. "Still, I know this is going to change our lives forever."

"Ja, but we trust in God for that too." Mormor straightened and put a hand to her lower back. "That's the last of it. There's a great pile now for Domar to figure out. He and Ilian can go through it this weekend."

"Ilian has been working to finish the Mackinaw boat while Morfar works with the dredging company. The boat is nearly done," Kirstin said, smiling.

"I think you have an interest in Ilian, ja?"

Kirstin nodded. "I do, but there are troubles too. I have always thought him very handsome and intelligent, but he has so much sorrow—and anger. He has to give those to God and, of course, work things out with his far. But I am definitely attracted to him." She gave a little shrug. "What girl wouldn't be?"

"Ja, that is true." Mormor laid a hand on Kirstin's arm. "Just give him time. You have plenty of it, and there is no rush to fall in love."

Kirstin felt her cheeks grow warm. "No. No reason to hurry such a thing."

"I wondered where you ladies had gotten to." It was Morfar.

"What are you doing here?" Mormor asked. "I thought they were pushing to get the canal open."

"They are," he agreed, "but the ground is not cooperating. The water might be thawed, but the ground is still frozen. John worries he'll ruin the dredger if he doesn't stop. Meanwhile, the folks from Superior have been there to harass us and cause us no end of grief. They've sent a man to St. Paul to file an injunction and force us to stop."

"What can we do?" Kirstin asked. "You cannot force the ground to thaw more quickly."

"Some of it we can. We can use black powder."

"That's very dangerous," Mormor said, "and it grieves me to know that such a thing will probably fall on your shoulders, since you've handled it before."

"Ja. It will be me, no doubt."

Kirstin could see the worry in her grandmother's eyes. She had no idea what all was involved in working with black powder, but she knew it was risky.

"I see you girls have been hard at work." Morfar glanced around the shed.

"We have been doing all we can. The things I didn't recognize or know what to do with we piled up for Domar to sort."

The old man laughed. "That sounds good. I don't suppose you want to come help *me* pack?"

"We will," Mormor replied. She put a hand to her braided crown. "I need a few more pins in my hair, but then I can come right away."

~⁓~

Ilian was more than pleased to put the final touches on the Mackinaw boat. The new owner planned to come for the boat in the morning, and Ilian knew his father would be happy to have the extra money.

"Afternoon, master boat builder," Domar said from the open doorway. The spring air had warmed things up a bit, and Ilian had left the doors open, hoping to disperse the smell of paint and stain.

"Come in. Aren't you a sight for sore eyes?"

"I'm worn to the core, but as for being a sight, I haven't looked in the mirror." Domar came toward him, and the two men embraced. "How goes it?"

"The boat is finished. And just in time. We will get paid for it and get it off the property in time for the move."

Domar frowned. "Where will everyone go?"

"Well, new houses are being built, but of course that takes time. Your mormor suggested a boardinghouse. Mr. Carson has hotel rooms available, and Far says a big tent put up on the property where they are building would remind the builders that we are waiting for a roof over our heads." Ilian motioned toward the stove. "Cold coffee?"

"No. I'm fine." Domar glanced around the room. "You've already packed most of it."

"Ja. And piled up what we don't want. Far said we could leave it to Mr. Webster to figure out what should be done with it." Ilian grinned. "And he was none too kind in his thoughts of what Mr. Webster might do."

"I'm sure. The man is ruthless, and I'm disappointed in the way the city helped him with his project, but I suppose it is spilt milk and we must move forward."

"Ja."

"I remember coming here after what happened in Sweden. This has been home—a place of welcome and safety." Domar shook his head. "I remember my grandfather teaching us how to feel the wood and imagine the life that could come from it."

"I remember that too. I thought it silly at the time, but years later working in the camp, it all came back to me. When we felled the big trees, I imagined what might come from that wood. Houses, furniture, fuel, whatever. It was all right there, just waiting for someone with the skill needed to transform it."

"Morfar always believed everyone had a purpose like that. You just had to surround yourself with the right folks to draw it out of you."

"And a willingness to be molded," Ilian added. "I found that part a little more difficult."

"So tell me, how is the leg doing?" Domar motioned to Ilian's thigh.

"I walk with a limp, and it sometimes aches. When the weather turns on us, I usually feel it before the storm even comes. I suppose now I understand when old people talk about feeling the weather coming. But I'll be all right. I have had to think hard about the fact that I can't return to the logging work, while still being grateful that I have two legs to stand on."

"That was something I hoped to discuss with you. The logging work, that is," Domar admitted with a sheepish expression.

"What is it?"

"Mr. Morganson wants to promote me to the job he would have given you."

Ilian felt momentarily gut-punched. He'd worked hard to prove himself and earn that position of authority. Domar had always been in the running for it as well, but they had both been confident that Ilian would be the one to receive the promotion in the end, and Morganson had agreed. Until now.

"You'll be good at it." Ilian forced the words out, still not exactly sure what to say.

"I won't do it if it has the potential to come between us."

Ilian frowned. He hated that Domar even thought that could be a problem. "No. Never that. I suppose it just reminds me that my entire life has been changed by one incident." He looked at the boat. "But I can't say that it is a bad thing. I enjoyed working on this Mackinaw. And, since I started seeing God in a different way—your way—" he paused and grinned—"I have to admit that everything else in my life has changed too."

"Mormor told me you've been reading the Bible." Domar's expression was admiring. "I can't imagine a better method to find your way."

"No. I suppose not." Ilian glanced around the room and shook his head. "This has never been a place of happiness for my family, and frankly, I like the idea of a fresh start. So you should have one too. Take the job and tell Mr. Morganson that I said he picked wisely. I know you will be a good leader and manager."

"Thank you." Domar pulled up a chair and sat down. "There is something else I'd like to talk about."

"I have something as well." Ilian chose a stool and joined Domar. "I have something to discuss that is very important to me."

"Go ahead. Mine can wait. What's this about?"

Ilian wasted no time. "Your sister."

"Kirstin?"

"Ja." Ilian stared at his hands. "I care for her."

"Does she know?"

"No. Not exactly, and certainly not because I've said anything. I've never been one to show a lot of emotion. I suppose Mor had so much for all of us that I preferred to remain silent and refrain from emotion. But your sister is kind and gentle. She has a heart of sincerity, and at the same time, she's not afraid to speak her mind. She's the only person who has ever fully stood up to me. Others, yourself included, come to a place where you realize my temperament is going to close the door to further conversation or reasoning, but Kirstin doesn't care. She just pushes that door back open and marches in to demand answers."

Domar laughed. "Ja, that's Kirstin."

"I never realized how much I need someone like that in my life. I never realized the benefit of being encouraged to move beyond my discomfort with something and strive toward resolution."

"That's interesting, but it doesn't speak to love. Do you love her?"

Ilian nodded. "I think I've loved her since I held her on

my lap after she fainted. All I've wanted to do was keep her safe and protected. I know the love is new and perhaps only strikes at the surface, but I believe firmly that in time it will deepen."

"Do you think she loves you?"

"I know she cares for me. Her tenderness in helping me while I was injured and her kind heart are there for all, but there was something about the way she would sit and talk with me or endure my bad moods that spoke of much more."

"But the two of you haven't spoken of love?"

"No. I wanted to talk to you first."

"I'm glad you did, because it applies itself nicely to what I hoped to talk to you about."

Ilian shifted on his stool. "Which is what?"

"Your father and my grandmother. I know they're in love, and you do as well."

"Ja. I know."

"Well, I think they are both of a mind to marry, and with this move, it would be ideal if they could arrange for one house instead of two. However, I don't think that will ever happen unless you and your father resolve your differences. I think the same applies to telling Kirstin that you're in love with her."

Ilian couldn't hide his frown. "What exactly are you saying?"

"You need to resolve the past with your far before you can move forward into the future. The pain and misery of your past will kill any hope of happiness for your future. You know it, and so do I. I don't want my sister hurt because you couldn't find a way to forgive your father for his part in your mother's unhappiness."

Ilian drew a deep breath. "I know it must be dealt with, and I intend to do so. I've been waiting for a good time to approach Far."

"There will never be a perfect moment, so you'd best just make the most of whatever moment presents itself. Until then, I'd just as soon you leave Kirstin out of it. She and I have a lot to deal with ourselves with writing to Mor." He patted his coat. "She's had a letter from home, and we're going to read it together tonight and then write to Mor and Far about my being alive."

"And you're sure that's what you want to do?"

For a long moment Domar said nothing. "I think what I want matters little compared to what is right to do. I think I've let this go on out of spite, rather than the hope of change. I convinced myself that it was for their own good to learn a lesson about false judgment, but I know now it was done more out of anger and a desire to hurt them."

"And will you forgive them?" Ilian asked.

Domar smiled. "I already have and wish I had years ago. The liberty I feel is like a stack of logs removed from atop me. I feel at ease even though I know there will be consequences to face. I will simply deal with those one day at a time."

"Will you go back to Sweden?"

Domar shook his head. "I don't think so, but I won't say that it will never happen, as I might have a few months ago." He got to his feet. "I've kept you long enough. We both have more than a little work to do."

Ilian reached for the table beside his stool in order to heave himself to his feet. The leg was still very weak at times.

"I'll speak to Far soon." He didn't know exactly how it might help, but he couldn't shake the feeling that this was the next step to making a better future.

~~~~~~~~

Kirstin sat down at the kitchen table with the letter and a stack of paper. She had her ink and pen prepared and smiled at Domar. "Do you suppose we will wake Mormor by working on the letters here?" Mormor had already gone to bed.

"I hardly think so. She's been working so hard these last few weeks. I was completely surprised to find you two had sorted everything into piles and stacks and now all that needs to be done is actually moving it."

Kirstin shrugged. "It had to be done. Mormor felt certain the sooner we arranged it, the better off we'd be. Now we're going to help Morfar finish sorting through his things." She rearranged her writing supplies. "But first things first. Are you ready to write your letter?"

"I already wrote it. I wrote it back at camp before I came to town."

"You did? How clever of you. Will you allow me to read it?"

"Of course." He reached into his coat pocket and placed the letter on the table.

Kirstin unfolded the single sheet.

Dear Mor and Far,

I know you are shocked to learn that I am still alive, and for the pain or anxiousness that this causes, I am sorry. When I left Sweden, you told me that I was dead to you, and when the ship sank off the coast of Nova Scotia, I thought it a perfect way to fix that solution more permanently. I was in a great deal of pain and anger for the way I'd been betrayed. That you would turn your back on me was crushing. I was still so much just a boy, and my family was everything to me.

Kirstin paused and glanced up. She didn't even try to hide the tears in her eyes.

"Go on," Domar encouraged.

She nodded and looked down at the page.

I felt God had given me a chance to teach a lesson about falsely judging people—believing the worst of them even when they denied their actions. The people of the village and my family, save Kirstin, were convinced of my guilt, and yet I knew in time they would learn the truth. When the list came out from the shipwreck and my name was among the dead, I saw no reason to change it. I considered it for some time, and no other conclusion came to me but to remain dead. I came to live with Mormor and Morfar and Uncle Per and told them what had happened. I threatened to leave—to disappear forever—if they told my secret. They agreed to remain silent. I know now that wasn't easy for any of them, but I was selfish, and my threat was real.

Then Kirstin came to America. I was a real shock for her, but seeing her so happy, it gave me pause to reconsider. She convinced me that I needed to let you know that I was alive—that I needed to forgive you and the others rather than spend my days trying to force a lesson that no one surely cared about anymore. So now I am writing to let you know how sorry I am for the years of pain I've caused. I am sorry that I gave no thought to how it might be for parents to suffer such a loss. I was only thinking of myself

*and my own pain. I hope you'll forgive me, just as I forgive all
of you for not believing me and for sending me away.*

There was little more to the letter, and Kirstin set it aside.
"It's very good. You were more than kind and generous."

"I'm glad to have it done. You may tell them I have no plans
for returning to Sweden. I started to mention it but couldn't
think of the right words."

"I understand. I will say something about it. Perhaps I'll tell
them about your job promotion. I was so happy to hear you
talk about it at supper. I still worry, however, that you might
get hurt like Ilian did."

"You care for him." It was more statement than question.

Kirstin nodded. "I do. There's something about him that has
attracted me from the start. We've neither one said anything
about our feelings. There's been too much to do, and romancing
each other is hardly appropriate when faced with such things.
I'm sure in time we can figure it out, however."

"Ilian has just managed to get back on his feet," Domar reminded her. "And his spiritual thinking has changed. He'll need
time to sort through that as well."

"Ja, and then there's his father. Ilian can hardly think of taking a wife before figuring out how to forgive his father for the
past. There can be no future without that matter resolved."

Domar smiled. "You're very wise. Here I was thinking I
might have to convince you."

"No." She shook her head. "I have spent my life listening
to wise council. I have taken to heart the things I've heard and
learned. There can be no peace in a man's future until he deals
with his past."

"I wish I'd learned that years ago. I've been frozen in place all these years because of my own unwillingness to learn that truth."

She covered his hand with hers. "Well, you've learned it now. Perhaps it will bring you more love than you ever dreamed possible."

"Maybe it will give me the courage to love."

Chapter 19

With the taste of spring in the air, it was full speed ahead on building the new Scandinavian neighborhood overlooking Lake Superior. Kirstin was excited to go and see the progress on the buildings. She knew her grandmother and Morfar had chosen lots they felt would be most beneficial to their needs, but until now she'd not seen them. So with Ilian riding beside her in the carriage and Mormor up front, Morfar drove them out to the new land.

"There is much to like about this property," Morfar declared as they drew near the area. "The view is a good one. Lena likes it a lot."

"I do," Mormor agreed. "It looks down on the water, but the trees help protect it from the wind. There are also some nice large rocks that make me think it will be sturdy in the years to come. Not only that, but the lot is set apart from the other houses and has a nice easy path to the water. Habram and Ilian should be able to get the Mackinaw boats delivered without any difficulty."

"Well, that remains to be seen. Speaking of which," Habram

said, looking over his shoulder, "I have an order to consider. We should talk about it later."

Ilian nodded. "I don't have a lot on my calendar just yet."

Kirstin grinned and nudged him gently in the ribs. "You have plenty to do. Mormor and I worried that you had completely overworked yourself last night, being over here with your far." She didn't add that they were also delighted that the men were working together.

"The place won't build itself," Ilian replied with a wink.

He was sitting very close, and Kirstin couldn't help but feel her heart beat a little faster. Mormor had always alluded to the possibility of a relationship between Kirstin and Ilian, but now that Kirstin was actually considering it, she felt shy and almost reserved.

"Well, neither do you two have to build it overnight. We have good men provided by Mr. Carson," Mormor scolded him. "We want you to recover from your injury first, Ilian."

"I am recovering just fine, as you well know. All thanks to you and Kirstin. You make wonderful nurses."

Kirstin could hear the workers laboring with their saws and hammers before she ever saw the first houses. She strained to see out of the carriage. There were two distinct rows of platted land. Someone had driven markers around each lot and tied string from stake to stake to show the various sizes.

"Mr. Carson had three separate house plans drawn up," Morfar told them. "One is for a small cottage with two bedrooms and a nice living area. The second has three bedrooms with two of them upstairs. The third is much bigger. That's the one your mormor chose, of course. She likes to have her space."

"I have family to share my house," Mormor replied. "The

key to a family happily living together is for everyone to have a little space all their own."

Kirstin smiled but said nothing about her grandmother sharing that house with a husband. "And you said the bigger house has three bedrooms upstairs?"

"Ja," Mormor replied. "And even a small room for storage. And there's a nice-sized bedroom downstairs, with another room that could be used for guests or sewing. The kitchen and pantry are at the back of the house, so when you walk in the front door, you just see the living room and stairs first thing."

"You'll see it for yourself in just a moment," Morfar assured her.

They pulled up to a place where there were two properties side by side. One had a house on it. The outside was already framed and in place. The other lot held a long rectangular building that looked more like a woodworking shop.

"What's that?" Kirstin asked.

"That is where the Mackinaw boats will be built," Morfar explained. "And at the back of it are a couple of rooms where Ilian can live. Until he needs something more."

Kirstin looked at the house. "And only one house?"

"We were thinking maybe one house is all we will need," Mormor declared. She glanced over her shoulder with a smile. "Come. Let's go see what they've arranged."

Kirstin looked at Ilian, who smiled and shrugged. "Let's go see," he suggested.

He climbed down from the carriage, favoring his leg. Kirstin waited until he was ready, then allowed him to help her dismount. She liked the possessive way he held on to her until he was certain her footing was sure.

"Did you know about the rooms for you off of the work-shop?" she asked him as the others set out across the yard.

"Ja, sure. Your grandmother suggested it when I told her I didn't feel right for her to plan on me living with her."

"She invited you to live with her?"

He shrugged. "I believe she's thinking of the future and being married to Far."

"And what do you think of that?"

He studied her for a moment. "Living in the workshop or your grandmother marrying my father?"

"Pick up the pace, you two. We want to show you some-thing," Mormor called over her shoulder.

They were fortunate that there had been a couple of dry days. Someone had thoughtfully laid down plank boards to walk on, but the ground had dried well, and Kirstin thought it easier to manage than the boards. "It will take a lot of work to make the yard pretty."

"Ja, but that can wait until we have a place to live," Mormor said. "Now, come. I want to show you something."

Kirstin followed Mormor and Morfar to the front of the house. "This will be our porch," Mormor told Kirstin, pointing out where several wooden stakes were planted.

"A real porch? Only wealthy folks have that." Kirstin grinned and turned to see the view behind her. "I can just imagine sit-ting here, gazing at the lake. Maybe we'll even be able to see the ice stacking in the winter."

"Perhaps." Mormor continued into the house. "It won't be a big porch, but large enough for a few chairs. Come see inside. They've already done so much more work than they'd accomplished last week."

"Do you come here often?" Kirstin asked. This was her first time seeing the new house, and she'd had no idea her grandmother had been making multiple trips.

"Habram and I come here every few days. He likes to help with the building. Ilian too."

Kirstin looked at Ilian. "I knew you'd been gone a lot."

"I helped put the woodworking shop together. We have to be able to earn our keep. As long as we have space to build the boats and get them to the water, we'll be able to pay the bills. A man has to be able to do that."

"Ja, I suppose that is true."

They walked through the house, giving a nod or hello to the workers. Mormor seemed quite content with the progress they'd made and told them so. One man told her they should be able to move in toward the middle of May.

"There will still be plenty to do," Morfar declared. "Painting and such, cabinets and shelves for the pantry, but we can do that ourselves."

Kirstin didn't press the obvious question. Did Morfar and Mormor intend to be married in the meantime?

"You and Domar will have rooms upstairs, and there will be plenty of space for us all," Mormor said, taking Kirstin's arm. "I like how it's all open to the upstairs. That will help it to warm much better in winter."

"It sounds very nice, Mormor. I'm impressed, but I hope you aren't spending too much money."

"No. We are being quite frugal. We paid in full for our land and house, thanks to the generous amount we got for our homes. We'll have plenty of work to do, and the house won't be completely finished when we move in. Habram and Ilian will do much of the finishing work. Habram told Mr. Carson that he preferred it that way. And because the shop requires nothing overly special, they were able to get that up right away, and the men will have it for their work."

Kirstin had never seen Mormor happier. "I'm still sorry they are forcing us from your home. You have lived there so long, and it was such a nice house."

"This is a new start for all of us, Kirstin. I refuse to give that joy away. I won't be glum and sad. I told my friend Metta that this was an opportunity for joy, and I would take it and cherish it. Already I prefer the view. Don't you?"

"Oh yes. I love the lake, and this is a nice rise to watch it from. I hope the other neighbors come and enjoy it as much as we will."

"Most are coming. Some decided to take their money and move away. They want to go be with family, and who can blame them? We wouldn't be able to do much if not for the generous nature of Mr. Carson and his Mr. Cooke. That Mr. Cooke has done so much for Duluth. I think we owe him a debt of gratitude."

Kirstin nodded. "I hope God blesses him greatly. I hope the town does well despite forcing us from our homes and giving in to the demands Mr. Webster made."

"Mr. Webster has money, and money always has a way of getting what it wants. Mr. Cooke is rich too, but he's using his money to better everyone and to build friendships. Mr. Webster is simply making enemies and buying his associates. It won't bode well for him in the long run."

Kirstin looked around and saw Morfar and Ilian were nowhere to be found. She pressed her question. "Have you and Morfar decided to marry soon?"

Mormor smiled. "We'll see. God wants Habram to speak to Ilian about the past first."

"I can see that as wisdom," Kirstin replied. "Ilian needs to settle the past."

"Ja. But it will be a painful ordeal. I'm glad you will be here to be his friend." Mormor's expression left Kirstin with a sense of dread.

"For sure, I'll be his friend." She frowned. There was something in the look on her grandmother's face that worried her. There was obviously something her grandmother wasn't saying.

Jordan Webster was a happy man. Happier than he'd been in some time. All of his life his father had berated him to take chances and do something to make his mark. Well, now he was doing both. The hotel and park he planned to build would bear his name, and people from far and wide would be impressed with all he had done.

He looked at the floor plans for the hotel lobby and marveled at the thought of white marble columns and fireplaces. The hotel would cost a small fortune—in fact, most of his personal fortune—but he would easily make back his money in a few years. The location would allow for arrival by water or train, and the plans he had for the finest of dining and personal amenities would leave people talking about it long after their departure. It would become a destination like the luxury places in New York and Europe. The Webster would be known as the showpiece of the Great Lakes, and he would finally win his father's approval, as his brothers had already done.

Of course, he'd upset a great many of the locals, but they were unimportant people who carried no weight in society. Jordan's father had often said that such people had faced hardship and disappointment their entire lives and were well versed in how to manage it. Therefore, there was no need to feel guilty or responsible when his actions caused misfortune. Besides, in the case of that miserable little Scandinavian neighborhood, Lucas Carson and Jay Cooke had already come forward to be the people's salvation. Jordan didn't like that they were looked up to in such favorable light. It only served to darken the town's view of the opposition, and Jordan still had to see to it that the community embraced his project.

He put aside the blueprints and shook off his concerns about being the bad guy in this situation. Those people had houses already being built for them. New houses, at that. They weren't having to face relocation to some ill-suited hovel. They were getting prime real estate overlooking the lake. Their fortunes had increased greatly. They should be grateful to him.

He locked his hotel room and made his way downstairs. He was hungry, and it was time to celebrate what he'd accomplished.

Ilian moved his checker and glanced up at Kirstin. "I think you can see that I'm about to win."

"Yes," she replied with a sigh. "That much is obvious. My mind hasn't really been on the game."

"Obviously not. Would you care to call the game and perhaps go for a walk instead? I could use the chance to strengthen my leg."

Kirstin smiled. "Of course. My grandmother and your father

are busy plotting and planning for the new property." She nodded toward the kitchen table, where they sat surrounded by papers and drawings. "They won't even miss us."

She got to her feet and fetched her cloak while Ilian grabbed his boots and started pulling them on.

"Are you two heading somewhere?" Lena asked.

"A walk to strengthen Ilian's leg," Kirstin answered before he could.

"That sounds good," Far replied. "I'm glad you're taking your recovery so seriously. You'll regain that strength before you know it."

Ilian was still hesitant when dealing with his father. After years of setting himself against the man, it was hard to allow that Far had Ilian's best interests at heart. So often his mother had told him that Habram Farstad cared about no one except himself. Now it was as if Ilian was allowing the scales to fall from his eyes.

"You two be careful," Mormor said as they made their way to the front door.

"We'll be fine," Kirstin declared, opening the front door. "Oh, it looks like you have company."

A man approached them and tipped his hat.

"I'm John Upham, and I need to speak with Mr. Farstad. I went next door, but he wasn't there. He mentioned he often visits here."

"Yes, he's here right now," Kirstin replied and stepped back. "Mr. Farstad, a Mr. Upham is here to see you."

Far joined them at the door. "Let him in. Good to see you, John. What can I do for you?"

"We need to dig that canal. Rumor has come up from St.

Paul that the government is going to stop us from putting it through. We have to complete it before the injunction papers can reach us."

Ilian took hold of Kirstin's arm, needing the support. She grasped his forearm. "Are you feeling weak?"

"I always do at first. The leg seems to have a mind of its own."

They left Far and Mr. Upham in conversation and headed down the narrow path, seeming to fit perfectly side by side. Ilian let the silence stretch. He just wanted to enjoy this time with Kirstin.

"I'll miss it here, even though I like the new location for the house," Kirstin said, glancing up at him in the fading light.

"Ja. It will be hard to leave. I grew up here, you know."

"I had forgotten. I suppose it's easy enough only to think of you as the man I know now."

Ilian wondered what she thought of that man. "This is the only neighborhood I have ever known. There were so many young children here, and I had lots of friends. They're all gone now—moved off to other places. Duluth proved too difficult for some and far too isolated for others. I sometimes wonder if they would come back now that we have the train and the city has grown a bit."

"I'm still imagining you as a child," Kirstin replied. "It's hard because you are such a serious man. You seem old beyond your years, and I can't imagine you ever being carefree."

"I don't think I was carefree. My sisters were. They were all about loving life and enjoying themselves. They had great senses of humor and played jokes on the family. My mother hated that and often punished them for their behavior, while our far would just excuse it with a grin. They were very close."

"Your sisters and father?"

"Ja. They were what Lena calls fun-loving."

"But not you?"

"No. Not really. My mor said they were fools laughing their heads off, and that one day it would catch up with them and they'd regret their silliness."

"And did they?"

"I don't think my sisters regretted anything. They married young and moved away, and as far as I've ever heard, they have loved their lives and choices. I like to imagine they have taught their children to play some of those same pranks on each other." He smiled as he considered it.

"I like the sound of their happiness—their joy. It's important to be happy, don't you think?"

Ilian had been without any real happiness in his life for so long that he wasn't sure he'd recognize it if it came along. Kirstin was probably as close to it as he had gotten.

"I'm trying to see it that way. Having grown up without it . . . well, I suppose it's all new to me. Your grandmother has probably done the most to throw a little my way."

"Mormor is pure joy. I've never met anyone who enjoys life so much and makes good situations out of bad. Do you know she's not complained once about Mr. Webster forcing her from her home?"

"Really?"

"She says that God is in charge of her life and that this must be His will for her. And if He has arranged all of this, she doesn't want to miss the blessing."

Ilian shook his head. "She really is something else."

They walked down the road that led to the water's edge.

Everything about Duluth seemed to lead back to the water. It was always there—always a part of life. Ilian had never really felt called to it like others had. He definitely favored the land, but he had a healthy appreciation for the water.

"How's your leg?"

"Weak but getting stronger." He didn't even try to pretend with her. He never felt the need. It was just one more reason he thought they worked well together.

"The exercise will see you back to normal before you know it. I'm always happy to walk with you if I'm free from other duties. I like our walks."

"I do too. I like your company."

"You didn't always," she said, pulling her cloak closer. She looked at him and smiled. "I like the way things are between us now rather than the way they were."

"You stopped being quite so bossy," he teased.

"And you stopped being so mean."

He stopped. She paused as well. "Was I really that mean?" he asked.

"Yes, and you well know it." She softened her tone. "But I know God is working on you, just as He's working on me."

His lips curved ever so slightly. "You don't need much work. I think you're pretty perfect."

Chapter 20

Domar showed up the next evening for his regular visit and a good meal. He looked exhausted, and even Mormor was worried he'd been working too hard.

"Well, the good news is that we won't be working much longer," he assured them. "At least not on our full schedule. The mud and muck is getting to be too much to deal with. That's why we've been pushing ourselves so hard."

"And how are you liking being the boss?" Kirstin asked.

"Being the boss isn't all it's thought to be. At least not for me. I miss the men and the friendships we shared. Everything changed when they started calling me boss."

Kirstin checked the water on the stove. There were four large pans of water, and each was boiling now. "It's hot, if you're ready for your bath."

"That's sounds wonderful." Domar suppressed a yawn as he looked around the sparse room. "You've really packed it all away, haven't you?"

Mormor chuckled. "We had to. We're moving in two or three weeks."

"Tomorrow I'll go through that pile of stuff you left me to sort. If it's good enough to keep, I'll rent a wagon and get it moved over to the new land. Speaking of which, I'm excited to see it."

"I don't know what we would have done without that wonderful Mr. Carson."

"As I understand it, he and Mr. Cooke have bought up quite a bit of land in Duluth. I hope it proves beneficial to them."

"Mr. Cooke is busy with his new railroad. The Northern Pacific," Kirstin declared. "I read about it just this morning in the newspaper. Do you know they have nearly one million acres of land for the railroad?"

"I can't even imagine," Mormor said, shaking her head. "The world is a much bigger place than I ever thought."

"Where are Habram and Ilian?" Domar asked, getting to his feet. "The house next door was dark."

"They're at the new place, working on it," Mormor replied. "You'll see it tomorrow. They've been quite busy getting it ready. We have to be off these properties by the twentieth of May, so they're doing what can be done to make at least a portion of the new house livable. They've also got the shop up and running to make Mackinaw boats."

"Together?" Domar asked.

"Hopefully." Mormor gathered the last of Domar's dishes. "They're working on making peace. Since Ilian decided to accept Jesus as his Savior, he's been quite thoughtful about making changes. Habram intends to speak to him about the past and explain things that Ilian has never been told."

Domar glanced at Kirstin. She gave him a nod. "Ilian says he wants to put the past behind him," she confirmed.

"That really would be a change for him. I'm glad to hear it."

Kirstin lifted the first of the pans of water off the stove. "I'll take this to the tub. Don't wait long, or it'll be cold."

"I'm coming."

She smiled and made her way to the bathtub. After three more trips, she had the last of the hot water in the tub along with a small amount of cold water. Morfar had talked about having running water in their house one day. Wouldn't that be something? For now, the pump was all they could count on.

Domar came into the room, stripping off his shirt.

Kirstin shook her head. "I should put more water on to heat. You're going to need it to wash off the layers of dirt you're sporting."

"Logging isn't clean work, that's for sure." He paused. "Did you send our letters?"

She nodded. "Mormor wanted to send one as well. She wasn't sure at first, but I waited to send ours, and she decided it was the right thing to do." She gathered the pans. "Now, you get in the tub before the water gets cold. I'll bring some more as soon as it's warmed."

Kirstin slipped out the back door and grabbed the bucket. She heard Morfar speaking to Mormor and knew he and Ilian had finally come back from their work. It couldn't be easy for Ilian to be on his leg for such long hours, but she admired his willingness to work alongside his father. Especially since she knew there was still much for them to overcome.

She'd nearly filled the bucket with water by the time the door opened and Ilian stepped outside. "Do you need help?"

"No. I just decided to heat some more water for Domar. He's taking a bath."

242

"So your grandmother said."

Kirstin started for the house with her pail, but Ilian stepped forward and took it from her. She gave him a smile. "And what about you and your father? Did you accomplish all that you hoped?"

"We met with a client who wanted to order two Mackinaw boats. He wants them by the end of June, which I think is impossible, but you know my father."

She grinned. "Indeed, I do. He thinks nothing is impossible."

"We'll have to ponder this and decide if we can take on the order."

They made their way back to the stove, where Kirstin took the pail and poured water into the pans. Next she made certain there was plenty of wood in the stove and stirred up the fire until the flames were burning bright. It wouldn't take long to heat the water.

She glanced over her shoulder. "Where are Mormor and your father?"

"He wanted to show her something at his house. Stuff he'd gathered together. I think he's trying to figure out what to take and what to leave."

"Has he said anything about them marrying?"

Ilian shook his head. "Not in so many words, but he did tell me that he wanted to talk to me about something. I figure it might be that. He probably wants to make sure it won't further damage our situation if he remarries."

"And would it?" She met his blue eyes and momentarily forgot about her grandmother and Morfar.

Ilian smiled as if knowing she was losing her heart to him. Could he tell? Was she wearing her heart on her sleeve? Maybe the time had come for her to say something. After all, her growing feelings weren't just going to go away.

"I want them to marry as much as you do." He leaned back against the pantry door. "I think they belong together."

"But what about the past?"

"What about it?" he asked, sounding irritable.

"I'm sorry. I shouldn't have asked that." She turned back to watch the pots of water heat. Her feelings confused her. She wanted to demand answers, but at the same time she was concerned about what those answers might be.

"Kirstin."

She turned to find him watching her. When he didn't continue to speak or attempt to move toward her, Kirstin raised her brows. "Say what you will."

He sighed. "I have a great deal I'd like to say to you, but the time isn't right. I'm not ready."

She shrugged. "I believe God has a proper place and time for everything." She tried to hide her frustration, however. For while she did believe in God's timing, it was her own timing she preferred at the moment. She wanted Ilian to speak to her of love—to tell her that he'd lost his heart to her. She wanted to return the favor and tell him that he had become dearer to her than she had thought possible. Of course, maybe it was too soon. Maybe she was just caught up in Mormor's romance with Morfar. After all, even if she had been helping to care for Ilian over the last few months, and even if they had spent more and more time together, and even if he was the handsomest man she'd ever known . . . maybe it was best to remain silent.

Mormor and Morfar returned in the midst of Kirstin's confusion. They were laughing about something, and she couldn't help but tease them.

"Laugh all night, cry in the morning."

"No," Morfar declared. "There will be no tears for us. Your grandmother always keeps me smiling."

"Are you having success with your canal?" Kirstin asked, trying to forget Ilian's nearness and all that she wanted to say to him.

"We made progress. Tomorrow we're setting off the black powder and nitroglycerin, however. The ground is still too hard to dredge, and we heard a rumor that folks from Superior intend to reach us by Monday with the injunction. We have done our best to get this thing dug, but now we will resort to desperate measures."

"Who will set the explosion?" Kirstin asked.

"I will, of course. Major John and I have worked together for far too many years. We know each other well enough to manage this together. He's hired more men to dig by hand, but he'll still handle the dredger. Together, I believe we'll join the waters tomorrow."

"That's very exciting." She turned back to the stove to find the water was just starting to bubble.

"I told him they needed a younger man to handle it," Mormor declared, "but he wouldn't even consider it."

"There's no one else we trust with the job. It's not going to be difficult. We'll plant it deep, and that way we can blow huge chunks out of the ground. We're so close, and it's going to be an exciting moment when we complete this. You should be happy. Duluth is about to have its own harbor. These are good days."

Ilian's sleep was restless that night. He dreamed of his mother and of a conversation they'd had just before he went off to war. She had been desperately worried that he would die and leave her alone in the world to contend with his father and sisters.

"You're the only one in America who cares if I live or die," she had told him. "My life means nothing if you are dead."

Ilian had hated her fear and sorrow over what he might encounter. He had promised her he would return. Promised to be careful. And, despite getting shot twice, Ilian had come through the war in one piece. Both of his wounds had been grazes that left outward scars but no inward damage. He'd been back on the field almost immediately.

But his mother hadn't been so fortunate. He hadn't expected her to contract whooping cough and die before he could return home to see her again. When his father's letter had arrived, telling him of her death, Ilian had blamed him. It had to be Far's fault. Everything was. According to his mother and all that he had ever been told, his father was to blame for all of the unhappiness in the world.

In the calming peace that was gradually growing in Ilian's heart, he could now reason that wasn't the case. His father had no doubt made mistakes, but Ilian no longer knew what to think about the marriage his mother and father had shared.

She'd been gone almost ten years, and in all that time, his father had said nothing bad about her. In fact, he'd not spoken of her at all except on rare occasions, and only after Ilian had brought her up. Even then, Far was kind and gracious. Why hadn't Ilian seen that before? Far never spoke against Ilian's mother. Not even once.

Sitting up in the pitch-black bedroom, Ilian rubbed his aching leg and listened to the rain hit the window and roof. It was quite the deluge, which made the pain he was feeling more understandable. Would it always be like this?

He got up and pulled on his robe. He figured he might as well check the fire while he was up.

"Couldn't sleep?" Domar asked as he reached the living room.

"No. Leg's hurting. Thought I'd come check the fire. What about you?"

"I woke up about an hour ago. As tired as I am, there was just too much on my mind."

"I'm here if you want to talk." Ilian took a seat in Lena's favorite rocker.

"We lost a man today."

"Lost him?"

Domar nodded in the soft glow of the firelight. "He fell to his death. He hadn't used the lines in the right way and lost his footing."

"That's a tough situation."

"The younger men were pretty upset. The more seasoned were upset but better at hiding it. All the while, I just kept thinking of how I was responsible. How I should have done more."

"Where's his family?"

Domar shook his head. "Don't know. He told us he was an orphan, but one of the men said he'd talked about leaving home on his sixteenth birthday and never looking back. Said he hated his folks and decided being an orphan was better than being a son." He met Ilian's eyes. "Sound familiar?"

"For both of us."

"I don't have any idea where I could even start to find his family. I thought I could run a death notice in a couple of big papers back East, but I doubt it would do any good. I don't even know where he was from or if the name he gave us was his real one. I keep thinking of how his folks might be really good people, and they're sitting at home thinking he's still alive and might one day come back to them."

"While your folks believe you're gone for good and will soon learn otherwise?"

"Yeah." Domar looked into the fire. "Lies really do cause a lot of trouble."

"They alter everything," Ilian replied in a whisper. "Even the lies we never know about."

Chapter 21

"So you've fallen in love with Ilian."

Kirstin looked up at her brother, thankful they were alone in the house. "I have. Is that all right with you?"

He laughed. "Would it matter?"

She considered it for a moment. "No."

That made Domar laugh all the more. "I didn't think so."

Kirstin took a seat at the kitchen table. "I didn't intend to fall in love with him, I will say that much. I think Mormor always wanted it, however. I remember her telling me about Ilian my first day here." She folded her arms over her pinafore apron. "It would seem to be something of my destiny."

"Has he declared his love for you?" Domar seemed very careful with the question, almost hesitant.

"No." She shook her head. "I think we're much too busy to worry about such things. Not only that, but he's just decided to embrace Christianity in full. I'm sure there is a lot for him to learn. I would like very much for him to declare for me, but as I've prayed for wisdom, I can see that it isn't the right time. Not yet."

Domar looked at her oddly, then took the kitchen chair opposite her and flipped it around backwards to sit. "You are something else, sister dear. I've never heard wiser words from any woman, save Mormor. You speak like a woman advanced in her years."

"I've long kept company with older women. At home it was my favorite place to be even before you left, but especially after I thought you were dead." She remembered it like yesterday. "I think their company was comforting to me because they knew what it was to contemplate death. Young people never want to think on it for long. Death is terrifying, reminding them that they aren't immortal—that they too will fade from the earth one day."

"But you kept company with death and had no fear of when it might come for you?"

"Why fear it? I know God. I know it's not the end of anything. There is great sorrow on earth in death. But that comes from our desire to still be with our loved ones. Or sorrow for what we might have left undone. We mourn the absence and what might have been, and well we should. Losing you was like losing a limb. I relied on you to be there—helping me through bad times, sharing laughter in good ones. You and I were so close despite your reckless behavior as you approached adulthood. Härse and Svena had little time for me, as they were caught up in their own lives, but you were there to tell me stories and help me deal with difficulties, and then without warning—you were gone. To lose you was devastating."

"And to have me back now?"

She smiled. "It makes me full of joy. Like the prodigal son— the lost has been found. I could never have believed we would get a second chance together. I still marvel at it. Who would not want a beloved family member returned to them?"

"I hope the others feel the same way. A lot of time has passed, and I still fear they will only be angry once the initial realization passes."

"They may be. I've battled with my anger."

"Anger at me?"

"Ja. Raging anger." She looked away. "I'm ashamed to admit it. I wanted to punch you in the nose."

"Maybe you should. It might make you feel better." He chuckled. "It might make me feel better."

Kirstin's head snapped up. "No. It would not. What made me feel better was remembering that God had given me a second chance. Had given us all a second chance. To be angry about it would be to focus on the past, and I no longer want to live in the past. I'm grateful to have you no matter the circumstance. I think I understand how Mormor could keep your secret and say nothing to the family. She loved you more than herself. She knew it would come at a price . . . and it will. The payments have only begun. But I believe the future will be better in the long run."

"Do you think Mor and Far will forgive me?"

"Ja. I know they will." She shifted her weight and met his gaze. "Will you forgive yourself?"

He frowned, and she could see the question had hit him hard. He shook his head. "I don't know. I never thought about it until recently. When I heard how much pain I'd caused our mother, it was nearly my undoing. I never meant to wound so deeply. How can I forgive myself when I'm only just coming to know the consequence of my decision?"

"We hopefully learn from our choices, work toward making the wrong right, and make better decisions next time."

"Sometimes it costs a life and you can't make the wrong right. I lost a good man at the logging camp, and I feel it's all my fault. How can I forgive myself for the loss of his life?"

"How was it your fault?"

"I was responsible for him. I should have taught him better. I should have checked to make sure he was doing things right. Somehow I failed to do what needed to be done to keep him alive."

"But you do not control life and death, Domar. You may have made mistakes . . . that much might be true. We all have and will again. But take a few moments, and you will see the truth of God's generous forgiveness. He is always welcoming us back, always forgiving us. Should we do any less?"

"I guess this man's death brought back all that I had done to Mor and Far. It's all entangled together in my mind. He had no family and died alone. I have a family but pushed them away and let them think me dead. I guess after all this time I've finally let it catch up to me. I finally let myself see the full picture of what I'd done. The lie I let be told—the wall I built between my family here and my family there. I was so selfish, Kirstin." His eyes dampened.

"I remember once when I was sitting with the old women during one of the festivals. They were talking about the significance of what they called sitting in the silence. Contemplating life and the fullness God had given. Thinking of the sorrow and what God would have them learn from it. They said that sitting in the silence was hard when they were young because life was much too noisy to ignore. There was so much going on in their heads and hearts that pausing for even a few minutes was difficult. But they came to learn it was the one place where God was always found waiting. They wished they'd known sooner the value of pushing aside everything else and just sitting quietly with God. I think that's what your soul longs for now, Domar. Go sit in the silence with God."

"What if He doesn't come?"

"He will," she assured him, seeing the desire for such communion in her brother's eyes. "Just wait for Him there. He will come."

⁓

"I need to give Mr. Jacobs an answer about the Mackinaw boats," Ilian's father said. He glanced around the old workshop.

"I think making two boats by the end of June with a move on top of that is too much." Ilian had considered the matter carefully and, being a cautious man, he felt they should say no.

"It is a great deal to consider. Frankly, I don't have the money needed to buy the boat supplies, even with the down payment from Mr. Jacobs."

"You already took his down payment?"

Far looked at him with a sheepish grin. "I didn't want him to ask someone else."

Ilian wasn't used to dealing with his father in this capacity. He studied the older man for a moment, then nodded. For most of his life, he had trained himself to feel nothing for this man, to question every thought he had and find fault. Ilian knew that his father was highly thought of by others. He was well respected by his peers and fellow workers. Even children loved him and always flocked to him for hugs. Ilian had never allowed himself to see this man—to know him.

Ilian felt he stood in a sort of doorway. A step back, and he could go on with things just as they had been. He could revert back to his anger and unyielding bitterness toward the man who had refused to take his wife home to her family in Sweden. Or one step forward, and he could forever break with the past and start anew.

Pastor Persson had told him God was all about the new creation He would make of a man's heart—the past was set aside. Ilian at least had to try to move forward. If not, he would never be able to be a part of Kirstin's life.

"I have some savings," he finally replied.

"Enough to buy materials for two boats?" his father asked.

"Ja, and then some. I could use it for our materials and get it back when the boats are completed."

"There would have to be some sort of interest paid. We would have to ask at the bank and see what rate would be fair."

"But if we're going into the boat-building business together—doesn't it stand to reason we'll be partners?"

Far's face lit up. "Ja. Partners sounds good. I like that very much."

"Then partners don't need to pay each other interest. At least not as far as I'm concerned," Ilian countered.

Far looked at him for a moment. "But it is a risk. Something could happen and you would lose your money, and then I will be to blame."

"Like usual?" Ilian asked without thinking.

His father nodded. "Ja. I don't think you need another reason to blame me."

The words were sobering to Ilian. "I never meant for it to be that way." His voice was barely audible. Apologizing felt so foreign. Would his father even believe him if he tried? Ilian looked up. "I want to do the right thing. This new understanding of God presses on me the need to do right, but I don't know how this works."

His father's expression softened. "God will help you, Ilian. He will show you what to do and how to speak."

"There's so much I don't understand." Ilian watched his father, uncertain what he could say or do that would make the situation easier.

"I see that. The Bible talks about a child being trained up in the way he should go. I'm afraid you were not. I failed you every time, and I regret that more than I can say."

Ilian could see a sincerity in his father's eyes that he had never seen before. But then again, Ilian had never looked for it.

"Mor didn't want us together. She wanted me for herself." Ilian could see the truth of that much.

"Ja. She said I had my girls, but you belonged to her."

"She told me you didn't care—that you never wanted a son."

Far surprised him with a bitter laugh. "She said that, huh? Well, now I must speak out. I always wanted a son. I wanted you, Ilian. I wanted us to be close."

"But it never seemed that way. Mor was always the one who came to me. Always the one who spoke to me."

"I tried, Ilian. I tried to share my work with you. I tried to share my heart. You wanted no part of it."

Ilian had to admit that was true. He nodded. How had he spent a lifetime convinced of his father's indifference? How had his mother kept him in such a tight spell of lies and hate?

"There is much I need to tell you," Far said. "You weren't ready to hear it before, but you are now. Come. We will sit, and I will tell you why your mother could never return to Sweden."

Domar sat in the silence as Kirstin had suggested. He'd taken a long walk to the area of the new house and found a rocky outcropping that looked down over the lake. Sitting there, he waited, as if God might at any moment stroll up and join him.

There were still quite a few men working on the various houses. The city hadn't given the people much time to move. It wasn't right, but no one had the money and time to fight against the city. The people of this neighborhood worked hard, and their jobs and family would take priority in their lives.

"Be still."

Domar heard the words so loudly, he glanced around to see who had spoken them. There was no one.

He drew a deep breath and looked back at the lake. It was calm today. The waves came in gentle laps as the fishing boats returned from their ventures. Down below on the docks, he heard the laughter of children and greetings from the men and women who welcomed the fishermen home. He spied a man lifting a child in the air. The little boy squealed in delight, reminding Domar of a time when he'd been little and Far had thrown him high in the air.

"Be still."

The voice came again. Domar once again looked around, but there was no one there speaking to him. What was going on? Was he losing his mind?

"Be still."

256

This time it was barely a whisper that seemed to come from deep within his soul.

Sitting in the silence. That was what Kirstin had called it. Domar was starting to see for himself, however, that it was more than just finding a quiet place. This place had its distractions, just as most places did, but it was more. Domar needed to still the noise in his head and heart.

What was it to be still?

He closed his eyes and waited. The noise seemed to fall away. His thoughts were less cooperative. He couldn't help but think of the young man who'd died. David. David Oberdean. Hardly even a man. Dead and without family even to claim his body.

"Be still."

The words beckoned him to let go of David. Let go of the accident. Let go of the anger and pain. Let go of his bad choices and the good ones as well. He needed to empty himself of what had happened at the logging camp—of what had happened a lifetime ago in Sweden.

He pulled up his feet and put his head against his knees. "Empty me, Lord. Please empty me. It's a terrifying thing, but I'm here, and I long to be emptied of me so that I might be filled with You." Tears came, and Domar did nothing to stop them. He was too exhausted to fight and too afraid of the emptiness. What if God didn't fill him up? What if God left him empty—broken—hopeless?

The world fell away, and Domar sat there, face against his knees, hands wrapped around his legs—bare before the living God of the universe.

"Forgive me." It was his only thought. "Please, God . . . forgive me."

Chapter 22

Ilian sat across from his father. The seriousness of the situation was evident in the lines etched on his face.

"Your mother was always a very busy person. When she was just a girl, she was teased because it seemed she was always moving about. Our folks knew one another through church. Her father owned a shop, and mine was a wainwright—as you know. They figured Sarah and I were a good match, and so the family struck a bargain to see us married. I was so much older—twenty-six to her ten years when my father sat me down and told me about his desires for the arrangement."

"She was only ten and you were a grown man?" Ilian found that hard to imagine. "I would never have agreed to such a thing."

"But you must understand, that was the way things were done back then. I hadn't yet married because my father had declared he would choose a bride for me. He found a lucrative arrangement in betrothing me to Sarah. To tell you the truth, I figured something would happen to break the arrangement before we ever made it to the altar. Things often did."

"But it didn't."

"No. But there were plenty of times I thought it would. I loved my far very much, so I agreed to do whatever he told me to do." His father's eyes narrowed as his expression became pained. "I wanted to please him and my mor. I wanted them to be proud. I agreed to the arrangement, knowing it would be years and years before we would marry."

"And Mor?"

"Your mother didn't understand much at first. She was a little girl playing with her dolls and sisters. Her parents were the kind of people who saw their daughters as commodities for sale, so they arranged lucrative marriages that either benefited them financially or socially. In my case, my father and Sarah's struck a deal that helped each man financially. That's just the way it was done.

"While she was young, Sarah and her friends thought it wonderful that she was engaged. Little girls were brought up to be this way, you know. They gathered together to make quilts and other things to fill their wedding chests. Meanwhile, as the husband-to-be, I worried about providing a home for us to live in. I worked hard, saved my money, and found a very nice little house in town to rent. I knew it would please Sarah."

"Did it?" Ilian was still trying to imagine his parents at that age.

"Ja. When we moved in after we married, Sarah thought it quite nice. It was one of the finest in town, and your mother liked fine things. Which I tried to provide. As the years went by, I did little things to win Sarah's love. Since she liked pretty things, it usually involved buying her something expensive.

She always seemed so happy with the gifts, but her love was just not to be."

"Did you and Mor court, or just marry when she was old enough?" Ilian knew his mother had said nothing about courtship.

"Ja, we courted. We started walking out and spending more time together when she turned sixteen. I was so much older, however, that she used to laugh and make fun of me for being an old man. I was thirty-two when she was sixteen. She told me she didn't want to marry—that I was too old. She had many friends—boys as well as girls—and she did not like the idea of being engaged. She wanted to get to know some of the other boys. I wasn't happy about that, but I understood. We had never been given a chance to choose for ourselves. I tried not to make her unhappy, but I knew our parents expected us to start focusing on each other. Sarah's family was quite hard on her about it. They would not tolerate her flirtatious nature."

"It's hard to imagine Mor being a flirt." Ilian shook his head. The idea of the hard, bitter woman he'd known being carefree and fun was more than he could bring to mind.

"Your mother was quite the free spirit." Far's voice was edged with sorrow. "She was always in trouble with her folks. Her father was very firm and would even beat her when she did something wrong. I remember once she came to me and begged me to tell her father a lie—to assure him that she had been with me all evening. I didn't want to see her hurt . . . so I lied for her. It was the first of many lies."

"Where had she been instead?"

"With another young man."

"You protected her even though she had been with another?"

Far looked at Ilian for a long moment. There was such regret and pain in his father's expression that Ilian wanted to take back his question.

"She fancied herself in love with him and told me she didn't want to marry me, but I couldn't release her. Our arrangement was such that I knew it would cause a great many problems if I dissolved the engagement. She went to her parents and begged them to end the betrothal, but of course they wouldn't and instead pushed for us to marry sooner than we'd originally planned."

"Obviously, you did marry."

"Ja. But it was not a happy day. I did what I could to make it one, but Sarah was most grieved. By the time we actually wed when Sarah turned eighteen, she had fallen hard for yet another young man, Lars Nyberg. He was handsome and related to nobility. The most powerful man in our village, a nobleman who owned most of the land, fancied Lars for a son-in-law and arranged for Lars to marry his daughter Frida. Still that didn't stop your mother from wanting him for her own. I think her father caught wind of this, and so for weeks prior to our wedding, he kept her under lock and key."

Ilian flinched. "That couldn't have been easy for her to endure."

"No. Nor for me. You see, I had come to love your mother even though she didn't love me. I lost my heart and hoped she would someday love me in return. I told her how much she had come to mean to me, but she told me she would never love me."

Ilian hadn't known this. It hurt to imagine the woman you loved assuring you she would never return that love. What if Kirstin felt that way about him? What would he do?

"I offered to let her go. I talked to her father and told him that while I loved Sarah with all my heart, I knew she did not love me. Her father thought me very admirable for being willing to lose what I loved in order to make her happy. He told me that he knew more than ever that he wanted me to marry his daughter because I would always forgive her and care for her even if she behaved badly. What more could a father want for his child?"

Ilian eased back in his chair and stretched his legs under the table. "So you married in spite of all the problems."

"Yes. I thought maybe in time things would be better. After all, we were married, and Sarah got with child right away. I hoped your mother would find great joy in our baby daughter, but she did not. She hardly paid the child any attention, so I had to. I asked my grandmother to come live with us, and she took care of the baby, since Sarah seemed to have no interest. Sarah spent her days visiting her sisters, who were all married with children of their own by this time."

Ilian shook his head. "I can't imagine Mor wanting nothing to do with Maja. To hear her tell it, you stole Maja's affections away from her. Sighne's too."

His father met his gaze. "Those girls were so starved for their mama's love that I had no choice but to give them extra. Your mother didn't want my children. She made that clear to me all the time. When she lost a baby between the girls, she told me she was glad."

Ilian couldn't hide his look of disgust. "You lie." He hadn't meant to blurt that out, but his father's words had so taken him by surprise that he couldn't hide his reaction. Ilian calmed. "I'm sorry."

"I wish it were a lie."

Ilian could see his father's pain. He had never heard any-thing about this from his mother. She only spoke of her own misery—of a loveless marriage that had been forced on her. Of never being loved by her husband. If he was to believe his father, then the stories Ilian had been raised on—the truths he thought he knew—were all lies.

"Of course, if that had been the only trouble between us, we might have found our way through. But your mor was still in love with Lars, who by now was another woman's husband. Our town was not all that big, and everyone knew most everyone's business. Your mother and her sisters were well-known for sharing gossip and creating plenty of their own. Your mother often spoke out against Lars's wife, Frida, which was in and of itself unwise. Her father, Bjork Carlsson, was the wealthiest and most powerful man in the area—a nobleman. He owned many of the businesses and houses. The farmland was his. People were obligated to him, including Sarah's father—your morfar—and me. He owned the place I rented for our home and business. He owned the freighting company that bought my wagons. He could easily ruin us."

Far bowed his head and fell silent for a moment. It seemed to Ilian that he was wrestling with something. Finally, he looked up, shaking his head. "I don't know how to say this to you in any other way but to be straightforward and honest." He clenched and unclenched his jaw as he sometimes did when something was particularly bad.

"Just do exactly that," Ilian replied. "I want to know the truth."

It was then that he realized he trusted his father to give him the truth. God had certainly brought him to this place, because Ilian knew he never would have come of his own accord.

"Sighne was just a year old when I was first told your mother was having an affair with Lars."

Ilian gasped. "Mor . . . committed adultery? I don't believe it." But even as he spoke the words, he knew somehow that what his father had said was true.

His father looked away. "I didn't believe it at first. I couldn't. I didn't even bother to ask her about it. I couldn't bear to know the answer. But the stories kept coming back to me, and one day Mr. Carlsson came to see me. He told me that Sarah was causing his daughter great pain and misery, and if I didn't control my wife . . . he would. I assured him I would speak to Sarah, that she was a good woman and would never want to hurt anyone. But unfortunately, I had to accept the situation for what it was.

"I spoke with Sarah that night and told her about Carlsson's visit. I didn't accuse her but told her what was said. She told me Carlsson was being ridiculous. Of course she talked to Lars, but that was all. Frida was just jealous because she knew Lars didn't love her. I allowed myself to believe her and begged her to be careful because Mr. Carlsson was so powerful." He shrugged. "She didn't listen to me any more than before."

"The rumors grew and grew. I knew what they were saying about your mother, but I didn't want to believe it. Finally, Mr. Carlsson's daughter had enough. She went to her father and begged him to do something. Mr. Carlsson came to me, money in hand, and told me I must leave Sweden and take my family to America and never return. If I didn't, he would accuse Sarah of being an adulteress and destroy our family. He would see to it that no one bought my wagons, nor my father's, and we would be shunned.

"But it was what he threatened against Sarah that worried me most. He talked of seeing her thrown into prison, and I couldn't bear that. I didn't want harm to come to her." He bowed his head. "I still loved her."

"So you moved to America." Ilian felt sick. All those years his mother had told him how selfish his father had been to force her to leave her family in Sweden . . . all those times she had said Far refused to take her home even for a visit because of his selfishness . . . all of it was a lie. She couldn't go back because of her own actions. Far had saved her life, in many ways.

But there was still that nagging doubt, that his father was wrong. That Mr. Carlsson and the others had been wrong. Perhaps it was only jealousy that made them say such cruel things about his mother. Surely she would never have slept with another man while married to his father.

"Mr. Carlsson was generous with the money he gave us. I sold him my business, except for my tools, and packed up my family. Your mother was livid. She argued and cried, and I had to sit her down and explain that I didn't believe Mr. Carlsson's accusations, but I did believe he would see her imprisoned or worse if we didn't leave."

"So you didn't believe Mor had . . . had taken a lover?"

"No. I thought she was a flirt, but I figured she was a good woman who honored her marriage vows." He fell silent for several moments. "I was wrong."

"How can you say that? How can you be sure? Did she admit it?" Ilian could hear the desperation in his voice.

"No." Far got up from the table. "I need to get something." He left the room.

What in the world was so important to get now, in the middle of this terrible explanation of why they'd come to America? Mor had never told him any of this. She'd always made it seem like Far did it to punish her, to make her suffer for some imagined wrong. Now Ilian was hearing an entirely different tale. His father had saved his mother from great shame and possible ruination. But how could he be sure this was the truth?

His father returned, carrying a picture. A daguerreotype, if Ilian wasn't mistaken. Far placed it facedown on the table and covered it with his hand.

"I know what I have said has been hard to hear. I know you have doubts that any of this could be true. I had my doubts too. I wanted to believe only the best about your mother. I wanted very much for us to be happy in America, but I knew it would never be. The arguments you so often heard us have were just as you believed. She demanded I take her to Sweden, and I refused. She threatened all manner of punishment for me, but she had already taken away my hope for our future and marriage. There was nothing more she could take."

Ilian saw the agony in his father's eyes. What could he say? All of his life, Ilian had believed his father was a heartless husband who cared nothing about his wife's needs, and now . . .

"As you know, you are the only one of our children born in America. Born not long after our arrival here. I didn't even know your mother was expecting when we left Sweden. When you were born, she took control of you and worked to turn you against me. I tried to fight for you, but it wasn't to be.

But you must know one thing, Ilian. I have always loved you despite everything."

Ilian could see his father wasn't done. There was still something that had gone unsaid. "What aren't you telling me?"

His father turned over the photo and pushed it toward Ilian. "You aren't my natural child. This is your father."

Ilian felt a tight band wrap around his gut. He looked down at the photograph and saw himself. It could have been a photograph taken days ago. It was so clear that Ilian could only stare at it in disbelief.

"That is Lars Nyberg, as you will read on the back. I found this in your mother's Bible after she died. I had my suspicions that you weren't mine. After Sighne's birth, your mother would hardly allow for my touch, but I told myself that I must have been wrong—that you were somehow my son. I wanted you to be my son—just as I will always want you to be my son."

Ilian picked up the daguerreotype and drew it closer. The resemblance was uncanny. Even the haircut was identical. Of course, Ilian wore his hair that way in honor of his mother, who had always styled it that way. Styled it after his real father.

Bile rose in the back of his throat as the truth settled on him. Far had always known Ilian wasn't his child and yet had stayed by his mother's side and raised him as if he were flesh of his flesh.

"Did Mor know you suspected I wasn't yours?"

For a long while there was no reply, and Ilian was afraid to look up. He kept his gaze on the photograph, hoping his father would answer and yet dreading it at the same time.

"No." The word came in a whisper.

"You never accused her of the truth even as you watched me

grow? Even as I became the image of the man she had taken in your place?"

"No."

Tears came to Ilian's eyes as he stared at Far. How bravely his father had borne his shame. How honorably he had treated the woman who wronged him.

"Why? You were well within your rights. You could have divorced her. You could have sent her back to Sweden to face whatever happened."

His father gave him a weak smile. "I loved her. How could I see her shamed and possibly harmed?"

"She shamed herself. Any harm that would have come to her would have been well earned. She committed adultery. She bore another man's child." He dropped his hold on the photograph as if it had suddenly become hot.

"I loved her," Far repeated. "I love her still. Just as I love you."

"But I'm not your son."

Far shook his head. "Perhaps not by blood, but in every other way possible. I chose you to be mine. I promised to be a father to you and care for you. I promise that still . . . if you want me to be. I realize that in telling you the truth, I may have lost you. I pray that isn't the case, but I felt you needed to know why I was so adamant we not return to Sweden. Your mother never knew what would happen to her or to you—I kept it from her. I had horrible thoughts of Carlsson taking you from us and giving you to his daughter, who had been unable to have children. Your mother never considered those possibilities, but I did."

"And I accused you and blamed you, and plotted behind your back to find a way to get Mor home." Tears trickled down Ilian's cheeks. How could one person have been so wrong about another? How could his mother have lied so completely, without feeling for either Ilian or her husband? Why had she never told him he wasn't Habram Farstad's son?

A sob broke from Ilian as he pushed from the chair. He moved to his father's side and fell to his knees. "I . . . I'm so sorry. I am . . . so sorry." He lowered his head against his father's leg. His entire life had been a lie that he not only believed but perpetuated in order to honor his mother.

Far put his hand atop Ilian's head. "Son, you are forgiven. You were never meant to carry the blame."

"I never . . . never . . . gave you . . . a chance," Ilian said, unable to stop his tears. The anguish of seeing the truth was almost too much. He had wronged this good man. He had tormented and withheld his love because of a lie he chose to believe. How could there be forgiveness for that?

Far caressed Ilian's shoulder. "The truth is hard, but it's given in love. I want you to know the truth so that you can be free of the past and we can start anew."

Ilian looked up. "How can you still want me? I've done nothing but hurt you."

Far smiled, and in his eyes was such love that Ilian felt the last of his anger and bitterness break into pieces. "You are my child—my son—and I love you."

Chapter 23

"We're going to break through today," Morfar declared at breakfast. "We're using black powder and nitro to blast it if need be, but the canal will be complete today. Or at least open to let the water flow. Superior can have their injunction, even though we've seen nothing of it yet."

"But if you go on building the canal with the injunction in place—won't they arrest you?" Mormor asked.

"They can try." He winked at Kirstin. "Besides, once we're through, the deed is done. We'll have our harbor entry." He finished off his coffee and got to his feet. "You should come and see. It's going to be quite exciting, and tomorrow we can sit in church and praise God for our success."

"I'm going to go watch," Ilian said.

"Me too," Domar agreed, glancing at his grandmother and then sister. "If you want, we could go together."

"That sounds like fun. I've never been around blasting," Kirstin admitted. "What's it like?"

"It's loud and shakes the ground to bits. It even knocked me on my backside once," Domar admitted. "It's powerful stuff and not to be trifled with."

"That's why they asked me to handle it." Morfar's voice was filled with pride. "John knows I can handle black powder with no problems."

"I need a few things from town anyway," Mormor said, getting to her feet. "Kirstin, let's take care of the breakfast dishes. We'll come down straightaway with the boys, Habram. When do you think you'll be breaking through?"

"There's no telling, but it'll be today for sure." The old man got to his feet and grinned. "It's going to be a day of celebration."

"That it will, Far," Ilian replied with a smile.

Kirstin hurried to gather up the empty dishes. For all the time she'd been in Duluth, she hadn't really cared much one way or the other regarding the canal, but she knew the longtime residents were anxious for this new waterway, so she was determined to be excited with them. However, the thing uppermost on her mind was Ilian. He was different. There was something going on between him and his father that had changed them. She longed to ask about it but knew it was hardly appropriate to do so now, with everyone gathered around.

But the Farstad men definitely seemed more at peace. Ilian's expression had softened when he spoke to his father—he'd even smiled. And there was respect in his tone. Turning to Jesus had no doubt helped Ilian think differently about Morfar, but Kirstin couldn't help but think it was something more.

"I'll be back for you ladies in half an hour or so," Domar said, kissing the top of his grandmother's head. "Ilian has asked for my help with a few things."

"That's just fine. You go right ahead." Mormor checked the stove's receptacle for water.

Kirstin waited until Domar left the house and it was just her and Mormor. "Something has changed between Morfar and Ilian."

Her grandmother looked up as she drew water for the dishes. "Changed in what way?"

"It's better. I can't explain it, but Ilian definitely looked at him differently. I think they must have had a talk about everything. Do you suppose they've decided to be friends?"

"I don't know about friends, but perhaps Ilian has decided to let go of the past. That would be to his advantage and help his spirit tremendously. Being unburdened of all that happened long ago will give him a freedom to enjoy the present."

"I've never understood his anger toward his father anyway. Oh, I could see the problems between them because of Ilian's belief that his mother was being mistreated. I should not be silent myself if I thought Far was hurting Mor. But Ilian's anger has always been such a powerful thing between them. Now it seems that is gone."

"God can work miracles, Kirstin. We must allow for His hand in all of this. Giving yourself over to God is a frightening thing, but it's also the most powerful and wonderful thing you will ever do. Ilian has always had a type of faith that believed in God's existence, but he didn't have a relationship with his heavenly Father. That makes all the difference. A great many people show up in church week after week. They believe that God exists and that He created the world, but they don't understand that God wants to be an intimate part of their lives. He wants them to surrender to Him in full so that He can remake them. Ilian has come to see that, and no doubt it will have a profound effect on him."

Kirstin thought about it for a moment. "Perhaps in coming to better know his heavenly Father, Ilian can now see the love of his earthly one."

"Perhaps. But remember, Kirstin, it is his path to walk, and if he chooses to share it with you, then all is well and fine. But if he doesn't want to . . . if he still feels too guarded to open up about it, don't make him feel bad about that. Don't push him."

"I wouldn't." She hadn't expected her grandmother's admonition. "I care too much for him."

Mormor smiled. "I know you do. It's just a gentle reminder, not a reprimand."

A lot of people were gathered to watch as Major Upham worked the dredge and tried to force the frozen ground to yield. Since it was Saturday, a lot of schoolchildren had come to see the operation as well. They were more excited than anyone, and with every bit of gravel and dirt that Major Upham pulled away, they cheered.

Kirstin studied the area and wondered how the people living on Minnesota Point were going to get to town once the canal was in place. She supposed they would need a bridge in time. For now, they would most likely use a ferry. She wasn't sure she would like being cut off that way. Lake Superior was so vast. It was very much like the ocean, going on and on for miles with nothing but water to see.

"What do you think?" her brother asked.

"It's quite the ordeal. I hope they'll break through without any more difficulty. Someone mentioned there's not another dredge like the *Ishpeming*. If it breaks down, we'll be hard-pressed to finish, and it's already been hours just working on it today."

"I know. They thought the ground would be more yielding, but they have the ability to bust up the ground with the black powder. I think we'll see it complete today, and I wouldn't worry about the *Ishpeming*. No one knows the risk better than Major Upham and Mr. Farstad. They'll be careful, believe me."

Kirstin raised her face to the skies, where the clouds had parted and begun to clear. They'd had some rain off and on—just enough to make the surrounding area muddier than before. "Maybe we'll have sunshine after all."

"I think even God is smiling at the thought of this canal finally being completed. The people here have wanted it for a long time. Having their own entry from the lake will change everything for them. They won't feel reliant upon Superior's good graces to get what they need, and they won't have to pay out large sums. This, along with the railroad, is going to put Duluth on the map, to be sure."

"Everything in America seems to be in some state of construction. I saw all sorts of building going on in New York City and elsewhere when I passed through on the train."

"America is definitely a busy place. It's been like that the whole time I've been here."

Kirstin touched her brother's arm. "Do you miss Sweden?"

He considered her question for a moment. "There are things I miss—people—but I've been here so long now that Sweden is no longer home. America is home. Duluth and this area are home to me."

"I think this will be home for me as well. I like it here very much."

"I think you like a certain person more than the place," he said with a grin.

"I do." She smiled as she met his gaze. "Have you noticed that he's changed? He and his father seem . . . better."

"I did notice that. I'm very glad for it. It's been a lifetime coming."

"I hope they'll be able to be close." The wind picked up and pulled at Kirstin's bonnet. She quickly caught it and tied the ribbons. "Uff da!"

Domar turned in surprise, then began to laugh. "I've not heard you say that since you arrived. I remember when you were little and said it so much that Mor threatened to wash your mouth out with soap."

Kirstin nodded. "I rarely ever say it. I can't even remember the last time. I guess that startled me."

Just then there was a tremendous boom, and from down below, rock and debris flew up into the air. The people cheered wildly.

With her mouth open in surprise, Kirstin looked at her brother. "Was that the black powder blowing up?"

"Ja. What do you think?"

She shook her head. "Uff da."

Ilian was more than a little nervous to have his father handling the kegs of black powder. He knew Far was good at most anything he put his hand to, but the dangers were worrisome, and he couldn't move as fast as he once could.

Getting around with the use of his cane, Ilian watched the procedure from the deck of the *Ishpeming*. Far had insisted it was the perfect place for a man with an injured leg to watch and wait.

A part of Ilian felt a great sense of frustration in being unable to do anything to help. Then there was a part of him that was still reeling from the information his father had shared. He'd been unable to think about anything else for more than a few minutes without the truth of his birth coming through to accuse him.

He was not Habram Farstad's son. He was Lars Nyberg's child. His mother had committed adultery and lied to him about the good man she'd married. She had destroyed any hope of happiness with her actions, yet Habram Farstad would have taken her back at any time and wiped the slate clean, because he loved her.

And he loved Ilian. It was without a doubt the most humbling thing Far could have said to him. Ilian didn't deserve his love. Especially after a lifetime of treating him badly. He had never honored his father, but instead had listened to lies his mother told. He had despised the man for the supposed pain and injustice he'd heaped upon them, only it hadn't been that way at all. Far had saved his wife's reputation. He'd given her grace when she had betrayed him.

Ilian shook his head and tried to refocus on where his father was at the moment. Danger was all around them, mingled with the excitement, and yet Ilian could only think of his own problems.

"What am I to do with this?" he murmured.

He gripped the side rail of the boat. What could he do? He couldn't very well go back to Sweden and meet his real father. That would bring definite shame to his mother's memory. His aunts still lived there, as well as a few cousins and others who might face heavy retribution when the truth was known.

His father had never so much as confronted his mother about her indiscretions. They had talked of the rumors, but his father had chosen to believe only the best of his wife. And even when he knew the truth regarding Ilian, or at least suspected it, he had continued in silence, accepting Ilian as his own.

The dredge was working again to move great bucketfuls of wet soil. There wasn't far to go before the bay and Lake Superior would be joined. Ilian glanced at the shoreline and saw the crowd continuing to grow. Groups of men had come down with their shovels and picks. No doubt they wanted to be able to say they had been a part of digging the canal.

Ilian had lost track of his father. He strained to see him through the vast sea of people. He made his way to Major John Upham, who was at the controls of the dredge. "Do you see my father?"

The major looked for a moment. "Can't be sure. He'll be setting that last blast in a moment." He pointed to the chart on his desk. "See the mark? That's where he should be."

Ilian studied the map. He didn't know exactly where the spot was, but knowing their objective, there weren't too many choices. "I'd like to make my way to him."

"I have to maneuver for the blast anyway. Let me get you closer to the floating dock."

When the *Ishpeming* was close enough, Ilian made his way to the dock. It was an awkward move at best, and when he landed hard on his injured leg, he let out an unexpected groan. Thankfully no one seemed too interested in what he was doing.

Ilian made his way along the temporary dock and then onto the plank boards that had been laid to help navigate the muck.

Men were busy working the ground and tossing up great shov-
elfuls of dirt. Ilian narrowly missed being hit as the work continued.

He moved past the crowds, surprised at how much the atmo-
sphere had turned into that of a party. People were everywhere.

Finally, at the very end of the line on the last strip of solid
ground before reaching the bay, Ilian found his father. He was
working to get a keg of black powder into place.

"How can I help?" Ilian asked, approaching his father's position.

"Nothing much left. This is going to open it all," his father
replied, looking up with a grin. "Let them bring their injunc-
tions. Once the waters are flowing, nothing is going to stop
Duluth." He motioned to the growing crowd. "Get everybody
back!"

Ilian nodded and hobbled up toward the first group of people.
"We're about to blow the powder keg. Everybody needs to
get back."

The people began talking all the louder and moving in ac-
cordance with Ilian's direction. They only went so far, so Ilian
pushed to get them back farther. "This is really going to be
dangerous. You need to get back!"

They moved a few feet but were too excited to go farther.

Ilian bellowed at them. "You're going to die if you don't
get back up on the road!"

This got their attention, and they scurried like rats deserting
a sinking ship. Ilian heard his father laugh. It made him smile.
Ilian wanted more for them than the misery and bitterness he'd
known before.

Far moved up the muck toward Ilian at a quick pace, waving people away as he came. "It's going to blow. Everyone get back." He slipped in the mud and went facedown.

Ilian jumped forward. His leg ached, causing him immediate pain, but he didn't care. He grabbed hold of his father and pulled him up. He nearly carried the older man the rest of the way to safety, but both men hit the ground when the blast knocked them forward. For a moment neither moved, and then Far began to laugh as though it were all a great joke.

Ilian pulled up into a sitting position and looked at his father. "What is so funny?"

"Ooh, there. I must've cut that one a little short."

Ilian met his father's humored gaze and smiled. "Maybe just a little."

People were yelling and cheering so loudly by now that the two men could no longer hear each other. They got to their feet and saw what all the excitement was about. Lake water was flowing across the cut from the east while bay water did the same in the opposite direction. The waters were mingling freely. Duluth had her canal.

Ilian patted his father on the back. "Looks like you did it, Far."

"It's a good thing. We'll be working on this for a long time to make it just right, but tomorrow we can celebrate in church and thank God for our new canal."

"Ja." He looked at his father with new eyes. "We can thank God for much."

"Are you two all right?" Domar asked, reaching them before Kirstin or Lena did.

Ilian turned from his father and found the ladies looking quite concerned as they arrived. "We're fine. Far cut the line a little short, and the blast went off before he expected it, but the ground broke our fall." He grinned and tried to wipe mud from his face.

"You promised to be careful," Lena scolded. "I say you should retire, now that your canal is dug, and marry me."

Far's eyes widened. "You are asking me to marry you? What a bold woman."

Lena smiled. "Well, I've waited long enough for you to make up your mind."

"Woman, I made up my mind a long time ago, but the good Lord told us both to wait. We had too much work to do first. Now all those things that troubled us so much have been resolved." He knelt in the mud. "Will you marry me?"

Lena grinned. "Oh ja, sure. I'll marry you, Mr. Farstad."

Chapter 24

All of Duluth celebrated that night. It was quite the accomplishment to build a canal that opened their town to the largest of the Great Lakes, and everyone knew it would forever change their future. The neighborhood decided it was the perfect excuse for a smörgåsbord and laid out an outdoor celebration second to none. Despite the temperature being rather chilly once the sun set, Kirstin thought the party was exactly what they needed. In just a few weeks they would have to vacate this land, and even though many were rebuilding their lives in a new neighborhood, it wouldn't be the same.

Bringing a big bowl of dilled potatoes to the table, Kirstin spied a group of men preparing to play music. This was something Mormor had talked about but Kirstin hadn't yet experienced. One man with a violin pulled the bow across a string, and everyone began tuning up. It wasn't long before six strong men brought a piano seemingly from nowhere. A short squat man Kirstin had only met once followed them with a stool. He sat at the piano and waited for the others to finish tuning their instruments. Then the little man ripped into the piano like he was searching for something. He played up and down the keyboard in a wild cacophony of notes that had everyone, even the old people, on their feet, clapping and dancing.

Kirstin found it very amusing and clapped in unison with everyone else. Mormor was soon at her side.

"Old Carl hasn't played like that since losing his wife last year. We've missed his skills."

"He plays so well. I never expected to hear such music."

"We used to have music and dancing almost every Saturday," Mormor declared. "We'd get together like this and eat and sing and dance." Her face glowed at the memories. "Your morfar was not a dancing man, but even he would do a jig now and then when Carl played."

"I like the music very much. I like it all," Kirstin admitted. "Especially the way they've hung lanterns in the trees and along the fences. It makes it seem like a fairy world."

"It's the way we would celebrate in the old country." Mormor continued to clap and smile as she gazed out across the party. "I shall miss it here, but I have a good feeling about our new home. Don't you?"

Kirstin nodded, although she wasn't sure what the future might hold for her. She knew Mormor would have her stay with her and Morfar even after they married, but frankly she wanted her own home and life with Ilian. She didn't mind if they all lived very close, as they had here in the neighborhood, but she wanted her own little house and the privacy a married couple needed to get to know each other. But she was getting ahead of herself. He hadn't declared his love for her yet. She hoped that would happen—and soon.

With everyone focused on putting together the celebration,

Kirstin hadn't heard another word from her grandmother about marrying. Hopefully Mormor wouldn't be offended by her curiosity.

"Mormor, when do you and Morfar plan to marry?" She figured the direct approach was best.

Her grandmother glanced over and smiled. "We figure to see what needs to be done to make it legal and then marry as soon as Pastor Persson can do the job. We aren't going to have a big wedding—just a simple ceremony."

"That sounds like you, Mormor. No frills. Just get the job done."

"What about you, Kirstin dear? When are you and Ilian going to wed?"

"I have no idea if we are. I like to think we will, but he hasn't asked me. He's had much on his mind, as you well know," Kirstin said.

"I do. Habram told me all about it, and I think you should give Ilian time to find his place again."

"So what happened? What did Morfar say?"

Mormor shook her head. "It isn't mine to tell. Ilian will surely let you know in time. Don't worry."

Kirstin always thought it silly when people told her not to worry. It merely reemphasized the fact that there was a reason to be concerned. She said nothing, however.

By now there were several older couples out dancing as the musicians continued to play. She looked around for her brother and Ilian but didn't see either of them. Usually Domar could be found by the food table, so it must have been something important that took him away.

"I'm going to see if I can find the boys," she told Mormor.

"I've come for a dance," Morfar announced, appearing behind Kirstin. She turned and found his gaze fixed on her grandmother.

"I will give my permission, but only if you dance very respectfully," Kirstin teased.

The old man laughed heartily. "Your mormor would pinch my ears if I did it any other way."

Kirstin stepped aside. "Then have fun. I'm going to see where the boys got off to."

"Last I saw them, Ilian was showing Domar something in the workshop."

"Thank you." Kirstin stretched up on her tiptoes and kissed his cheek. "I'm so glad you're about to be my grandfather."

"Or better still, your father-in-law, eh? I think that boy of mine is finally getting his head on straight. I told him he'd better ask you soon, or some other good man would steal you away."

Kirstin felt her cheeks grow hot and was grateful for the dim light. She left without saying anything more, knowing that if she opened her mouth, she might very well insert her foot.

The workshop had few windows, but light radiated from within, leaving Kirstin no doubt the boys were there. She wondered if they would mind her intrusion. Would it be possible to get Ilian to share his heart with her about his father and whatever had happened between them?

The door was already open, but Kirstin paused just inside all the same. "Mind if I come in?" she asked, spying the two men sitting across the room.

Domar laughed. "Your timing is impeccable. Ilian was just saying he needed to tell me something but wanted to do it when he could explain it to us both at the same time."

She breathed a sigh of relief that she hadn't annoyed them with her interruption. "Well, I'm happy to oblige and hear anything Ilian wishes to say."

Ilian got up from his chair and offered it to her. "Sit, and I will try to explain. It's all so new to me that I will probably make a mess of it."

She looked into his face and found his expression edged with worry. "I'm sure whatever you have to tell us will be just fine. Don't worry about the presentation. Just speak."

Ilian nodded, and Kirstin took her seat. She couldn't imagine what weighed on him so heavily, but she whispered a quick prayer for God to give him strength and that she would have understanding.

"My father . . ." Ilian began, then hesitated and fell silent. He seemed to consider his words, then began again. "My father and I had a long talk the other day. He felt it was time to reveal the truth to me about my mother and her unhappiness." He began to pace and then stopped. "I'm sorry. This is a difficult thing for me—a confession, of sorts, that I feel is very necessary yet painful."

"Go on," Domar encouraged. "You are with friends who will not condemn you."

Ilian gave a hint of a smile. "You needn't bother. I've thoroughly condemned myself. But thank you. You have always been a good friend to me, Domar. Strangely enough, I feel the things my father told me tie you and me together in a way that makes our relationship even stronger." He drew a deep breath. "As you know, I always felt my mother was treated badly by Far. I sympathized with her and held such anger and bitterness toward Far. I thought Far selfish and mean-spirited. All Mor wanted was to go home to Sweden."

Kirstin heard the regret in his voice. Everyone had their missed opportunities and sorrows, and she wondered if Ilian's would always be centered around his inability to take his mother back to her native land. Poor man. After all, there was nothing to be done about it now.

"Far never spoke against her. Even when I was hard on him and confrontational. Even after all these years of my anger and unwillingness to discuss the past. Far had wanted to explain himself before now, but I wouldn't hear it. I was wrong, and I want to confess that here and now. I let the devil keep spite and malice in my heart toward a good man." He looked at the floor. "I wronged Habram Farstad. He is a good man. A better man than most know."

"But you've made it right," Domar interjected. "You've come to see the truth."

"I could have seen it years earlier if I hadn't been so stubborn." Ilian held up his hands and looked at Domar and then Kirstin. "That's neither here nor there. The fact of the matter is that my father had every right to have nothing to do with me. To put my mother and me out of his house and never look back."

"How can you say that?" Kirstin asked.

Ilian wasted no more time. "Because I am not his son. My mor was unfaithful. My father lives in Sweden, married to a nobleman's daughter."

Kirstin was stunned. She shook her head. "How can this be?"

"My mother was in love with this man, Lars Nyberg, despite them both being married. The nobleman found out and came to my father with threats of charging my mother and seeing her imprisoned for adultery. He demanded my father take his family and leave Sweden for good. He even gave Far money for the trip so that we would be gone and his daughter could have peace of mind once again.

"Far forced Mor to leave Sweden, telling her of the threat but not believing it for himself. He thought her simply flirtatious and foolish. But when I was born a few months later in America, Far knew what she'd done. He never confronted her about it. He told me he had no wish to shame her. He loved her. Even after everything she did to refuse him . . . he loved her."

Kirstin heard the emotion in Ilian's voice, and it brought tears to her eyes. She could see how much it hurt him. He had believed his mother's lies. He had blamed the wrong person for their misery.

Ilian held out a daguerreotype. Kirstin took it. It was a picture of Ilian. She looked up in confusion.

"That is my father."

Her hand went to her throat. It was the exact image of Ilian. She shook her head and handed it to her brother. "It could be you."

"It is me, in a way. It's my blood," Ilian declared.

Domar studied the picture for a moment. "It's uncanny."

"Yes, but absolute proof that everything Far said was right."

"What do you plan?"

Ilian shrugged and leaned back against the carpentry table. "Nothing. I can hardly go back and declare myself without bringing greater shame on my mother. Her family is still there to bear the brunt of gossips and maligners. Not only that, but the only father I've ever known—or needed—is right here. Far told me he has never cared that I wasn't his by blood because he chose me to be his by love."

Tears trickled down Kirstin's cheeks. "How beautiful. I've

always loved your father, but now I love him all the more. He is a good man."

"He is an amazing man," Ilian continued, "and sadly I am only now seeing it. When I think of all the wasted years, it grieves me as nothing else can."

Domar handed back the photograph. "Why are you telling us about this now?"

"Because I wanted you to know, first of all. I want no more secrets between us. When I put all the pieces together, I thought of how uncanny the similarities were in our lives. The prices we paid for the indiscretion of others. The betrayals and wrongs done changed everything for us."

"And neither of us handled it well," Domar murmured.

"No. No, we didn't, but we are making it right now. We are working toward restitution and reconciliation. We are willing to let go of the past thanks to God's grace. A grace I might have missed but for your family."

Kirstin dabbed her eyes with the hem of her apron. "I'm just so sorry you've both had to endure such pain. You're good men, and you will become even better men with God's help, but these are painful wounds that I wish you did not have to bear."

"We will be stronger for them," Ilian assured her. "But it was important for you to know the truth because of my second reason."

"And that is what?" Kirstin looked at him, wondering what else he might have to say.

The edges of his lips turned up in a smile. "In your far's absence, I want Domar's permission to court you—to marry you."

Kirstin's mouth fell open in a gasp of surprise. She looked at

Domar and then back to Ilian. She had anticipated his declaration but hadn't thought it would come in this old-fashioned manner.

Domar laughed and got to his feet. "You know my feelings on the matter. I only wanted you to get your life in order before proposing to her."

"You knew he cared for me?" Kirstin asked.

"Of course I knew. How could I not? Every time he thought no one was looking, he watched you with such intensity that I thought he might lose all other rational thought." He went to Ilian and hugged him close. "I don't care whose son you are, but I will cherish you as my brother."

Ilian hugged him, then let go. "I'm Habram Farstad's son. He's the only father I've known and the only one I care to know." He smiled. "And I feel as though I've been your brother for more years than I can remember. We will always be brothers."

Domar nodded. "I think now is the moment that I should take my leave, *brother*, and let you speak to my sister. I'm sure she's longing to hear all your flowery declarations of love." He winked at Kirstin. "I hope you know what you're doing."

"I've got a pretty good idea." Kirstin smiled as Domar came to embrace her. She rose and held him tight for a moment.

Domar said nothing more before leaving. He'd always been a man of few words, and his lack of them now did not surprise her.

"I hope it didn't bother you that I spoke to Domar about my feelings for you before I told you," Ilian said.

She looked up to find him watching her. "I don't mind. It's very old-fashioned, and so am I."

He smiled and closed the space between them. "I think

I've loved you since you fainted into my arms and then sat on my lap afterward as if it were nothing at all. I thought *I* might faint."

She couldn't help but laugh. "I honestly thought nothing of it. I wasn't thinking of love or propriety. I was so shocked to find Domar alive. But when you were brought to the hospital all broken and hurting, my heart went out to you. I can't say I fell in love then, but it pushed me in that direction."

He took hold of her hands. "And now? Is there love in your heart for me, Kirstin?"

"There is so much love there that I can scarcely breathe. I think of you all the time and long for the day we might be married."

"And you don't care about the past and the circumstances of my birth?"

"No." She shook her head. "You are a story of grace. Of mercy and love. I will always think of that when I think of your birth. I am sorry that it took so many years for you to know the truth and find peace."

"There are other things to consider as well. I am still rather crippled."

"You are getting stronger every day and have little trouble working on the Mackinaw boats. I think one day you'll have quite an industry with it, if you want one. And if you want something else, I've no doubt you'll figure that out as well. You aren't crippled anymore."

"But I've still much to learn about God."

"And so do I. Let us learn together." She squeezed his fingers. "Or are you trying to talk me out of loving you? If so, it won't work."

He shook his head. "I want you forever my own without any secrets between us."

"And I want the same."

He lowered his head to kiss her. Kirstin put her arms around his neck and pulled him close. This was her first kiss, and she intended it to be perfect.

It was.

Chapter 25

Kirstin and her grandmother stood on either side of Domar as Pastor Persson asked if there were any objections to the marriages that were about to take place. Kirstin gazed at Ilian, who stood before the altar with his normal stoic expression. If it was the last thing she did, she planned to see that he smiled more. She hoped she might always give him something to smile about.

"It isn't every day that I perform double weddings," Pastor Persson began, smiling. "And I don't believe I've ever married fathers and grandmothers while also marrying their family members, but I'm quite honored to do so today. Who gives these lovely ladies to be married?"

"I do," Domar declared.

The pastor nodded. Domar handed Mormor off to Habram Farstad and then gave Kirstin to Ilian.

"You'd both better take good care of them, or you'll answer to me." He smiled and went to sit in the first pew.

Kirstin held fast to Ilian's arm. She was determined not to repeat their first meeting and faint, but she was overwhelmed by the meaning of this day. She was about to become a wife.

Five months earlier she had just arrived in this country, eager to help her grandmother and craving adventure. Now she had learned her dead brother was alive, helped Ilian recover from a near-fatal accident, packed up an entire household to move across town to a beautiful new house, and was about to marry. Mor had always said she was a person of action. When she set her mind to accomplish something, Kirstin always forged ahead full speed.

Pastor Persson chose to read through the entirety of the wedding vows for Mormor and Mr. Farstad first. There was an impish grin on the older man's face. Mormor was going to have her hands full with that one.

"Well, Ilian and Kirstin, it's your turn now," the pastor finally said, turning to them.

Kirstin looked up at Ilian and smiled. She wished her father and mother could have been there to experience the wedding. She tried not to think about when they might receive her letter telling them about Domar, but she prayed they'd be happy.

She made her vows to Ilian and he to her, and soon enough he was giving her a chaste little kiss before escorting her from the church. The minute they were outside the door, he loosened the tie he'd worn and drew a deep breath.

"I thought maybe you'd be picking me up off the floor. It was warm in there."

Kirstin grinned. "You were just nervous. Are you worried about me being a difficult wife?"

He stopped walking and gave her a serious look. "I never had a good example of a happy marriage. What if I'm no good at this, Kirstin? The last thing I want to do is hurt you."

She took his hand. "We've talked all of this through. One

step at a time is all God calls us to. We'll work through it if bad times come. We've promised each other to be tolerant and loving. You've always been a man of your word, and I expect you always will be."

He rubbed his thigh. He'd chosen not to use his cane today, and Kirstin worried it was too much.

"Would you like to sit for a while?" She looked around, hoping there might be a stump or rock nearby that he could use.

"No. I'll be fine." He glanced back toward the church, where his father and Kirstin's grandmother were just emerging. "I wish we didn't have to worry about the party and that I could just whisk you away and keep you to myself." He smiled and touched her cheek. "I can scarcely believe I've married. I never intended to wed. It seemed like such a miserable institution. But then I met you. All spit and sass, a strong woman to match my own . . ."

"Spit and sass?" she replied with an impish grin.

"Temperament," he countered. "So much has changed since we first met."

"It's almost frightening." Kirstin shrugged. "But then I remember I have you to bear it with me, and I'm not afraid."

"What are you two discussing?"

Kirstin startled. She hadn't realized Ilian's father and her grandmother had joined them. "I think we're still in shock that we've done this," she declared.

"You're not regretting it, are you?" Mormor asked.

Ilian chuckled. "Not at all. Just amazed."

"Well, I think we should return to the new house and show Kirstin the surprise. You can be amazed the rest of your life," Ilian's far said, pulling Mormor close.

Ilian gave a nod and pulled Kirstin to his side as well. "Come, wife. I have something to show you."

They made their way back to the new neighborhood in a leisurely fashion. There, gathered with Domar on the little porch of the new house, they found all of their friends, who had gone ahead to prepare the reception. Domar looked like he was about to make a speech.

"Three cheers for the newly married couples!"

The crowd let out a whoop and cheer. Kirstin laughed. She gave a wave, not knowing what else to do. When the people had concluded their greeting, Domar raised his hands.

Mormor and Morfar drew up to the front steps of the house with Ilian and Kirstin staying a little farther back. Kirstin knew the house wasn't complete, but they'd agreed to finish it together as time permitted.

"We have a surprise for you," Domar said, grinning from ear to ear.

Kirstin looked at Ilian. "Do you know what this is about?"

He shook his head. "No idea."

"While you four have been off planning your wedding and then getting married, we took it upon ourselves to finish painting and staining and readying your house for your new life here. This morning we moved the last of the furniture from the old place into this house, and it's more than ready for your wedding night."

The crowd made teasing sounds of approval, causing Mormor to blush. Kirstin laughed, but she was afraid of what lay in store for her.

"Welcome to your new home and new life," Domar continued. "We have prayed for you to be blessed here, and we know that God will always be present at every meal and celebration, every heartache and tragedy."

"Amen," Ilian's father said. He pulled Mormor with him and climbed the steps to where Domar stood. "Thank you for this gift. I am honored and blessed to have such a fine young man in my life." He turned and looked down at Ilian. "Did you have a hand in this, son?"

"No. As you'll remember, we had our own project to tend to."

"That's right. There's a surprise for Kirstin as well," Domar said, motioning toward the workshop building. "I think you'll be very happy, little sister."

Kirstin could see how pleased he was with himself. "I'm sure I will be. I find my happiness is overflowing today."

"Let's go investigate and see what everyone has been doing," Morfar told Kirstin's grandmother. She nodded and headed for the door. "Wait just a minute," he said, stopping her before she went inside. "I will carry you across."

"No you won't," Mormor countered. "I am too plump, and you will drop me."

"I won't drop you. You are as light as a feather."

Everyone roared with laughter as they argued back and forth until Habram finally just threw his new wife over his shoulder and forged ahead into the house.

Kirstin laughed so hard that tears came to her eyes. She loved finally seeing those two together. They belonged together and were long overdue all the happiness that it was possible to have.

From inside the house, Kirstin heard her grandmother's joy. "Oh, just look and see what they've done!"

Kirstin looked at Ilian as some of the neighborhood folks followed the old couple into the house. "Do you want to go in?"

"No. I want to go home, where I can have you to myself." He pulled her toward the workshop. Kirstin glanced over her shoulder to see that they were all but forgotten for now.

"I think you're going to be pleased. I've worked very hard with Far and even Domar when he had time."

"Worked on what?"

They reached the back of the workshop and moved to where there was a small stoop and door. Kirstin hadn't remembered that the building had two large windows on either side of the door, but truth be told, after agreeing to marry Ilian, she'd been rather preoccupied. Ilian opened the door and then, without warning, scooped her into his arms and carried her inside.

"Welcome home." He lowered his mouth to hers and kissed her long and passionately.

Kirstin's arms went around his neck as she held him fast. What an amazing and impulsive man, her husband.

He pulled away and lowered her to the floor. "More of that in a moment. What do you think?"

She looked around for the first time and found they were standing in a small but very nicely arranged living area. There was a large stove in the middle of the room to heat the place. To the side, Kirstin saw a little kitchen area with white cupboards.

"It's . . . it's wonderful. I thought it was just going to be a large bedroom."

"It was. But when I decided that we would marry, I thought it better to at least give you a little house of your own. I couldn't afford much because I put most of my savings into what we needed for the boats. But Far and I—Domar too, when he was around—we figured we could at least add a little kitchen and living room for us. I know it's not much, but in time I will build you a grand house all your own. Meanwhile, I know your grandmother and my father intend for us to take meals with them and be one big happy family."

Kirstin couldn't hide her emotions. She wrapped her arms around Ilian. "It's so perfect. We don't need much space, after all. It's just us two."

"For now. I hope in time we will need a much bigger place," he said, causing Kirstin to look up. "I know we haven't really discussed it, but I would like a big family."

"I would too." She felt rather shy at the thought. "I want a house full of laughter and love," she added quickly, hoping to calm her nerves.

Ilian took her hands. "For now and forever, I just want you." He pulled her back into his arms and bent her slightly back as he kissed her again. "You're forever my own, and I am yours."

Epilogue

Duluth, Minnesota
September 1871

"That was quite the storm last night. I hope and pray everyone is safe," Mormor said as she served up breakfast. There were thick slabs of ham and a heaping bowl of scrambled eggs, as well as pickled herring and rusks.

"I think it shook the house right down to the foundation," Morfar said, helping himself to the eggs.

A hard pounding on the front door caused Kirstin to jump. She looked at the others, who seemed just as surprised. "Who could that be at this hour? The sun isn't even up."

"I'll get it," Ilian said, getting to his feet.

He left the room, and Kirstin could hear him speaking to someone at the front door. When he returned, he had the strangest look on his face.

"You will need to don your coats and boots. Apparently there is quite the sight down at the canal."

"What is going on?" Mormor asked.

"Well, if I understand correctly, Mr. Webster's hotel is floating away."

"What?" Kirstin shook her head and got up from the table. "How can a hotel float away?"

"I have no idea. That was Mr. Sandberg. He said a huge part of the construction broke off, and a good portion of what used to be our old neighborhood just floated away from the shoreline."

"I'll bet you, by golly, that it is a floating island," Morfar said, going to his boots. "When we first got here, there were a lot of them. Some got built on, and some would break up when the weather got bad."

"A floating island?" Kirstin asked, pulling on her boots. "How could people not know it wasn't solid land?"

"Sometimes they knew but built anyway," Mormor said. "I remember one man put up his house and bought a few cows and lost it all because the land tore apart in a storm."

Morfar was dressed first and helped Mormor with her coat. Kirstin loved the way he took care of her. Since they had married, she hadn't known any two happier people unless it was Ilian and herself.

"Well, let's go see this sight. I remember the man Lena is talking about. That was quite the experience, watching his house disintegrate and those poor cows swimming for all they were worth," Ilian said, helping Kirstin with her coat. "I was just a boy, and it fascinated me. I remember wondering if the rest of the land would do the same thing. I was glad Far had taught me to swim the year before."

The foursome made their way outside. The horizon was just showing pink hues as light filled the eastern skies.

"Be careful, it's slick in places," Ilian said, taking Kirstin's arm. "I don't want you getting hurt." His expression was filled with love, and she couldn't help but smile.

"If I fall now, I'll be taking you with me."

"That's all right. At least you'll be safe."

"Unless you happen to land on top of me." She chuckled and sidled closer to her husband.

They reached the canal about fifteen minutes later and stood looking down at the great amount of debris passing through the narrow opening. Other people had gathered up and down the roadway even though it wasn't yet six thirty.

"Will you look at that?" someone cried out. "That chunk is as big as a ship."

They all looked as a piece of the island maneuvered into the canal. The lake was already churning from last night's storm. It seemed to greedily accept the new offering coming from the bay and then chew it to bits. The pieces of island continued to float and break and swirl as they moved away from the city. It appeared Mr. Webster's dreams were soon to be at the bottom of Lake Superior.

"It's a good thing the hotel was just being built," Kirstin murmured. "How tragic it would have been to have guests wake up to find themselves being swept away."

Mormor reached out and took her arm. "It could have been us."

"Ja, she's right," Morfar said, shaking his head. "That's the old neighborhood. We didn't know we had built on such dangerous ground. Everything seemed solid and firm."

The sun was just coming up, and Kirstin could see the shock on his face as he continued.

"It could have been us scrambling in the dark to find our way to safety. We would have lost everything—maybe even our lives."

The realization hit them hard. They looked at one another as the full implication settled on each one of them. The storm had come in the night, and the disturbance caused the currents to shift, no doubt weakening the foundation of the land.

"That was our neighborhood," Mormor said, shaking her head. "God has saved us from a terrible fate."

Kirstin shivered more from the thought of what could have happened than the cold. Ilian put his arm around her. "I think it's much too cold to stand out here watching this terrible thing. Let's go home."

He led her back up the road, and his father and Kirstin's grandmother fell in step behind them. The shock of it all and the realization that they might have been killed had caused them to fall silent.

Once they were back in the house and rid of their coats and boots, the foursome reclaimed their seats. For a long while no one spoke. Kirstin kept seeing the demolished structure and land float past her and disappear into the lake. How very fragile was their world.

"I just stand amazed at how God has saved us from complete devastation," Mormor said, picking up her coffee. "That would have been us in our houses. It would have destroyed everything. We might not have even had time to save our lives, but for sure we would have lost all that we owned."

"God is good." Morfar leaned back in his chair. "We couldn't see the good when Mr. Webster and the city forced us to sell. We wondered why God would allow such a thing. We mourned having to leave, and yet now we see the outcome of it all."

"At least it was still being built," Ilian reminded them. "There should be no loss of life, and hopefully if anyone was hiding out there or using it to get away from the cold, they had time to run for safety. I can't imagine such a thing happened in silence. Breaking apart a building and the ground beneath it would have to be a noisy affair."

"We are blessed." Kirstin looked at each person at the table. "We are safe, and all of our friends are as well. God let the truth be known about the dangers of that land. He let it be known before anyone else could live or work there and be killed."

"It's a lesson I won't soon forget," Ilian said, reaching out to hold her hand. "When something happens in my life, I must ask God to show me what's best and what I am to do rather than look at the situation and protest the trouble it's causing me."

"Ja," his father agreed. "We have many things in life that we bemoan. We complain and grumble and fail to understand why it must be, yet we forget that God has already ordained our days."

"We forget that we've given Him charge over us—trusted Him for our future even when we do not understand it," Mormor added.

Kirstin smiled. "You bore this entire thing with patience and praise, Mormor. I was amazed at how calmly you took the news. You didn't like what was happening—that Mr. Webster was forcing us to leave—but I remember you told me we would praise God anyway and look to see what He had planned."

"And His plan was life. Where ours was death." Mormor

put her cup down. "We must give thanks and praise, for God has saved us yet again."

"Ja," Morfar said, nodding. "He has given us so much."

Kirstin looked at Ilian and smiled. "There is one more thing He has given us that Ilian and I wanted to tell you about this morning. The news about Mr. Webster's hotel sidetracked us, but it's of no matter." She couldn't contain her joy. "We're going to have a baby."

Mormor met her gaze, and Kirstin could see the happiness in her eyes. "Oh, how wonderful. When?"

"The doctor believes it will be in April. Just about the time Mor and Far will arrive." They had received a letter back in August, responding to the news of Domar. Her mother and father had been in great shock over the letters they'd received, but as time passed, they were elated and more happy than they could even put into words. Mor's letter had been more of a praise to God than comments on what had taken place. They wrote to say that they were going to arrange to come to America in the spring. They would sell everything, if need be, and leave the old country for good if it meant they could be reunited with their son—even for a short time. Brita would come with them, and perhaps in time the others siblings would as well. What a joy that would be. Kirstin could only hope they might all be reunited, but for now it was enough to know they would be able to make things right with Domar. Domar seemed just as pleased.

"Congratulations. This is such good news. Good news and joy unspeakable," Morfar said, reaching over to squeeze Ilian's shoulder. "May this child be the first of many blessings on you and your household."

"We thought if it is a boy," Ilian said, meeting his father's gaze, "we would like to name him after our fathers."

Kirstin nodded. "Habram Albrit Farstad."

Her father-in-law's eyes grew damp as he looked from Kirstin to Ilian. "Ja. It's a good name."

"Ja." Ilian met his father's gaze. "A family name."

Author's Note

I have found the history of Duluth to be quite fascinating. The Duluth canal was a project that, as the story tells, was opposed by the folks in Superior, Wisconsin. They did indeed work for an injunction to stop the canal and got it in June of 1871—months after the initial completion of the canal. The story of the canal was exciting and truly did change the course of Duluth. For more information you can read about it at

http://zenithcity.com/archive/parks-landmarks/the
   -duluth-ship-canal/
http://www.duluthport.com/port-history

As for the story about the floating islands, while my land was fiction, the concept was true. There were pieces of land that looked like regular islands and some that had connected to shore over years and years. Fremont, Minnesota, (not to be confused with the current-day city near Rochester) was one of the early townships on the edge of Duluth. In 1873, due to storms and changes in currents, it broke loose and floated through the canal. I thought it would be fun to show something like that in the story as I tried to imagine this township floating off to self-destruction in Lake Superior. What a shock that must have been to the people living on or near it. You can find more information in *Duluth and St. Louis County, Minnesota: Their Story and People* by Walter Van Brunt or at: http://zenithcity.com /archive/duluth-history/fremont-township/.

An excerpt from

Waiting on Love

TRACIE PETERSON

Book 3 in the

— Ladies of the Lake —

series

Chapter 1

Elise Wright watched her sister Caroline as she greeted the wedding guests. Caroline was five years her junior, and Elise wanted to be happy for her, but she found it difficult. Caroline hadn't sought their father's advice, or even Elise's, about her marriage. Of course, Elise's sister had been so distanced from the family that when Mama died the year before, Caroline hardly even seemed upset. Elise had tried not to hate her for her callous attitude, but it had required a great deal of prayer. Now Caroline wanted Elise and their father to be happy about her marrying into New York society to a man none of them really knew.

Still, Caroline seemed happy as she moved effortlessly in her ivory wedding gown of lace upon lace and satin ruching. The long train didn't seem to slow her in the least, nor did the trailing tulle veil. She was radiant and full of energy. Maybe she truly had married for love rather than money and position.

"She is beautiful, isn't she?" their father whispered against Elise's ear.

"She is. And she seems so happy. Nelson must be the right man for her." They'd only just met Nelson Worthington a few days prior to the wedding.

Her father nodded. "I had my doubts, but your uncle James assured me he was from a good family. They're in church every Sunday. Your mama would be happy to know that."

"I don't know that it would be enough. Mama used to say that Satan himself is in church every Sunday. The purpose in being there is what really matters."

Her father smiled. "You're so like her. How I miss her." His joy seemed to fade.

"I do too, Papa." She let him hug her close despite her very tight corset and uncomfortable clothes. She knew her father was just as miserable in the fancy suit that Uncle James had let him borrow. As if reading her thoughts, Papa loosened his tie.

"It's been a little more than a year, and yet it seems like she was here just yesterday," her father whispered. "Other days it feels like she's been gone forever."

"I know, Papa. It's that way for me too."

He gazed out across the garden reception. "She would love seeing your sister get what she wanted for her wedding."

"It would have been nice if Caroline had given more consideration to what you and Mama wanted." Elise struggled with the anger she felt toward her sister. Caroline had hurt their parents so much with her choices. She never seemed to think of anyone but herself.

"We used to talk about you girls getting married. We worried about whether we'd have enough money to give you a nice wedding. I regret that your uncle is paying for this. I offered him money—what I could—but he said it was their delight to give this wedding to Caroline. What could I say?"

"Well, you won't have to worry about giving me this kind of wedding. I can scarcely breathe, much less enjoy myself in restrictive gowns like this one." She looked down at the lavender creation. "I feel completely out of sorts. Especially with this bustle. Goodness, but whoever created such a thing?" She glanced over her shoulder and then gave her father a smile. "Besides, I don't intend ever to marry. I'm married to the *Mary Elise*," she said, referencing their ship.

Her father roared with laughter, causing a great many of Oswego's social elite to gaze their way. It would no doubt be a terrible embarrassment to Caroline, who hated that she was from a ship captain's family and spoke very little of it. Elise had heard from her cousins that Caroline told people their father was quite wealthy and chose to captain a ship for pure pleasure. Elise had heard her sister say their father took to sailing because it was his favorite thing to do and he was very eccentric.

The truth was, however, that Elise and her sister had both grown up on ships, and money was often scarce. When Uncle James got into the shipping business just six years ago, he had helped Papa buy the *Mary Elise*—a three-masted schooner named after Elise and Caroline's mother and grandmother. Elise loved life on the lakes and had helped their mother in the galley, but Caroline had enjoyed when they stayed with Uncle James and his family. She had taken to the life of a wealthy socialite and never wanted to return to their shipboard life. More than once she had made their mother cry, and Elise hated that Caroline had been so heartless. Her sister was only a child at the time, so

Mama had encouraged everyone to be patient with Caroline, but as the years passed, the tantrums only increased. Caroline would cry for hours at a time. She would take to her bed and swear that ship life was killing her. By the time she was fifteen, Mama and Papa had given up. They allowed her to live with Mama's wealthy brother and his family.

Uncle James had been Mama's support throughout the years, and even when she ran away to elope with Papa, he had been the one to make it all possible. Therefore, when he offered to let the girls come live with him and his family, it wasn't a surprise. He had told his sister that the girls would never get good husbands if they weren't finished properly. Mama and Papa left it up to Elise as to whether she wanted to join her sister. She didn't.

"Are you enjoying yourselves?" her cousin Louis asked, interrupting her thoughts.

"It's everything I expected it would be." Elise gave him a smile. "And what about you, Louis?"

"I'd rather be anywhere else in the world," he answered, returning the smile.

"You mean you don't like dressing up in tight-fitting suits?" Papa asked.

"As much as any fellow ever has at these occasions. Being here just reminds every would-be bride that I'm eligible to marry." Even though he was three years younger than Elise, at twenty-two, Louis seemed to have a most stable outlook on life.

Elise giggled. She had watched a bevy of frilly young ladies flock around her male cousins all day.

"Go ahead and laugh, but it's torment for me. At least Caroline and her young man seem happy. A father could hardly ask for more." Louis looked at Elise. "She did, however, step out of line and marry before her older sister."

"Oh, I am not finding her position enviable," Elise replied, hugging her father's arm. "Besides, being married hasn't seemed harmful to your brother Randolph. He looks quite content." She nodded toward the tall, handsome man who stood smiling down into the face of his wife.

"Oh, they're absolutely gone over each other. It's most embarrassing, but our mother's greatest triumph . . . well, at least until now, with Caroline. Mother just loves pairing us all up." Louis grinned. "If Elise sticks around, Mother is convinced she can get her married off as well. She loves having people to fuss over. I suppose they're like china dolls to dress up and arrange."

"Well, I'd just as soon Elise stick around with me awhile longer," her father declared. "After all, if she were gone, who would cook for the men on the *Mary Elise*?" He winked at her.

"Also, I'm afraid," Elise said, trying to keep her tone sweet, "I would make a very poor china doll. Besides, the *Mary Elise* is my life. I don't intend to add a man into that equation."

"You are a strange one, just as Mother said." Louis bit his lip. "I didn't mean to say that. It's not exactly what Mother meant."

"It's quite all right. I know I'm not what passes for a normal female in her world." Elise did her best not to reveal the hurt his words had caused. Why should her aunt call her strange just because she enjoyed a life on the lakes with her parents? Since Mama died the year before, however, Aunt Martha had nagged all the more for Elise to come live with them.

"It looks like that dashing Mr. Casper is coming our way," her father whispered. "No doubt he wants to dance, Elise."

"Oh, please send him away. He stepped on my foot three

Harrison County Public Library

times in our first dance. I have no desire to repeat the performance, and I'm sick of dancing."

"I'll take care of it," Louis declared. "I know Charlie well. I'll take him to see my new horse. The man loves horses more than anything else on earth. Charlie! Wait until you see my new mare." He headed off to intercept the man whose face was lighting up as Louis explained his plan.

"What a sweetheart." Elise would have to find a way to pay him back. "How much longer will this go on?"

Her father shrugged. "I have no idea. I've never been a part of higher society. In my experience, the party's over when the liquor runs out, but since these folks have enough money to keep that flow steady, I'm not sure what will bring things to an end."

"Perhaps someone will announce it, as they do for dinner." Elise smiled, imagining a well-dressed butler announcing that the party was over and everyone needed to vacate the property.

"They seem to have announcements for just about everything else. Why not the end of a thing?" her father replied.

"Do you suppose if we just sneak off to our rooms to change, they will leave us to our rat-killing?" Elise asked with a grin. *Rat-killing* was her mother's favorite phrase for any odd task that needed to be done. "We could slip upstairs when no one is looking."

"I honestly don't expect we'll be missed. Not even by your sister." There was an edge of regret in Papa's voice. "Besides, I need to check on Joe and see what the doc said about his leg."

Elise knew neither of them expected the news to be good. The *Mary Elise*'s first mate had injured his leg nearly a month ago, but no one knew about the wound until he started limping.

By that time, the leg was putrid, and red streaks were moving up the thigh.

"Let's just go, then. We can tell Caroline good-bye and pray with her on our way out the door." Elise pulled Papa in the direction of her sister. She didn't want to give him a chance to refuse. He didn't even try.

Elise waited for her sister to finish speaking to some of her guests before tapping her shoulder. "Caroline, we must be on our way."

"But you can't! Not until you help me change. Come on. I was already looking for an excuse. Nelson said we had to keep to our schedule."

Elise looked at her father with a shrug. "I guess Caroline needs my help. I'll be back as soon as possible, and then we can go."

Caroline all but dragged Elise up the stairs. "Everything was beautiful, wasn't it?"

"Yes. Quite lovely."

"The garden was perfect for the reception. I was so afraid there'd be no roses because of the cold spring, but they were in full bloom, and the gardeners were able to get additional flowers to weave in." Caroline opened the door to her bed-room suite.

Elise gazed around the large room. There was a sitting area by the fireplace, a dressing area, and of course the beautiful four-poster bed with elegant gossamer curtains draped from its frame. It was hard to imagine calling such a place home.

"Unfasten the buttons in back," Caroline commanded as she removed her veil.

"What about *please*?"

"I'm used to servants, and you don't say *please* and *thank you*. It's their job."

"But Mama always encouraged us to be polite even to the lowliest servant."

"Well, you aren't Mama," Caroline snapped.

"I'm also not a servant."

Silence hung heavy for a moment. Caroline gave a little huff. "Would you please undo my buttons?"

Elise began the task of unfastening thirty-six pearl buttons. "Why did you make that comment about Mama?"

"Well, ever since you and Papa arrived, you've done nothing but mother me. You've even talked to me like Mama. I'm sure you must feel the need to step into her shoes, and while that might be acceptable regarding cooking for Papa and the boys on the ship, it's not for me. I'm perfectly capable of seeing to myself."

"Including your back buttons?"

Caroline sighed. "Very well. Etta!" she called, not even seeming to notice whether Elise had continued with the buttons.

The uniformed maid appeared. "Ma'am." She gave a curtsey.

"Bring my new traveling suit and help me dress." Caroline glanced over her shoulder as Elise finished with the last of the buttons. "Please."

Elise smiled and watched the maid hurry away. "That wasn't so hard, was it?"

Caroline rolled her eyes. She worked at undoing the buttons on her sleeves. "Etta can help me now. Why don't you go downstairs and wait with the others? I know they plan to throw rice."

Elise waited as Caroline finished with the buttons. Stepping close, she surprised Caroline with an embrace. "I just want you to know that I love you. I hope you have a wonderful trip . . . and marriage."

Caroline hesitated, then finally hugged Elise. "I'm certain I will, so you can stop fretting." She stiffened and gave a little push. "Now, let me get back to this."

"We were close once." Elise hadn't meant to whisper the words aloud.

"We were children," Caroline countered. "And we had no choice. There was no other person to confide in or play with. We only had each other."

Elise saw her sister in that moment not as a wealthy bride but as a little girl. "I liked it that way. We knew we could count on each other always to be there. Now you have other obligations. I will continue to miss you."

"Oh, bother. Where is that girl?" Caroline went to the open door that led to her bathing room. "Etta?"

"Coming, ma'am." Etta returned carrying a forest-green traveling suit. She placed the outfit carefully at the end of the bed, then went immediately to Caroline and helped her rid herself of the ivory gown.

Elise slipped from the room, knowing that neither woman needed her nor cared for her company. Her sister's attitude only worked to stir her anger. How could she be so heartless? Didn't Caroline have any feelings of love toward the family? Maybe money and prestige were all she loved now.

An hour later, Elise waited in her uncle's borrowed carriage outside of Joseph Brett's apartment. Her father's first mate lived in a modest part of town. Elise knew that despite Joe's being a better paid seaman who didn't drink or gamble, he was still hard-pressed to keep his family fed and clothed, so the tiny duplex came as no surprise.

Joe had a family of five children and a wife who had once been quite pretty. Since the wife had been on her way out the door when they'd pulled up to the curb, Elise had decided to wait outside and let her father and Joe visit privately. The two women had exchanged hellos, but then Joe's wife had to be on her way to retrieve her children from her sister's house.

Mrs. Brett had at least shared the news that Joe was doing better. The doctor had given him medication for his wound and strict orders for tending it. She was certain he'd be back on his feet soon.

It was good to hear. Joe had been her father's first mate for as long as Elise could remember. Papa relied on him heavily. It was hard enough to be without Mama onboard, but losing Joe would be sheer misery. Elise knew her father would be relieved to hear the good news.

While she waited in the carriage, Elise fidgeted with the bodice of her dress. At least it wasn't quite as fancy as her wedding clothes, but it was just as snug. Probably two sizes smaller than she usually wore, thanks to the tightly tied corset beneath it. She could scarcely draw breath, and given the day's heat and humidity, she actually worried she might faint dead away. How ridiculous! Why did women put themselves through such torment? A well-fitted corset tied in a reasonable manner was a useful thing, but the practice of securing them as tightly as possible was absurd.

There was some sort of commotion going on down the street,

and Elise looked up just in time to see a freight wagon veering out of control. The horses pulling the wagon were driverless and headed straight for her. All she could do was brace herself for impact as her uncle's driver struggled to get the carriage out of the way.

"Miss. Miss, are you all right?"

Elise slowly opened her eyes and gazed straight up into the worried expression of a very handsome man. He was freshly shaved, and the cologne he'd used had a pleasant aroma.

"What . . . what happened?" She was lying on her back, and her vision seemed rather blurred.

The man smiled. "Your carriage was hit by a freighter. It threw you to the street. You have a few scrapes on your chin. Are you hurt anywhere else?"

"I don't know." Elise put her gloved hand to her chin.

"Are you able to sit up?"

She tried with his help, but pain cut through her back. "Oh, I don't think so." She was grateful when he lowered her back to the ground. She turned her head to see where she was. She spied Joe's house through the growing crowd.

"My father . . . he's in number twelve-twenty-three." How had she remembered the address? "He's visiting Joseph Brett."

"I know Joe," another man said. "I'll fetch her father."

The man who'd tried to help her sit up glanced around. "I think I'd best lift you rather than leave you lying here in the street."

"Yes. Thank you."

He put one arm behind her back and another under her legs. He was so very gentle.

"What is your name?" she asked.

He smiled. "Nicodemus Clark, but most call me Nick."

"Nick. Thank you again."

He frowned. "You might want to wait to thank me. This will probably hurt."

"I know." She drew a deep breath. "Go ahead." She gritted her teeth, determined not to cry out.

"Elise!" Her father appeared. "Bring her in the house. I'm sure Joe won't mind," he instructed Nick. "They said the freight wagon hit you. How do you feel, darlin'?"

"Confused, dizzy, and in pain." She smiled. "How are you?"

Her father chuckled. "Much the same without the aid of a freight wagon."

Nick placed her on the empty kitchen table. This time the pain wasn't quite as bad as before.

"I'm a doctor," a man said, pushing past several of the by-standers who'd followed them into the house. "If you aren't related to this young woman or live here, then I want you to leave." Several people filed outside.

Elise's father grabbed her hand. The look on his face nearly broke her heart. He looked at the doctor. "Can you tell if her back is broken?"

"My back isn't broken," Elise assured him. "It hurts, but look—I can move my legs and arms, and with a little help I can sit up." She looked to the right and found the same man who had helped her earlier. "Would you lend me a hand?"

"It's best you don't stress your body at this time, miss," the doctor declared. "I've already sent a man to bring round the ambulance."

"That was hardly necessary." Elise knew her protest fell on deaf ears.

"The carriage was totally demolished, Elise," her father added. "We'll need some form of transport for you. The young man who was helping you has no wagon either. We can't very well expect him to carry you home."

Elise tried to swallow her embarrassment. She shrugged, and it hurt from the base of her neck down the back of her legs. She didn't so much as grimace, however. Papa was already worried, and she didn't want to give him something else to worry about.

The doctor forced a large spoonful of medicine into her mouth. "Take this. It will help with the pain."

She swallowed the bitter medicine and couldn't hide her displeasure. "I don't know what that was, but I believe the pain was less difficult to bear. That tastes terrible."

Her father laughed. "Good medicine often tastes bad."

"It will make the ambulance ride more bearable."

She felt a wave of dizziness. "Well, I've never ridden in an ambulance. I suppose there are first times for everything." She forced a smile and looked at the man who'd helped her. "What did you say your name was?" The medicine was making her sleepy.

"Nick."

She fought to keep her focus. "Yes. Nicodemus. Such a wonderful name." She closed her eyes. "Thank you for helping me."

"I would say it was my pleasure, but I'm not sure that's exactly the right word."

She smiled. "Nor would I. But I appreciate no longer lying in the middle of the road."

"The ambulance is here," someone called from the open door.

Elise wasn't at all sure how long she'd been unconscious, but now she felt like falling asleep for a good long time. Two men with a stretcher appeared. They spoke to the doctor, then maneuvered the stretcher beneath her without any apparent concern for her comfort and lifted her from the table. She couldn't help but moan.

Her father gave them Uncle James's address, then followed them. She had no chance to bid good-bye to the man who'd rescued her. He'd been so nice.

Tracie Peterson is the award-winning author of over one hundred novels, both historical and contemporary. She is often referred to as the "Queen of Historical Christian Fiction," and her avid research resonates in her stories, as seen in her bestselling HEIRS OF MONTANA and ALASKAN QUEST series. Tracie considers her writing a ministry for God to share the Gospel and biblical application. She and her family make their home in Montana. Visit her website at www.traciepeterson.com or on Facebook at www.facebook.com/AuthorTraciePeterson.

Sign Up for Tracie's Newsletter

Keep up to date with Tracie's news on book releases and events by signing up for her email list at traciepeterson.com.

More from Tracie Peterson

After smallpox kills her mother and siblings, Gloriana Womack is dedicated to holding together what's left of her fractured family. Luke Carson arrives in Duluth to shepherd the construction of the railroad and reunite with his brother. When tragedy strikes, Gloriana and Luke must help each other through their grief and find their lives inextricably linked.

Destined for You • LADIES OF THE LAKE #1

You May Also Like . . .

When Madysen Powell's supposedly dead father shows up, her gift for forgiveness is tested and she's left searching for answers. Daniel Beaufort arrives in Nome, longing to start fresh after the gold rush leaves him with only empty pockets, and finds employment at the Powell dairy. Will deceptions from the past tear apart their hopes for a better future?

Endless Mercy by Tracie Peterson and Kimberley Woodhouse
THE TREASURES OF NOME #2
traciepeterson.com; kimberleywoodhouse.com

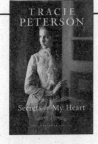

Reunited with childhood friend and lawyer Seth Carpenter, recently widowed Nancy Pritchard must search through the pieces of her loveless marriage for the truth behind her husband's death after his schemes come to light. But as Seth and Nancy pursue answers, their attraction to each other creates complications, and dark secrets reveal themselves.

Secrets of My Heart by Tracie Peterson
WILLAMETTE BRIDES #1
traciepeterson.com

Nate Long has always watched over his twin, even if it's led him to be an outlaw. When his brother is wounded in a shootout, it's their former prisoner, Laura, who ends up nursing his wounds at Settler's Fort. She knows Nate wants a fresh start, but struggles with how his devotion blinds him. Do the futures they seek include love, or is too much in the way?

Faith's Mountain Home by Misty M. Beller
HEARTS OF MONTANA #3
mistymbeller.com

BETHANYHOUSE

More from Bethany House

After turning the tables on a crooked gambler, Larkspur Nielsen flees her home with her sisters on a wagon train bound for Oregon. Knowing four women will draw unwanted attention, she dons a disguise as a man. But maintaining the ruse is harder than she imagined, as is protecting her sisters from difficult circumstances and eligible young men.

The Seeds of Change by Lauraine Snelling
LEAH'S GARDEN #1
laurainesnelling.com

With more children on their way from England who need caring homes, Lillian and Grace Walsh must use every ounce of gumption to keep their mission alive. But when startling information about the past surfaces and a new arrival comes via suspicious circumstances, they'll have to decided what is worth fighting for and what is better left in God's hands.

Sustaining Faith by Janette Oke and Laurel Oke Logan
WHEN HOPE CALLS #2

On a trip west to save her ailing sister, Greta Nilsson is robbed—leaving her homeless and penniless. Struggling to get his new ranch running, Wyatt McQuaid is offered a bargain: the mayor will invest in a herd of cattle if Wyatt agrees to help the town become more respectable by marrying . . . and the mayor has the perfect woman in mind.

A Cowboy for Keeps by Jody Hedlund
COLORADO COWBOYS #1
jodyhedlund.com

◈ BETHANY HOUSE